# PRAISE FOR NINA LAURIN

"Debut novelist Nina Laurin has created a memorable character in complicated, flawed and endearing Laine Moreno. From the very first page, *Girl Last Seen* jettisons the reader into the life of a crime victim trying to outrun her past."

—Heather Gudenkauf, *New York Times* bestselling author of *The Weight of Silence* and *Not a Sound*

"*Girl Last Seen* hooked me so quickly I might have whiplash. This is a sharp, twisting, intense thriller, the heartbreaking and fast-paced story of a woman who bears the scars of a trip to hell and back but who refuses to be defeated. Don't miss this smashing debut!"

—David Bell, bestselling author of *Bring Her Home*

"*Girl Last Seen* gripped me from start to finish. Lainey Moreno is a riveting heroine, a kidnapping survivor who will only escape her demons if she faces her greatest fears, and Nina Laurin brings her vividly to life. Psychological suspense doesn't come much grittier or more packed with satisfying twists and turns."

—Meg Gardiner, Edgar Award–winning author of *Unsub*

"*Girl Last Seen* by Nina Laurin is a chilling suspense about two missing girls whose stories intertwine—perfect for Paula Hawkins fans."

—EliteDaily.com

"Every good thriller has a shocking plot twist. *Girl Last Seen* has many. Author Nina Laurin's eerie novel will stay with you for days, months, even years to come."

—HelloGiggles.com

"A well-written and compelling novel that offers more than suspense; it offers a deeper understanding of how sexual assault can leave its victims broken. Ms. Laurin is to be congratulated for her achievement."

—NYJournalofBooks.com on *Girl Last Seen*

"4 Stars! This debut novel is a gritty thriller with dark twists you won't see coming. The heartbreaking, heart-racing journey... will keep you guessing to the nail-biting end."

—TheSuspenseisThrillingMe.com on *Girl Last Seen*

"Laurin creates a compelling, vulnerable central character."

— *Publishers Weekly* on *Girl Last Seen*

"Laurin's novel is nearly as compelling as it is depressing in detailing Lainey's story to a hair-raising, violent climax. A promising debut."

— *Booklist Online* on *Girl Last Seen*

"Disturbing and suspenseful... provides a great twisty ending that will satisfy."

—*RT Book Reviews* on *Girl Last Seen*

# WHAT MY
# SISTER KNEW

ALSO BY NINA LAURIN

*Girl Last Seen*

# WHAT MY SISTER KNEW

## NINA LAURIN

**GRAND CENTRAL**
**PUBLISHING**

NEW YORK   BOSTON

Copyright © 2018 by Ioulia Zaitchik
Excerpt from *Girl Last Seen* copyright © 2017 by Ioulia Zaitchik

Cover design by Lisa Amoroso
Cover photos by Elisabeth Ansley / Arcangel (trees); Carmen Winant / Getty Images (woman)
Cover copyright © 2018 by Hachette Book Group, Inc.

Grand Central Publishing
Hachette Book Group
1290 Avenue of the Americas, New York, NY 10104
grandcentralpublishing.com
twitter.com/grandcentralpub

First Edition: June 2018

Grand Central Publishing is a division of Hachette Book Group, Inc. The Grand Central Publishing name and logo is a trademark of Hachette Book Group, Inc.

The publisher is not responsible for websites (or their content) that are not owned by the publisher.

The Hachette Speakers Bureau provides a wide range of authors for speaking events. To find out more, go to www.hachettespeakersbureau.com or call (866) 376-6591.

Library of Congress Control Number: 2018935574

ISBN: 978-1-4555-6904-5 (trade paperback), 978-1-4555-6905-2 (ebook)

Printed in the United States of America

LSC-C

10  9  8  7  6  5  4  3  2  1

# WHAT MY SISTER
KNEW

# CHAPTER ONE

APRIL 10, 3:44 A.M.

A sticky thread of saliva runs from the corner of my mouth down to my earlobe, cool across my cheek. My vertebrae feel like a bunch of disconnected Lego pieces but I manage to hold up my head.

Humid April wind howls through the car. That's not right. Then I realize there's no windshield and the gleaming uncut diamonds scattered all over the passenger seat are glass shards.

My temple throbs with hot, clean pain, and I realize I need to call someone: Milton, or better yet, an ambulance. Why didn't the airbag work? The light from the car—the one surviving headlight, like a beam of a lost lighthouse in the night—shines into emptiness filled with stray raindrops, catching the side of the tree that I wrapped my car around.

When I raise my hand to my forehead, my fingers come away coated with slick, shiny blood. More of it is already

running down my neck under my collar—foreheads bleed
a lot. An ambulance sounds better and better, but I don't
know where to even begin looking for my phone. Was I
texting when I crashed? Checking my email? They're going
to ask that, and I have to say no. I sometimes use my phone
as a GPS, but not tonight. I've taken this route a million
times. When there's no traffic, and there's never any traffic,
it takes me forty-five minutes to get home.

The door is stuck, and for a few moments, I tug and
push and pull on the handle, consumed by ever-growing
panic. But then, once I give it a kick, it comes unstuck and
swings open. Getting out is a feat. I unfold my aching body
and have to hold on to the car door to keep from falling
over. After stumbling through the usual debris on the side
of the highway, I breathe a sigh of relief when there's finally flat, solid asphalt beneath my feet, the yellow stripe in
its center curving into the dark distance. I follow it. Down
the road, there's a gas station. If I were driving, it would be
right there around that curve. I don't know how far it is on
foot but, hopefully, not that far.

I take one step after another until the road steadies itself
beneath my feet and stops swaying. Next thing I know,
when I turn around, I can no longer see my car. The one
headlight went out, and now it's just me and the sky and
the road.

My heart starts to thunder, which makes my forehead
bleed more—or at least it feels like it, that little throbbing
pulse intensifying. Maybe I should have stayed and looked
for my phone in the wilted grass of the ditch. Anything
could be out here on this road. The darkness is alive.

I wrap my arms around myself and do my best to walk faster, but a rush of dizziness stops me in my tracks. When I close my eyes, an image flashes in front of them, a shadow. A figure. Except this isn't imagination—it's memory. It's vivid, fresh. I'm driving, twin beams of my car's headlights intact, my hands firmly on the steering wheel, my mind calm in that dull way it is after a long, late shift. I'm thinking about a bath and a bowl of ramen noodles in front of the TV I will only half watch because nothing good is on that late.

The shadow flickers out of nowhere, my headlights snatching it out of the darkness. It's the silhouette of a man, standing stock-still in the middle of the road, right over that yellow line.

I open my eyes, and there's nothing—no car, no lights, no figure. A glow in the distance suggests that I'm getting closer to the gas station and, hopefully, a phone and an ambulance. At the same time, the dizziness settles in, and I fight the temptation to sit down, just for a moment. Or better yet, lie down, right here on the side of the road. This means I have a concussion, which means I need to do precisely the opposite, as I learned in my mandatory first aid courses.

A spike of headache drives itself into my temple, and when I flinch, the image springs back up, like a movie I paused in the middle of the action. I'm careening toward the figure at eighty miles per hour. When I react, it's already too late to slow down, to give him a wide berth. The car's headlights bathe him in bluish light, erasing facial features, bleaching out everything except a strange harlequin pattern of splotches and spots that look black against his ghostly skin. Just as I swerve the steering wheel and hit the brakes, I have time to see that I was wrong—it's not black. It's red, red like ripe cherries and rust.

Then the world spins, the road is gone, and so is the figure. My eyes snap open just as everything explodes. *Bang.*

I'm panting and need to stop to catch my breath, hands on my knees. The gas station is finally in view, deserted but all aglow like a church on Christmas Eve.

Only a few more steps and I've reached salvation.

\*　　　\*　　　\*

What follows is a blur but somehow I find myself on a gurney with a blanket around my shoulders, and an ambulance tech is shining a flashlight into my eyes. Whether I have a concussion or not, the cut on my temple keeps oozing blood so they tape a gauze pad over it. I expect someone to ask me what happened but no one does. Through the open doors, I watch the ambulance lights bounce off the rain-slicked road. Is that what happened? Did my car skid? Maybe I fell asleep at the wheel.

"Ms. Boudreaux?" the ambulance tech is saying. They already know my name, which means they ran my car's plates. Then I see my open purse just sitting there in the middle of the wet road, my wallet splayed open next to it. Oh. How did it get here? I don't remember grabbing it as I got out. "We're taking you to Saint Joseph Hospital, all right? For observation."

I hate that soothing tone, maybe because I've oftentimes

used it myself, on frightened teenage runaways who show up at the shelter where I work. But whether I like it or not, it has the intended effect: He could be saying literally anything in that calm, measured voice. It's the intonation and timbre that have the effect.

"We'll notify your family," the tech says. It's that word that wakes me up, overriding whatever he just shot into the crook of my elbow. I make a clumsy move to grasp his forearm.

"Wait. There's someone else there." I must have hit my head harder than I thought—I can barely get the words out, slurring and misshapen.

He frowns. "Someone else?"

"I saw someone. Maybe they're hurt."

"You mean you hit someone?"

I give a vigorous shake of my head. I'm disoriented as hell, but this I'm sure of. Certain. Although when I think about it, I have no reason to be so certain, considering I still go to AA meetings once a week. "No. I saw someone." I didn't drink, I didn't take anything, I haven't even smoked a joint in months. That part of my memory is crystal clear. I wasn't wasted, and I didn't run anyone over.

But there was a man, covered in blood. And by the time I came to, a few minutes later—or maybe hours later, for all I know—he was gone.

# CHAPTER TWO

This is what they tell Milton when he gets there: I was driving home from work, crashed my car, and hit my head. They think I have a concussion. They don't hook me up to any machines, only an IV and a heart rate monitor. I'm in a room with four or five other people. I can't tell exactly how many because the space is separated by white plastic curtains that smell faintly of cleanser. When all of them are closed, the space I have to myself is just big enough to accommodate the bed itself and the plastic chair next to it.

My health insurance through work only covers the most basic stuff. In retrospect, I should have swallowed my pride and let my adoptive mother put me on the family plan. The family plan includes separate rooms. And probably a monogrammed bathrobe as a souvenir. That same plan once gave me braces for my teeth and laser treatments for the burn scars on my chest, neck, and upper arms. The braces did their job; the laser treatment . . . not so much.

Far over my head, positioned at an angle above the curtains so that everyone in the room can see it, is a TV screen. It's hard to watch without painfully craning my neck, and anyway, the channel is fuzzy with static.

The curtain crinkles, and its metal rings clink against the curtain rod, alerting me that Milt is back. I lower my head onto the flat hospital pillow and try to look appropriately injured.

He's brought me sour candies and a can of the exact no-name orange soda I like, presumably from the vending machine downstairs. There's nothing like favorite childhood junk foods to make you feel better but right now I can barely bring myself to look at the treats.

"Quick," he says, tossing me the bag of sour candies. I catch it in midair. "Before the nurse comes in and sees you." He winks, and I do my best not to cringe.

Few people wear their name quite as badly as Milt does. My gorgeous, six-foot-two, blond, blue-eyed, college soccer champion fiancé—pardon, ex-fiancé. It's easy to forget. Even when I still had the ring he gave me, I hardly ever wore it, not because I didn't appreciate it but because I'd never think of wearing a two-carat diamond to work at the homeless youth shelter. When the ring disappeared, my first logical thought was to tell him that someone stole it.

Milton wasn't my type until I met him. In fact, he was the opposite of my type. I always liked the dangerous boys, dark eyes and hair in need of clippers, a tattoo peeking out from under a collar or sleeve. When we met, I was at a party where I barely knew anyone, pursuing one or another such boy—I don't even remember which anymore. I remember getting stupid-drunk on those canned, premixed, malty-tasting sex on the beach drinks because the boy failed to show.

It wasn't a love-at-first-sight thing; Milt was there with somebody else. I never really knew who that girl was or what happened to her, because the next time Milton and I met, I pretended not to remember that party. It was more than a year later. I'd had time to grow out my ugly haircut and realize that black lipstick wasn't for me. I hoped he wouldn't recognize me, but I underestimated his ability to notice details. Because he recognized me, all right.

And within another two years, I somehow had not just Milt but also the diamond, the town house, all those things so normal and conventional it made them magical somehow. Everyone sort of expected me to die in a ditch, and here I was, with a mortgage and a reluctant subscription to a bridal magazine.

Of course, it couldn't have lasted. Just as we were already deciding on venues and caterers, I went and fucked it all up. Milt doesn't have the heart to leave me, so we're not broken up—we're taking a break. Same word, different formulation, but he doesn't see it's essentially the same meaning. He let me have the town house while he lives in his parents' summer residence.

I tear open the packet, and sour candies go flying all over the pale-blue hospital sheet. I snatch them up and pop two or three into my mouth at once. My taste buds writhe in acidic agony, and my eyes start to water, but I figure, with a mouthful of chewy high-fructose corn syrup, I can't be expected to talk.

"So you're going to tell me what happened?" Milt asks. He's not angry with me. It's not really in his nature to get angry. He's anxious, although he tries hard to hide it—it's not so easy to hide things from a psych major, even one who only made it to the end of senior year on a prayer.

"I'm fine. It's just a concussion." I have a feeling like I just said the same words less than five minutes ago. I gulp down the half-chewed sour candy that sears the back of my throat. "Where's my phone?"

His gaze darts back and forth. "I don't know. I checked at Reception. They gave me your coat and purse, but I don't think your phone is in there." He clears his throat, which is one of his tells. "Maybe, er, the police—"

"I wasn't texting," I say. I feel like I already said this too. "And I wasn't drunk."

Have they taken my blood to test for alcohol and drugs? My upper lip breaks out in beads of anxious sweat. They have no reason to do that, do they? No one else got hurt. Even I didn't get hurt...too badly. Besides, even if they did the test, I have nothing to worry about.

"So what happened?"

"Milton," I say. I catch his wrist and feel the muscles in his forearm, sinewy and ropey through the sleeve of his jacket. They tense and pop as he instinctively pulls away. This is bad. I hold on but my grip is weak. "Milton, you do believe me, right?"

"Of course I believe you." Milton sounds sad. Milton knows more about me than almost anyone—because I told him things I've told very few people who weren't shrinks. And also because his parents hired a PI to look into my background when we started dating, and he accidentally blabbed about it months after the fact. "It's just, you're a good driver."

For just a moment, I consider telling him the truth. Blink, and it's gone. "The road was slippery. Or maybe...maybe I fell asleep. I don't know, okay? I was exhausted. I don't remember exactly. I hit my head."

"Yeah." He finds it in him to grin and ruffles my hair. "You're going to look like a football for a while. Completing your gangsta cred?"

I chuckle. I want him to keep touching me.

His look turns serious. "I believe you, Addie." He knows I hate the nickname, but the more I protested the more he made it sort of a playful tug-of-war until it stuck, whether I liked it or not. "But I have the right to be worried. And your airbag—it didn't deploy."

"My bad for buying a crappy used car." Last year, he did offer to buy me a brand-new sedan, one with the top safety rating in its category. But I always had an issue with accepting his money—by extension, his parents' money— ever since I found out about the PI.

I can handle the fact that they hate me, but investigating me is another thing.

"Have they told you when they're letting me go home?"

He shrugs. "I tried to ask at Reception but they barely acknowledged I was there, so..." He gives me a guilty smile. "Can I at least get you something to pass the time? A magazine from the lobby? A book?"

Yes. As a matter of fact, you can get me a phone, hopefully one with a signal and a full battery and an internet connection. But I just return his smile in a properly pained way and shake my head.

"I'll see if I can find a nurse. Or someone who knows what's going on." He makes a motion to leave but slowly, reluctantly, as if he's hoping I'll ask him to stay.

"Milton," I blurt, like it's my last chance. For all I know, it is. "Wait. There's a . . . thing I think I remember. Or maybe I imagined it. Or dreamed it, if I really did fall asleep."

Alarm crosses his features. He doesn't have time to hide it, and I nearly change my mind but realize it's too late to go back. "I saw something," I say, swallowing. My mouth immediately goes sandpaper dry. "On the road, someone jumped out in front of my car. I didn't have time to see. A figure."

Milton's brows, a few shades darker than his sandy-blond hair, knit as he frowns. "Addie," he says, "have you told anyone? Have you told the police?"

"Police?" I stammer. "Why would I—"

But in that moment, I'm miraculously saved from the mess I got myself into. I hear rapidly approaching clacking steps that don't sound like a nurse's orthopedic sneakers, and a moment later, someone yanks the plastic curtain out of the way. No *hello*, no *are you decent*.

"Jesus Christ, Andrea. Not this bullshit again. What on earth where you thinking?"

With maroon lipstick at seven a.m. and fury blazing forth off her gold-rimmed bifocals, the formidable Cynthia Boudreaux has arrived.

"I wasn't drunk," I say through gritted teeth. "I fell asleep at the wheel." I don't glance at Milt, and he keeps mum, thank God. The mysterious-figure-in-the-middle-of-the-road version of events has been forgotten for now.

The woman who raised me from age twelve dismisses me with a wave of her hand. She probably already knows I wasn't in a DUI-related accident—the nurses or the police would have told her, because no such nonsense as patient confidentiality ever got in the way of Cynthia Boudreaux. I don't understand why she's here. Certainly not out of concern for me. Even if she had any, once upon a time, I sure did everything in my power to make sure this was no longer the case.

"They'll be releasing her soon," she says over my head at Milt. "I'm going to take her *home*."

The ominous way she says the last word, with a subtle but present emphasis, tells me she doesn't mean the town house.

"No way," I protest.

"Did you get her stuff from Reception?" Cynthia's icy gaze doesn't waver from Milt, like I don't even exist.

"Here," he says, complying, handing her the plastic bag with all my belongings. I'm stricken speechless by the betrayal unfolding right before my eyes, and Milt studiously avoids looking at me. She snatches the bag out of his hand and peers in.

"Is her phone in there?"

"No."

She fishes unceremoniously through my things, unzips my purse, and plunges her veiny hand with its gold rings into its depths, retrieving my wallet that she flips open and fleetingly inspects. "Anything else missing?"

"Why would anything be missing? Mom?"

For once, the *m* word fails to get her attention.

"Go check at Reception again," she says to Milt. "Make sure we have everything. Her car keys. Where are her car keys?"

Milt looks uncertain. He opens his mouth to say something but cuts himself off, silenced by my adoptive mother's sharp glare. The second he vanishes on the other side of the white curtain, Cynthia drops the act—it's an instant, head-to-toe flip, a shape-shifter changing form. She takes her glasses off and rubs the bridge of her nose where the little plastic pads have left two kidney-shaped red marks in her foundation. Her shoulders drop, relaxing from the perfect politician's wife posture; even her face itself seems to fall an inch or two, a mask with loosened strings.

"Do you think I don't know what you're up to?" she says in a hoarse, loud whisper. "Do you think you're the only smart person around here? And if I can figure it out, so can the police." She heaves a noisy sigh that smells like her herbal supplements and mouthwash. "I knew it would come back to bite you. I knew it."

I lift myself up on my elbows. "Mom, what are you going on about?"

"Don't *mom* me," she snaps. "We're well past that, Andrea, and you really should have thought about it when—"

"I wasn't driving drunk, and I wasn't texting. I swear." I make a move to catch her hand, which she eludes. "Why did they take my phone? Was it the police?"

"And they have your thermal cup too," she says dryly. "They're analyzing the contents."

A thought flits through my head: *Good, let them think I spiked my coffee with some dregs of cheap whiskey I confiscated from one of my shelter kids; let them think I swallowed pills, whatever.* I don't let the thought show on my face.

"But that's not the point," Cynthia adds. "Anyway, we're going home now; I already called our lawyer, and if they want to talk to you, not a word without him present, understand?"

"I'm not going to your house," I say, struggling to contain the anger that fills my chest. "I'm going home. I'll ask Milt to drive me."

"Milton is coming too," she says, not missing a single beat. "Just keep in mind, your sister is there, so at least have the decency to behave."

At the news that my adopted sister is home, an electric tingle of alarm shoots down my spine, and I know that whatever it is might not have anything to do with the crash after all.

And it must be really, really bad.

"Mom—"

A nurse comes in, her bulky presence overfilling the small space, all canned hospital cheer and smell of disinfectant. Cynthia puts her glasses back on and reluctantly steps aside, letting the nurse yank the catheter needle out of my arm and disconnect me from the heart rate monitor. For better or for worse, I'm being let go.

The nurse is professional and efficient, and before I

know it, I'm seated in a wheelchair, a piece of folded-up gauze stuck to the crook of my elbow with clear tape. The whole time, she manages not to look me in the eye once, and whenever she speaks, I feel like she's talking at me, not to me. Like Cynthia's been giving her lessons.

Just as she hands me over to another nurse, a short Filipino woman, I turn and glimpse at her over my shoulder—in time to catch her looking. An expression races across her face but vanishes before I can make anything of it, facial muscles relaxing and eyebrow creases smoothing back to a waxy neutrality.

I recognize this look, or one like it, from many years ago.

From after the fire. When I forever became That Boy's Sister.

# CHAPTER THREE

*The woman whose friends knew her as Cassie hid a difficult start behind her cheerful, optimistic demeanor. Photos from her youth show a beautiful, smiling girl with piercing green eyes and long, glossy brunette tresses, teased up per the dictates of late eighties fashion. But by the time her children, Andrea and Eli, were born in 1990, that smile had faded.*

*The children's father had an extensive arrest record for felonies ranging from petty theft to battery and assault. Cassandra had lost touch with her only remaining family, an elderly aunt, and dropped most of her friends. Her coworkers reported that she showed up with bruises poorly concealed by makeup.*

*When the twins were only two years old, she finally snapped. After a particularly violent episode, she pressed charges against her first husband and spent several months at a women's shelter. She could have easily gone down a familiar path: more dysfunctional relationships, alcohol, drugs, and eventual tragedy. But instead, things took a good turn. She found a job, which allowed her to leave the shelter and move into an apartment with the twins. For several years, Cassie worked long hours on minimum wage, still managing to support herself and her children. Eventually, she got a cashier job at a furniture store, and shortly after that, she married the store's owner, Sergio Bianchi.*

*Now a housewife living in a spacious suburban home, Cassie's future looked as bright as ever. But everything was shattered when tragedy found its way back into Cassie's life, from the place she least expected it.*

—*Into Ashes: The Shocking Double Murder in the Suburbs* by Jonathan Lamb, Eclipse Paperbacks, 2004, 1st ed.

## FIFTEEN YEARS EARLIER: BEFORE THE FIRE

Crouched on the brick border of a flowerbed across from the school playground, Andrea stares at the face of the hot-pink watch around her wrist. She wiggles its translucent strap with bits of glitter trapped in the plastic. It's uncomfortable, even on the loosest setting, too small for a twelve-year-old, and the buckle leaves a sweaty red welt in the plump, pale flesh of her wrist. That's why she keeps the watch hidden under her sleeve at all times.

Other girls don't wear watches with cartoon characters anymore. Other girls paint their lips in front of the bathroom mirror during breaks and smoke during lunch, perched on the windowsill next to the window that only opens a smidgen. Andrea thought she might like smoking: The smell of it, whenever she dashes in and out of the bathroom unnoticed, tickles her nostrils in a way that's not unpleasant, and it makes her ponder other exciting possibilities like stealing sips of Miller beer at a high schoolers' party, or even making out with boys. She's not entirely sure what making out consists of and how it's different from just kissing. But she knows these are the things she's supposed to want, even though she can never quite get a clear mental image.

And besides, the cigarette smoke makes her think of Sergio, her mom's husband. Sergio is supposed to have quit, but she knows he still sneaks cigarettes on the balcony when her mom isn't home. She caught him once, when she came home from school fifteen minutes early. She felt strange watching him, leaning on his elbow on the balcony railing as he exhaled smoke through flared nostrils. He looked different alone, lost in his thoughts as he tapped the ashes over the railing. A tiny spark detached itself from the glowing tip of the cigarette, drew a luminous orange arc in the air, and winked out gracelessly to a black point. She felt like she was seeing something she wasn't supposed to. Like watching scary movies through a crack in the door.

He caught her looking after only a few seconds, but

he must have thought she'd been standing there for a while. He didn't look alarmed. He waved her over, and she trudged through the backyard, right through the snow Sergio was supposed to shovel from the pathway but didn't. Now it had developed a grayish crust that crunched under her boots. Sinking to midcalf, she stumbled over.

"Let's keep this a secret, hmm, kid?" he said. "I'll get you something you want, and you don't tell Mom, all right?"

This was when she could have asked for one of those charm bracelets, or a new set of gel pens, or a Discman, or bedazzled jeans with the butterflies above the hems like the other girls had. She would have gotten it—she was fairly sure—because if she told her mom about the cigarette, there would be yelling, and there was a chance Sergio wouldn't get to be her dad anymore, which was not what she wanted. She still isn't sure why she didn't ask for something nicer.

Now she glances at the watch, and the long, thin hand with the jumping pink heart on it seems to twitch and jerk in one place without ever moving. Only ten minutes are left until the lunch hour is over, and Andrea considers going back, slinking along the wall to wait in front of the classroom even though you're not supposed to before the first bell. Bathrooms have been her respite until this year, but now the lip gloss and cigarette girls have claimed them as their fiefdom, and she'd sooner throw herself off the roof.

A noise, and her head snaps up. It's a wrong noise. It's coming from the fire exit by the gym where she snuck out. The door wails and groans as someone swings it wide open, and then it crashes shut. She hears giggling and excited shrieks. She knows who she'll see before they come into her range of sight.

Andrea is twelve, and the girls are thirteen. Her December birthday not only shortchanges her on birthday gifts, which double as Christmas presents, but it also makes her one of the youngest in her grade. And in those few months that feel like a chasm she'll never be able to get across, all the others seem to have picked up on things intuitively, things Andrea still has no clue about. Andrea isn't a pretty girl. She's not rich enough to compensate, and she's never been smart. She's just a strange, lonely girl, in an age before smartphones, before the internet was ubiquitous, before strange, lonely girls had online friends to confide in and blogs to fill with bad poems.

She is, however, smart enough to know what they're here for. Under the sleeves of her sweater, yesterday's bruises make themselves known, and her right ribs throb with every inhale. The girls are coming. There's one especially, Leeanne, who is the worst of them all. Whenever Andrea thinks of her, even when she's not at school, even on Saturday mornings when Sergio is making pancakes for all of them, her stomach twists with dread. Her heart starts to race like when the teacher makes them run laps in gym.

The laughter and voices grow closer and closer, and Andrea knows she must hide. A panicked glance around confirms that she has nowhere to go, only open space everywhere; the playground won't hide her. So she does the only thing she can: She ducks behind the brick border and flattens herself against the earth. She lets herself think that maybe, just maybe, the border is tall enough to hide her. Maybe if Leeanne doesn't see her right away, she'll think Andrea is hiding somewhere else, and Leeanne and her posse will leave.

The ground is mind-bogglingly cold, and damp seeps through Andrea's gray sweater, the one Leeanne called a dishrag last week. Andrea stuck it in the trash once she got home, but her mom fished it out and made her wear it again. Her jeans are black, and the mud won't show as much, but the sweater will be ruined. Andrea presses her cheek into the earth and flexes her fingers in the dirt. It's so cold that her hands go numb at once.

The steps grow closer, and Leeanne's peals of laughter ring out right over her head. She squeezes her eyes shut.

"Oh my God. Look at her. What is she doing?" The voice belongs to another girl, and every word drips with disdain.

Andrea barely has time to draw a breath. A hand grabs the back of her collar and pulls her up as if she were a kitten.

"Eww! Let her go, Leelee. So gross," says the first voice.

"You disgusting little pig," Leeanne's voice sneers, so close to Andrea's face that she can smell her strawberry gum. "Look at yourself. You're repulsive."

The other two girls start to make oinking noises. Andrea's collar cuts deep into her neck. She tries to steady herself on the brick border but her hands slip off it. Tears are stubbornly sneaking from under her shut eyelids.

"What a shame. You got mud all over that nice sweater. What will Mommy think?"

Andrea opens her eyes to see Leeanne's rapturous grin just inches from her face. She has a little bit of glittery pink gloss on one of her front teeth. The light of day brings out the pimple on her forehead that she coated with concealer. She wears that cropped puffy coat with the white fur trim that all the girls envy. Leeanne's parents are rich, and she has everything. Lip gloss, platform shoes, bedazzled jeans, rabbit fur collars.

Suddenly Andrea knows what to do. Leeanne is leering while her two cronies keep on oinking, pressing their fingertips with pink-polished nails into their noses to turn them up. Andrea raises her hand, unclenches her fingers, and plants the handful of mud into the dead center of Leeanne's white coat.

For a moment, everyone is stunned into silence. Then Leeanne's shriek nearly splits her eardrums. The girls yelp *oh my God* and *look what she did* and *what a little bitch*. Leeanne's grip loosens on Andrea's collar, and just as Andrea draws in a lungful of air, Leeanne's palm connects with her right cheek.

The slap goes off like an explosion and sends her flying right back onto the muddy lawn. The world tilts as she lands on her side, the impact knocking the wind out of her.

"You bitch! You'll pay for this," shrieks Leeanne. Andrea realizes her mistake, but all she has time to do is curl up on her side, pulling her knees up to her chin. Leeanne's pointy-toed boot digs into her side, right into yesterday's bruise, drawing a gasp from her. Her mouth fills with mud as more kicks rain down from all directions. Suddenly, they stop, and she realizes the ringing isn't inside her skull—it's the bell far overhead.

When she opens her eyes again, the girls are gone. But

she can't go to class—she knows that. She barely finds the strength to sit up. Tears are running down her face freely now, and she smears them along with the mud all over her cheeks.

"Hey! Addie."

She spins around and sees a lone, lanky silhouette sauntering toward her. She wants to call out to him, but if she opens her mouth, she knows she'll start to sob.

"What happened?" He crouches to be at her face level, and she turns her head away. "Shit. Leeanne again?"

"Mom will kill me," Andrea murmurs, surprised that it's the first thing that comes to mind.

"Why? It wasn't your fault."

"For the sweater."

Her brother's face blurs with the tears in her eyes. Eli is everything Andrea is not, like he'd leeched all the bright colors out of her when they were still in the womb, and some of the girls are already starting to look at him in *that* way, giggling behind their hands.

"Don't worry about the sweater. I'll switch with you." Their mom buys their clothes at Walmart, and he's wearing the same gray sweater with fitted cuffs, except scrupulously clean. "Come on, Addie. Let's go get you cleaned up."

She lets go of a tiny sob. Eli grins and picks up some of the mud at his feet.

"Hey. Look." Under her puzzled gaze, he smears the dirt along his hairline and down his cheek. She can't help but giggle. "Feel better? Come on. We'll be late for class."

"You're not going to go to class like this," she says.

"Sure I am. Boys will be boys, right?"

# CHAPTER FOUR

They smuggle me out the back like some celebrity after a stint in rehab. So it really must be that bad, I think, trying not to let myself panic.

Milt takes the back seat on the passenger's side, next to me, in Cynthia's black, shiny Cadillac SUV. The morning is obscenely bright and sunny, and the car is stuffy like a toaster oven from soaking up the sunshine in the parking lot. I watch my adoptive mother jab the buttons irritably with her manicured finger until the fans start their quiet hum in the four corners of the car. My sweat cools on my upper lip. Here, in the gauzy aroma of Cynthia's lilac air freshener, I notice the sour, stale smell wafting from me. It can't be coming from the clean clothes Milt brought me from home, my favorite old jeans and a sweatshirt I'd left thrown over the back of a chair in the bedroom, in another life. It seems to seep from my very pores, and I detect my own fetid breath, which means it's even worse than I can tell. I smell not too unlike my charges when they show up at the shelter, hoping for a place to turn in for the night, or at least for a cup of coffee and five minutes in a tepid shower.

As soon as I'm home, I'm going to run a bath, I think automatically, my mind on the oversize oval tub in our town house. Except I'm not going home and there will be no bath, not for a little bit.

"Can I have my phone now?" I pipe up.

"You don't have a phone anymore," Cynthia says flatly. My snappish retort dies when I see her eyes in the rearview mirror. Her regular Botox appointments maintain her face in a pleasing, smooth expression, but in spite of all that paralyzing toxin, her glare manages to convey murder. So I decide to keep quiet.

When we turn the corner onto the quiet street where the house sits at the very end, I sit up straight and look around. My adoptive parents used to live in an honest-to-God gated community, right up until the out-of-nowhere divorce that came as a surprise even to me. The ensuing move from the McMansion to the neat Victorian-style cottage in an upper-middle-class area was a comedown Cynthia never got over. That was when Cynthia's own biological daughter began to hate her. I, for one, was glad to be out of that mansion. Maybe it's all the memories of life right after the fire that I was glad to leave behind. Maybe I just liked the cottage that smelled like home—not my home, maybe, but a home.

Right now, there are cars—not our neighbors' quaint Toyota SUVs and dated Jeeps, but other cars, vans splashed with logos. One or two have that telltale tower sticking out of them, like something from a cartoon.

"Milton," Cynthia says in that reserved voice that nonetheless manages to be commanding. He nods, shrugs out of his jacket, and throws it over me. It's big enough to cover me entirely, like a large, warm tent that smells like him. Except right now it's anything but comforting.

"What the hell is going on?" I ask, peering out from under the collar.

He gives me a look so apologetic it borders on pity. "Come along, Addie."

We make our way through the swarm of reporters, and all I can see are legs and feet: my own once-white work shoes, Milt's brown leather boots, Cynthia's maroon stocky heels and massive nylon-clad calves in front of me. And other shoes, crowding in from all sides: loafers, sneakers, pumps. Voices descend on us, overwhelming despite the coat that covers me from head to midthigh.

"Do you have any comment, Andrea? What can you tell us about what happened?"

Milton yells at them to get the fuck away from me, or something like that—I don't make out the actual words. Cynthia's shrill voice chimes in: *Please disperse; she will not be talking to anyone right now.* Finally, the front door opens, swallows us up, and shuts behind us. I throw the coat off me with all the violence my painkiller-weakened muscles can muster, just in time to see Cynthia turn the two locks and slide the latch into place too.

"I was afraid it would be worse," Milt is saying.

"Worse?" Cynthia hisses. "How can it possibly be worse?"

That's when I realize I've had enough. "One of you is going to tell me what the fuck is going on," I snap. "Right fucking now."

They turn to me as if on command, and their faces soften, expressions shifting.

"Addie," Milt says in that pacifying tone, the same one he used when we had The Talk months ago about taking a break.

"You should go to your room and rest," Cynthia cuts in. "You have a concussion, for goodness' sake. You're not thinking clearly."

"I think I'm the only one here right now who's thinking clearly."

Cynthia looks at Milt, half-pleading, half-exasperated. He steps forward, tiny steps like he's about to tame a wild horse, and tries to take my arm. I throw him off. He grabs it again, more insistent this time, and I'm reminded that he's an athlete who still works out five days a week, and the heaviest thing I've lifted in years is a beer can. He leads me along to the staircase up to where my old room used to be, next to my sister's.

"I hate to say this, Addie, but this time, you should listen to her," he mutters into my ear.

"What happened? Don't lie to me, Milt. Not you too. Please. What happened?"

"Nothing you need to worry about. Nothing that has anything to do with you."

"Did I do something?"

"No."

"Did I . . . did I run someone over? Did I kill someone?"

# CHAPTER FIVE

The door of my old room closes behind Milt and me, and it's like we've fallen through time nearly ten years back. I only lived here from about sixteen until I turned eighteen, and I was sure that the moment I moved out, Cynthia would tear everything down and turn the room into a nice, faceless, prim "guest room" for hypothetical guests who would never arrive. But she never touched it. Not that I had been very keen on decorating and personalizing. The wallpaper is the same as when we moved in, pale blue with tiny silver flowers. There's a single bed with a gray bedspread, a vanity, a dresser with drawers, and one of those built-in wall closets nothing ever fits into, with a latticed door that doesn't close all the way. And most importantly, the TV on the dresser, half facing the bed. A TV that Cynthia forgot about, thank God.

The remote has been lost years ago so I use the power

button on the TV itself—it's one of those boxy old ones you can only find on the curb nowadays. Once upon a time, when I came to live with the Boudreaux family when I was twelve, it was still considered something special to have a TV in your room. My sister even had a computer.

The TV flickers on with that satisfying hum, and the sound appears before the picture. It's not like in the movies and TV shows when you fall on the news report you're looking for right away—I have to browse through infomercials and before-school cartoons before I happen on a news channel.

They're talking about something else, some economic crisis in some part of the world that's important indeed, I'm sure, but right now it makes me want to smash the TV in frustration. Behind me, Milt clears his throat.

"Addie..."

"Don't call me Addie."

"Andrea. You sure you want to do this?"

I don't bother answering him.

"Andrea, turn off the TV."

"I'll find out anyway," I snarl. As if on command, the screen flickers and changes, and the next thing I know, my brother's face splashes across it, life-size.

It's a shock that makes my breath catch. The old TV screen distorts his features a little, turns clean lines blurry, bright colors murky. This is my brother as an adult, a sharp contrast to the image of him from fifteen years ago that's still engraved on my memory: covered in soot, wild-eyed, clutching the lighter in his hand still, his knuckles stark white against the dirt and ash.

Everyone always said he'd grow up to be a heartbreaker. I don't know if I'd describe what I'm seeing as a heartbreaker. His face that promised to be chiseled with cut-glass cheekbones like our mother's has gone gaunt and angular instead, his nose aquiline and lips thin, pale, and pressed together so they almost disappear. His hair is too long, in need of a cut, but that only underlines the sharp M shape of a hairline that's starting to recede before its time. Even its coppery-gold color, inherited from the birth father we never knew, seems to have faded, leeched out by time or lack of nutrients or a hard-luck lifestyle. The stubble on his cheeks and chin is patchy, unhealthy looking, and his eyes look dull and dark, like windows of an abandoned house long after the last lights have gone out.

My first thought is that it's all been a mistake, that it's not him. Not my beautiful brother whom everyone loved, the golden boy. Yet as soon as I met Milt's gaze and saw that look in his eyes back at the hospital, I knew who this was about. Deep down, I've always known this would eventually happen.

What did you do, Eli? What the hell did you do?

My knees buckle, and I find myself sitting right on the floor at the foot of my old bed.

The face flickers out, and in its place appears a close-up of a ramshackle duplex-type building. Police tape is strewn about everywhere, like Halloween decorations.

" ... currently wanted by police after a young woman's body was found inside an apartment in northeast Denver. If you know anything about the suspect's whereabouts, please call ... " The image changes once again, to rows of information and a scrolling phone number in an urgent red font. And before I can release my breath, the newscast moves on, the image changing back to the anchor.

Numbly, I watch her frosty-pink glossed lips move. She could be talking about anything. I'm no longer listening.

So that's it, then?

Milton groans, and I realize I spoke out loud. "What do you mean 'that's it'? He killed someone."

"We don't know that," I say automatically.

"Yes, we do. At least the reporters on the front lawn sure do."

"They creamed their pants the moment they heard the name," I snap. My gaze is still riveted on the TV. Waiting for what I know is to come. "That's all. It doesn't mean it's true."

Milt sighs. "What I don't understand is why you're defending him right now."

"I am not defending anyone. Maybe you think I should just jump to conclusions, like everyone else?"

As if on cue, the TV flickers back to my brother's picture. Except this time, it's a different picture, one I remember and recognize, and it makes my heart clench with raw pain, like taking a bullet. It's the school picture the year we turned twelve—the hazy lilac-and-blue background they hung up in the gym blasted by two powerful lamps that brought out every single stray hair and adolescent blemish, that cruelly bounced off braces and glasses, sealing our fate onto glossy photo paper for all eternity. But Eli looks wonderful. He's not facing the camera head-on like in that other, newer photo—a mug shot? His head is turned just barely to the right, and the corner of his mouth curls in a knowing smirk, a cute kid about to become a handsome man.

That photo did the rounds back then, the talk shows, the press. That awful true crime book used it as a cover image, cropped and altered with the colors changed to more sinister, foreboding red and black tones. Every time I looked at it, I wondered if he already knew in the back of his mind what he was going to do. Had he already planned it? He always had his secrets, even from me. Especially from me. They never found the lighter he used, not even after combing through every inch of the smoking pile of ashes, extracting charred "clues" to inspect and catalogue as irrevocable proof of my brother's guilt. He never did tell anyone what happened to it, how he got rid of it.

"Eli Warren last came into the public eye in connection with a fire that consumed a suburban home in 2002. After believing the cause was electric, the investigation team soon discovered that—"

She drones on and on, repeating the story I know by heart. It seems to me that everybody knows it by heart. Every time someone looks at me oddly, or a stranger's gaze lingers a millisecond too long, or a cashier takes a beat too long before she gives me my change, I think to myself, *They know*. But in truth, of course, to most people the story was just a morbid curiosity, something they read about in the paper. Maybe they even picked up that true crime paperback at the airport or at Walmart, skimmed it in a couple of hours, and left it on a bench.

But that was years ago, and they've long since moved

on, turning to other crimes real and fictional to take them away from their humdrum lives for a few minutes at a time. Nobody remembers who we are. Especially who I am, the afterthought, the faint supporting character in the background. The silent sister.

I only remember that Milt is still there when his shape blocks the TV screen. He reaches out and turns it off.

"No!" I protest.

"Yes. It's enough. Why do you even care what happens to him? He already killed your parents."

The words, spat out like an accusation, paralyze me. I open my mouth to answer but no sound comes out. We face each other, me sitting on the floor, him towering over me, glaring down from the height of his six feet two inches. It's unfair.

"Let him be," Milt says. "He got himself into some shit that's nobody's fault but his own and that of the people dumb enough to let him out of prison. He's not your problem anymore."

"Don't say that."

"Why? He wouldn't have done the same for you."

The door flies open and bangs against the wall, like a gunshot. We both turn around. Cynthia is in the doorway. Doesn't she ever fucking knock?

"Andrea, there's a detective downstairs. She wants to talk to you."

# CHAPTER SIX

*Dating Sergio Bianchi was an undeniable step up for Cassandra. You could almost call it a Cinderella story. Born in Denver to Italian immigrant parents, he was fifteen years Cassie's senior. After graduating with honors with a degree in business management, he opened a furniture store in suburban Denver. Sergio offered great working conditions and was beloved by all his employees. "He would never, ever leave anyone in trouble," one of his employees, who wished to remain anonymous, told me. "And he would even help with money if he could. He was a generous soul." So when a chestnut-haired beauty came in for a job interview with two kids in tow because her sitter cancelled at the last second, he was moved. He hired her on the spot. The rest, as they say, is history.*

*—Into Ashes: The Shocking Double Murder in the Suburbs* by Jonathan Lamb, Eclipse Paperbacks, 2004, 1st ed.

### *FIFTEEN YEARS EARLIER: BEFORE THE FIRE*

Eli brings home a complaint from one of his teachers, written on yellow notepaper. Upstairs, in the room they share, Andrea asks him to show her the paper, and when he tosses the folded yellow square onto her lap, she freezes up a little. Gingerly she unfolds it and reads the lines of text in a teacher's loopy scrawl, in red ink: *Unacceptable, dirty attire, unsuitable for a learning environment.* Her lips move silently as she makes sense of the cursive letters, and when she looks up, she meets her brother's gaze—he's been watching her the whole time, an amused look on his face. She gets up to hand the paper back to him.

"What are you going to do?" she asks.

"Do? Absolutely nothing." With a shrug, he crumples the paper in his fist and tosses it into the wastebasket with a flourish.

She barely holds back a terrified exclamation. "But—you have to show it to Mom!"

"No, I don't. Don't be such a dork, Addie. No wonder no one at school likes you."

She tries not to show how much the remark hurt her.

She has known what her brother is like from a young age, and she has learned how this works. He hadn't even meant to get to her—he simply said what he was thinking, with no regard for the consequences. He's not like that with other people, only with her. Because they're twins, he says. They're like two sides of the same coin. They can't have secrets from each other and they can't lie to each other, he says, not even white lies.

And while what he said may be true, she does wonder, sometimes, why that is. She had a friend once, when she first came to this school. Almost. A girl was friendly to her—hardly the most popular girl in class, but Andrea didn't care. It was nice to talk to someone. Then, overnight, the girl started to act like Andrea was invisible. She felt hurt and confused. Then, a few weeks later, she realized everyone in class gave her the same peculiar look.

Eli, in the meantime, casually made friends with everyone. She knew, on a subconscious level, that he said something to the girl, and to the others, told some crazy story that made her seem like a freak or loser. But she never had proof. She never even learned what the story was.

Eli stretches his arms over his head. When it was time to leave after the last bell, he'd managed to get changed—the dirty sweater had vanished, and instead he wore another, clean one, with a little brand logo over his heart. Borrowed from someone? Nabbed from an open locker after gym class? Andrea doesn't dare ask.

"Leeanne and the other bitches bothering you again?" Eli bounces a little on his narrow bed. Andrea flinches at the *b* word.

"What? It's true. That's what she is. Do you know what the guys say about her?"

Andrea has no idea why "the guys" would say anything about Leeanne. The thought makes her nervous somehow, uneasy, the same way she feels when she catches other girls from her class doing things she hasn't even thought about yet, rolling up their skirts, plucking their eyebrows. Her chest constricts, and there's an uncomfortable, pulling sensation in her stomach. It's not fear, exactly. More like foreboding and dread. She knows she's about to enter a whole different game, very different but also very much the same as the elementary school version where the one with the coolest stuff and the most friends wins. And she knows that, just like the old version, she'll lose this game the same way, maybe worse. Except now there's going to be a lot more at stake.

"What do they say?" she asks cautiously.

Her brother gives her a look that borders on exasperation. Like she's supposed to know.

"Theo said she blew him behind the bleachers," Eli starts, and she presses her hands over her ears, which makes him huff with laughter. "Okay, okay. No more icky stuff," he mouths exaggeratedly. She drops her hands by her side, feeling defeated.

"I see her smoking in the bathroom," Andrea says meekly, feeling like a pathetic baby. They're the same age—he is actually a few minutes younger than her—but for as long as she can remember, he's seemed older. Always one step ahead.

"She's what we call a slut. She gets weed from a guy

who's in high school in exchange for..." He gives her a clever sideways glance. "Well, you know. Oh, and her mom is the head of some youth abstinence committee program thing. Use that info as you see fit."

The only thing for Andrea to do is to nod. She wants him to think that she knows what to do. He sure does. Doesn't he always know what to do in any situation? There's nothing you can't do with the right dirt on the right person, he'd often say to her.

For some reason, her mind goes back to that Saturday afternoon not so long ago, when she had to stay home while her mom, Sergio, and Eli went to the movies for the weekly family outing. Eli had hogged the computer all morning, and she bugged and bugged him to let her use it, whining that it was her turn and it was unfair and she'd tell Sergio. Up until she got on his nerves and they had a fight, with her pushing him off the computer chair just as their mom walked in. Mom got mad and made Andrea stay home as punishment. Andrea remembers how peaceful and quiet the house became with everyone else gone; the computer stood there on the desk in the basement rec room, all hers for the next two to three hours. Somehow, by breaking the rules, she'd gotten exactly what she wanted. It was a discovery that mystified her because, try as she might, she couldn't think of ways to repeat the feat. Her brother seemed to pull this off so often and with such ease.

She had climbed into the big, cushy computer chair that Sergio had bought a while back and turned on the computer. The machine took a few minutes to boot up, and before it had loaded all the way, she impatiently clicked on the browser icon, opening a window.

Her brother spent more and more time on the computer lately, and she had to know what he was doing. Once or twice, she woke up in the middle of the night and saw that he wasn't in his bed. When she went to look for him downstairs, she saw the light under the door of the rec room. She knew it was sex stuff. If only she could find proof, she'd tell her mom, and she'd banish him from the computer for good. Andrea would have it to herself as much as she wanted, to draw multicolored squiggles with Paint or to play online games, colorful and primitive versions of pinball and Battleship that could keep her occupied for hours on end.

With a few clicks, she found the browser history, her eyes roaming the columns of links, greedily soaking up forbidden sightings. She had to reread the top three several times before the meaning began to sink in. They were searches on a search engine. She reread them nervously one more time, to be sure, and then clicked on the top one. The page loaded in moments. The top two links were purple instead of blue. Her hand sweaty on the computer mouse, she clicked the first one, went back, read the second.

The last question her brother had typed into the search field less than an hour ago burned in her mind. *What happens if—*

There had to be some mistake. She read the header of the page she found herself on. It read, in blocky, austere black letters, SIGNS OF CHILDHOOD SEXUAL ABUSE: SPOTTING THE TELLTALE BEHAVIORS.

She squeezed her eyes shut, opened them again, and the page was still there. Exhaling noisily, she clicked Back, again and again, until she was back on the blank browser page. She opened the history one more time and reread the top query.

rape what happens 12yo

Then, underneath it:

molest accusations child

And finally:

what happens if you rape a 12yo how long u go to jail

With a little more clicking around, she found the option to erase the browser history. Without hesitation, she clicked it and watched it all disappear.

If only wiping what she had seen from her mind could be as easy.

# CHAPTER SEVEN

It's a feeling I know all too well. When I set foot onto the first step, terror and dread are warring within me, my mind in disarray, but by the time I get to the last step, my nerves have calmed, falling back into well-memorized patterns, my protective shell settling back into place seamlessly, even after all these years. The knot in my stomach is familiar, a part of who I am, like a limb.

Downstairs is like a scene from a bad Lifetime movie, reminding me uncomfortably of another scene in the same living room, my so-called intervention that Cynthia staged six months earlier. Except this time, there are police. At the other end of the room, in the doorway, I notice a familiar tall, portly figure—my stepfather, Jim Boudreaux. I feel an uncomfortable chill. What is he doing here? Now, of all times.

That's when he looks up, as if sensing my gaze. Our eyes

meet for just a moment, and he gives a short shake of his head, so subtle it's barely noticeable.

In the living room, Cynthia circles around, chattering with her well-practiced, overly loud politician's wife cheer. She may never have gotten to be a real politician's wife after all, but old habits die hard. At the center of her attention are two detectives, a man seated on the couch and a woman hovering in the periphery. An untouched cup of coffee is already sitting on the table in front of the man, next to the sugar bowl and creamer. They're both wearing civilian clothes, him in trousers, button-down, and suit jacket, her in a sweater and baggy jeans.

Cynthia focuses her attention on the man, naturally. She asks him if he'd like anything to eat with his coffee and bravely attempts small talk. He responds with the tight-lipped smile of a saint. Cynthia either doesn't realize it's fake or doesn't care.

So it's the woman I need to watch out for, then. I know it in my bones the moment I set eyes on her. She has a look I recognize, a half frown that seems to have become the default setting of her face, her eyes quietly watchful, wary, taking in everything around her. She's a woman who fades into the background, and she knows it. But while others might try to overcompensate with flashy clothes and makeup, she chooses to turn it into her advantage.

I know something about that.

She is the one who sees me first, while I hover on the bottom stair. Her eyes, of an indiscernible color that looks plain dark at this distance, zero in on me, her gaze sinking into my skin like a hook. It will not let go, not without rip-ping out a chunk of flesh. I instinctively hide the shudder that courses through me.

Then, as if on cue, Cynthia and the man turn their heads and see me. Cynthia purses her lips, but the man breaks into a smile.

"Ms. Boudreaux," he says.

The woman steps forward. She's not here to waste time.

"I'm Sergeant Detective Figueroa, and this is Detective Childs." She barely acknowledges him with a nod. Her voice is deep and melodious—the voice of a much more beautiful woman. All of us plain girls have that one thing—with me, it's my eyes, or so said the drunk guys in bars who tried to hit on me. They're not bright blue like Eli's, but without him around, there's no one to com-pare to, and my gray eyes with dark lashes can pass for beautiful.

I should say something—hello would suffice. But instead I stand there and look from one to the other, in what I hope passes for bafflement. They don't know that I've just seen the newscast, I remind myself. I have every reason to be surprised to have detectives show up at my mother's house.

"Why don't you have a seat," Childs says. I try to puz-zle out how old he is. In contrast to her, he's probably considered attractive, with close-cropped black hair and dark eyes. "We understand that you just got out of the hospital."

"She has a concussion," Cynthia chimes in, a hysteric edge to her tone.

Figueroa doesn't even look at her.

"Andrea, do you know why we're here?"

"She doesn't," Cynthia says, in a much softer voice.

I make a split-second decision. "I do."

Cynthia turns livid. I know this look of hers, the one she gets in private when the Stepford-wife mask drops. Her furious gaze jumps from me to somewhere above my shoulder, and I remember that Milton is here, right behind me, hovering protectively. Sorry, Milt, I think as the knot in my stomach tightens. You can't protect me from this.

"Milton," Cynthia snaps in a low voice, "I thought I was clear. I said—"

"She would find out eventually," Milt says. "And she has the right to know, doesn't she?"

Figueroa, in the meantime, is observing the whole soap opera with what I guess to be amusement, as far as I can tell by the look on her face. The hint is the corner of her pale lips that turns up a touch.

"Andrea, your brother is wanted for murder," she says, making it all true. Not something on the other side of a TV screen, not something I may have dreamed up because of the concussion. "Sit down. Let's talk."

"Andrea, you don't have to say anything," Cynthia murmurs. She casts a quick glance at her ex-husband as if silently pleading with—or commanding—him to step in.

"You don't have to talk to anyone," he says at last. "Not without a lawyer present."

"They're right," Milt chimes in behind me, sounding apologetic for agreeing with Cynthia for the second time in as many hours.

Cynthia looks triumphant.

"He'll be here any minute. Can it wait?" Jim still manages to sound like he has authority, influence, like in the good old days. When I get a closer look at him though, I'm a little shocked at how much older he looks. He's stooping, as if all the disappointments of his life are pressing down on his spine, an enormous, invisible weight.

"It really can't," says Detective Childs.

Feeling everyone's gazes on me, I walk over to the couch and sit on the very edge. As if ready to jump to my feet any second. "It's all right. I can talk, because there's nothing to say. I haven't seen him since . . . since last time."

Figueroa nods. I can inspect her up close at last. She isn't wearing a stitch of makeup, and her dark, curly hair sticks out in flyaways around her head. Lines are starting to etch into her forehead and in deep brackets around her mouth. Her lips are chapped.

"And when was the last time?" she asks. She manages to intimidate without looking her victim straight in the eye.

"After the fire. As everyone knows."

"Who's everyone?"

"It was in all the papers."

Figueroa smiles, a smile that doesn't get anywhere close to her slate-gray stare. "If you don't mind, I'm recording this." She points at her phone, on the coffee table next to the cup of coffee for Childs. And what if I do mind, I think. I'm guessing it doesn't make a difference.

"Tell me about last night. Walk me through it."

"I crashed my car on the way home," I say.

"I know that. I'm talking about the part up until the crash."

"I was working. At the Relay Youth Center, out by the refineries. My shift ended at three a.m., like always. I got in my car and drove home."

Figueroa nods along with each clipped sentence. "I already verified all that."

"I crashed my car on the stretch of the road before the gas station," I say. "As you probably know too. It must have been about three fifteen. The next thing I knew, I came to, the car was wrecked, and there was no one around. I couldn't find my phone so I had to walk to the gas station for help. I don't know how long I was unconscious. I guess I was lucky I woke up—it would have been morning before anyone found me."

"Lucky," she echoes. "Definitely. I saw pictures of the car. It could have been a lot more serious. You could have been badly injured, or worse."

"Yeah."

"It was almost four when the clerk called the ambulance. So you would have been unconscious for a half hour."

"If you say so. To me it might as well have been five hours. I was completely out of it."

Cynthia sighs loudly, reminding us all of her presence. Milt clears his throat. "I always wanted to get her a newer car," he says, speaking up. "I knew that sardine can would kill her one day."

Figueroa acknowledges him with another cold smile. "I'll speak with you another time, Mr. DeVoort. You can tell me all about it then." The smile widens. "If it's necessary, that is."

"Is it going to be?"

I hear the old confrontational note in Milt's voice and silently pray he shuts up.

"What does any of this have to do with anything?" I say, raising my voice. "I just want to know. What exactly did E—did my brother do?"

"I'm getting to that."

"It's the only reason I'm talking to you right now," I say, throwing a sideways glance at Cynthia. "Without a lawyer. I want to know what happened to my brother."

Somehow, a look of satisfaction appears on Figueroa's face, unmissable, the first genuine emotion she's shown so far, and what's more alarming is that she's not even trying to hide it.

"Your brother murdered a young woman."

"What young woman? How can you know—"

"That it was him? The body was found in his apartment; his neighbors heard a fight and screaming; his prints are all over the place...Do you want me to go on?"

So far, it sounds circumstantial at best.

"You don't even know who she is yet." I meant it to be a question, but it doesn't come out that way.

That satisfied look flashes over her features once more. She reaches into a square bag by her side and takes out a black portfolio.

"See, your brother made it difficult for us." The zipper hisses as she opens the portfolio. My chest tightens when she takes out a stack of four or five photos the size of a printer page. She puts them down on the table with a thump of finality.

Cynthia makes a sound midway between a moan and a shriek. Milton draws a breath through his teeth.

What reaction does Figueroa expect from me? To fold over and vomit right on Cynthia's gleaming floor? Scream, maybe? Throw the pictures in her face and demand how dare she show me such traumatizing things? But I can't bring myself to do any of that. I just sit there like a doll at a pretend tea party, not moving a muscle.

The girl in the top picture—I know to call her a girl only because Figueroa just told me it was—doesn't have a face to speak of. Just a pulpy, bloody mass, like something out of a B-grade horror flick, a mess of fake blood and gelatin and fake bones and teeth thrown in for realism. I can't even tell the color of her hair, matted as it is with blood and gray matter. I try to imagine how much rage you'd need to muster such violence, how much adrenaline to summon enough strength. You'd have to hit her again and again until she was dead, and for a while after.

You'd have to hate someone more than you've hated anyone in your life.

I'm trapped in my bubble of numb shock when Figueroa flips to the next photo with a flick of her hand. The next picture I can't even identify—it's just a limp piece of bloody meat not attached to anything. As I peer closer—not like I could look away even if I'd wanted to—I see five bloodied stumps with grayish-white bone poking through in places.

"Her hands." Figueroa's jarringly melodious voice reaches me from far away. "He smashed them and crushed her fingers so we can't identify her with prints. We can't use dental records either, with her teeth almost all knocked out."

"Why are you showing me all this?" I finally bleat.

Figueroa catches my gaze in hers and holds it, for an agonizingly long time.

"Because you're the key to finding him."

# CHAPTER EIGHT

"I think you're mistaken," I say, carefully weighing every syllable. And I mean it. If she thinks I can help her, she's crazy.

"I don't think I am," Figueroa says.

"Why? I haven't seen him in fifteen years—I already told you that. I haven't even spoken to him. I—"

"Maybe so," she says. "You might not even know it, but you can help me find him."

"You want me to help you hunt him down." The words escape from me before I realize how they sound.

But Figueroa sighs patiently.

"Not quite. I have reason to believe that, while you cut off all contact with your brother after the fire that killed your parents...he might not have done the same."

I draw a breath to speak, but the words won't come. First of all, I want to say, a fire didn't kill my parents. Eli killed my parents, and I don't see why she's being delicate about it now, of all times. "You're saying he's been spying on me."

Infuriatingly, she won't say yes or no. But she holds my gaze again. "You are his only remaining family, after all."

"So you think he intends to finish what he started," I spit. Milton exhales with a hiss.

"Let's talk more about your car crash," Figueroa says, and I clench my fists, forgetting that my hands are placed neatly on my thighs, in plain sight.

"I already told you everything there was to tell. You have to tell me what you know about Eli. You—" I almost say *you promised* except, of course, she didn't promise jack shit. She threw out only a few shocking facts that I was supposedly the first to learn. Except those same facts will probably make the evening news, if not today then tomorrow, since certain gore-hungry tabloid papers and channels thrive on this stuff. But I stumbled into the trap, thinking we had some kind of rapport.

"There's something you said to the paramedic who showed up on the scene," Figueroa says.

I swallow nervously. "I was out of it. I don't remember. My head hurt like hell, and blood was in my eyes, and—"

"You said something about a figure."

*Of course.* "I must have...It could have just been a shadow. Or nothing at all. It was all very sudden. I—"

"Did you swerve and drive off the road because you saw this figure?"

"It was three a.m. I was dead tired."

"But I think that's exactly what you saw. A surveillance camera near the crime scene caught your brother crossing a parking lot. It was only for a couple of seconds before he was out of the camera's range. But it's clearly visible that he's covered in blood. Just like he would have been if he'd bludgeoned this young woman to death with such force."

"So you're saying that..." I don't know what I think she's saying. My head is spinning.

"He tried to contact you, to come see you. Which means he knew where you worked, and what time, and what road you took home. Which in turn means that he must have been keeping an eye on you for some time."

Milt has had enough. He steps forward and takes my hand. His palm is dry and hot, in contrast to my clammy, icy grip, but I gratefully take it and intertwine my fingers with his.

"Does this mean Andrea is in danger?" he asks forcefully.

"Not necessarily. If he wanted to hurt her, he already had a chance. Although now that he's wanted by the police, he's cornered and desperate. It's better that Andrea stay someplace safe and keep the door locked."

I shift uncomfortably, wishing they wouldn't talk about me over my head like this.

"That's ridiculous. I'm not in danger," I say, surprised at how powerful my voice is. "He wouldn't hurt me."

"You don't know that." Figueroa studies me with interest. "He did kill your parents without a second thought."

But he dragged me out of the fire, I almost say. My hand pulls out of Milton's, and I stop it midair, an old habit awakening—the need to touch the rippling burn on my neck, to feel the new skin, smooth and pearly pink like the inside of a shell.

"I think it's best that you take a leave of absence from work," Figueroa is saying. I can't take a leave of absence. There's no one to fill in for me because no one wants to work so late in the bad part of town with the most difficult subjects of all—the ones who fall through the cracks, the runaways, the drug addicts who come to the shelter as a last resort.

"There's no need," I say, but she silences me with a glance.

"And Andrea, I need you to think very hard. About anything from last night, anything out of the ordinary. And the preceding couple of weeks, maybe even a few months."

A few months? She thinks that's how long my brother might have been spying on me?

"If anything jumps out at you, get in touch with me at once." She folds her hands in her lap. "And don't worry— I'll talk to your boss. You can have that leave of absence and your employment will not be in danger."

I'm supposed to thank her. That's what Milt and Cynthia do, he with a subtle nod and she profusely, her hands clasped in front of her ample chest. But to me, the promise to talk to my boss sounds more like a threat.

"Oh, one more thing," Figueroa says lightly, too lightly. "You can have this back. We have no further need for it."

She nods at Childs, who reaches into his satchel and comes out with one of those plastic evidence bags, on which something is scrawled in untidy Sharpie marker. He hands it to Figueroa, who tosses it on the coffee table with seeming carelessness. It lands with a clack, and after looking at it uncomprehendingly for a couple of beats, I finally identify the murky dark rectangle inside. My phone.

"Is that all?" she asks.

"I'm sorry?"

"Your things," she says patiently. "You have everything back?"

"There was a thermos," Cynthia chimes in. I grit my teeth.

"That's okay," I say quickly. "I don't need it back."

Figueroa nods graciously. Cynthia hides the fact that she's fuming. Then they're leaving. That's all. It's over.

Except one thing is missing. It's not in my purse or in the pockets of my coat, and I'm willing to bet it's not in the wrecked remains of my car.

And I have a pretty good guess where it is.

# CHAPTER NINE

*Her twins were Cassie Bianchi's blessings, she said. Occasionally she would bring them to the store with her when she had weekend shifts. "They were great kids," a coworker of Cassie's, who wished to remain anonymous, said in an interview. "Never caused any trouble. And she loved them—everyone could tell. Everyone loved them, especially the boy, Eli. He'd follow us around to see if we needed help with anything, and we'd give him little tasks like gluing on discount stickers, just to keep him busy. And he looked so proud of himself, that he was helping out."*

*The elementary school they were attending during that time didn't report anything out of the ordinary. Eli was well liked, had no trouble making friends.*

*When the twins were ten, Cassie married Sergio
Bianchi, moved into his house, and transferred the
children to a smaller school closer to home.*

*That's when the golden child began to show a dark
side.*

—*Into Ashes: The Shocking Double Murder in the
Suburbs* by Jonathan Lamb, Eclipse Paperbacks,
2004, 1st ed.


### FIFTEEN YEARS EARLIER: BEFORE THE FIRE

Andrea has never ventured into this corner of the school
before. The hallway here is deserted. The only indication
that the school is full of children is the faraway din. But
here, her steps send an echo rolling right up to the tall door
at the end of the hall, her destination. The peeling plaque
next to it reads SCHOOL COUNSELOR. She's never heard of
anyone coming here of their own free will, and she wilts
inside to think of what would happen if any of her class-
mates got wind of it. With every step she takes toward the
door, her rib cage squeezes with fear. Her bladder seems to
shrink three sizes, and she has to stop and press her knees
together, cowardly.

The temptation to make a run for it turns from a nagging
little voice in the back of her mind to an irresistible, magnetic force. *What do you expect the counselor to do, anyway?* it rumbles in her ear. *Even if she does something, then
Leeanne and the others will figure out that you snitched,*

*and then things are only going to get worse. This isn't going to help, Andrea. No one is going to help you.*

The voice sounds suspiciously like her brother. *No one's going to help you. You have to take care of it yourself.*

If only she had any idea how.

The door is open a crack, and if she leans closer, she can see inside. To her surprise, the counselor is not a woman with gold-rimmed glasses and a bun like she imagined. It's a man. He reminds her a bit of Sergio, right down to the knitted sweater and the shirt collar peeking out of it. There's also a whiff of tobacco so subtle she wouldn't have noticed if she wasn't accustomed to it—it's forbidden to smoke on school grounds, and he probably goes outside to light up but the scent follows him back in. It puts her somewhat at ease.

She clenches her sweaty hand into a fist and knocks. She only sees half of him from where she's standing. He glances away from the boxy computer monitor on his desk with mild surprise and tells her to come in.

The office has a lot of books in it. All the walls are book-cases, and there are the colorful spines of schoolbooks, of course, but also others, thick tomes with those reddish-brown leather spines, gold-embossed letters gleaming.

"Is something the matter? . . . " the counselor—a plaque on the desk identifies him as Mr. Ainsworth—asks her. His gaze searches her face. She decides to help him out.

"Andrea," she says. "My name is Andrea Warren."

"Your lunch break is almost over. Class starts soon."

"I can go," she blurts out and turns around, ready to make a beeline for the door.

"No, wait up. If you're here, then you must have a good reason."

Her face turns painfully crimson. He just confirmed her guess: Not many others waltz in here to share their misgivings with him. Especially not that many seventh graders, who are mostly at the age where they've become disillusioned about the adults' abilities to solve their problems.

"I'll write a note for your teacher if needed. Have a seat."

He's sitting in a computer chair that looks ancient but comfortable. For her, there's a little plastic chair, just like the ones in the classrooms. She throws a glance over her shoulder at the door, which is half-open. They never close the door, she knows, because she's heard other girls' whisperings about incidents. Apparently, a few years back, a girl made up a story about a teacher, and there was a scandal. So now all the doors are open.

"So what seems to be the problem, Andrea?" he asks once she's perched on the chair, sitting on her hands because she doesn't know what else to do with them.

Andrea gulps. "There are these girls," she says. He nods encouragingly.

"They're giving you a hard time?"

She forces a terse nod, and her thoughts go to all the bruises past and present, to the ruined sweater. But when she opens her mouth to tell Mr. Ainsworth about it, she closes it with a clack of teeth. There's nothing to tell, because Eli took the sweater and Eli is the one who got in trouble for it. The sight of the crumpled note on top of the trash pops into her head, followed by the search history. A sudden flash of guilt twists her insides. Her problems with Leeanne don't seem so significant anymore.

"Can you tell me what happened?" Ainsworth prompts, pulling her back to the present moment. His kind patience makes her eyes burn. None of the teachers are particularly nice to her, when they notice her at all. Her grades aren't good by any measure but never bad enough to get her undue attention, not at a public school. She peeked at a report card they mailed to her parents last term. It read *Andrea could be an average, perhaps even good, student but she's easily distracted, and I often catch her daydreaming in class and spacing out when she's called on.* For her, average would forever be the only thing to aspire to.

She looks him in the eye, gulps, and instantly knows she won't tell him about Leeanne. Something tells her he already knows anyway. A lot of them know. They won't do anything about Leeanne because her parents donate to the school, and with government funding getting tighter and tighter every year (if her parents' conversations are to be believed), they can't afford to get on their bad side. Leeanne never listens in class, but they always pad her test scores.

Andrea's decision is split-second.

"It's not the girls," she says, breathless with her own courage. "It's something else. What are you supposed to do if you think a friend is being abused at home?"

She barely wraps her tongue around the last words. She never imagined she'd ever have to utter such a thing out loud. These things only happen in those melodramatic, preachy books from the library.

The shift in Mr. Ainsworth is instant and, she suspects, irreversible. The warmth is gone, replaced with laser focus. And she's in the crosshairs.

"Abused? What makes you think that?"

There's nothing she can say that won't give away who it is: either her or Eli, because she doesn't have any friends she's that close to. Not close enough to share that sort of thing with her.

"Did they confide in you?" he asks carefully.

Stricken mute by regret and wishing she could go back, she can only shake her head.

He sighs and rubs his chin, another gesture that makes her think of her stepfather.

"Andrea," he says in a carefully measured voice. Dread creeps into her chest when she realizes he thinks it's her—and the whole "friend" thing is just the oldest tactic in the book. "Can you wait here for a minute? Don't go anywhere, okay?"

It's the last thing she wants to do. But in that moment, an idea glimmers dimly in her mind. "Okay," she says.

He exits the office, not in a hurry but without wasting time either. She's alone now, and it's her chance to slip out unseen. She hops off the plastic chair and is about to dart for the door but something stops her, a strange, voyeuristic impulse. Instead of going in the opposite direction, she takes a step closer to the desk and peers across it. On the computer monitor, she catches a glimpse of a game of solitaire right before the screen saver kicks in, the school logo crawling across the screen. There's also a ledger of some kind and a pretty bowl of tinted cut glass like amber, the kind you keep candy in. She peers into it, and indeed, there are a few hard candies, looking old, their once silver-and-gold wrappers scuffed. She cringes. There are also keys, paper clips, erasers, and other odds and ends she has no use for, but one thing that glints beneath it all catches her eye.

A glance at the door—no one is coming yet—and she reaches into the bowl, her heart thundering with excitement. She grabs it, sticks it in her pocket, and leaves the office as quickly as she can.

# CHAPTER TEN

"I'm going home, Cynthia," I say, feeling like I'm once again on the cusp of thirteen, bewildered by my new family and their house and the regulated existence I'm forced to endure, like zoo animals, eating and sleeping at designated times and constantly, constantly watched. Except instead of a charity case meant to bring her husband votes, I'm now the source of her disgrace. I don't know why she would object to my leaving.

"Out of the question," she says. The moment the door closed after the detectives, her demeanor did a one-eighty. The shaky voice, damp eyes, knitting brows all vanished without a trace, and Cynthia as I know her was back, the same Cynthia I saw at the hospital—no-nonsense, fully in damage-control mode. And damage control doesn't allow for excessive emotions. Unless the right people are there to witness them, of course. "If there are journalists here, can you imagine the swarm that's already waiting for you at your door?"

So this is what it's all about. Not my well-being. Or my safety.

"And I need to buy a new phone," I say. Mine, predictably, is no longer working. Figueroa only told me she found it in my car, under the passenger seat. I could have sworn I looked for it there, but then again, I was out of it, and blood was pouring into my eyes. I told her and Childs as much. There are cracks on the screen, but I've seen phones in much worse shape still working as good as new. Did she do something to it? I have no illusions about that. If she gave it back, it means there was nothing more she could extract from it.

"I'll get you one," Milt volunteers. There goes my excuse to leave the house.

"You'll stay in your old room," Cynthia says, pretending he hadn't spoken.

I don't have any of my things here, not even a change of clothes.

"Until at least the end of the week."

She's got to be joking.

"It's not necessary, Mrs. Boudreaux." I hate how he always calls my adoptive mother that. You'd think we were fourteen and he's come to take me out on a date that lasts past curfew. "She doesn't have anything to tell them, and they know it. They'll leave her alone eventually."

"Yeah. I'll believe that when I see it," she says.

"This is ridiculous," I mutter, which makes my adoptive mother glower at me.

"Andrea." Milt takes my arm, carefully, like I might turn on him and bite him. "Come on. Let's go upstairs and talk."

He leads me without leading me—I could pull my arm away at any moment but instead I follow him without arguing, feeling Cynthia's heavy glare on my back the whole time.

Upstairs, he closes the door of my old bedroom. I plunk down on my bed like a petulant teenager.

"Andrea," Milt starts, "are you okay?"

"That's a broad question, all things considered." I only manage half a smirk.

"You know what I mean."

"No, I really don't," I say, crossing my arms on my chest. "Why did you play along with Cynthia? Why did you let them all hide it from me? You should have just told me. Immediately."

Every time I look at him, I still can't believe he was ever mine, even for a relatively short time. Even though it all went to hell and it was all my fault. I throw a glance at the shut door and catch myself subconsciously licking my lips. In spite of everything, all I want right now is to jump on him, devour his lips with mine, sink my fingers into that wheat-colored hair, like I used to do when we were together, when I was determined to get my fill of him before he moved on. I was sure that any day now he'd find someone else, someone who's a better fit, someone gorgeous and rich and unburdened by an infamous last name. And then this hypothetical someone would take him away from me and the rightful order of things would be restored.

But there was no leggy blond undergrad or smoldering lingerie model or pampered heiress—in the end, it was me who put a definitive end to it by pawning that family-heirloom rock he gave me at a shitty pawnshop in downtown Denver.

"What I mean is, are you going to be okay? Can I let you go home by yourself? Or are you going to—"

Pour wine on my cereal and sprinkle it with cocaine, he means.

"I'm fine," I snarl. "I just got my two-month chip."

"You have to keep going to your meetings," he says. He lowers himself to my level—for him it means kneeling on the floor next to my bed. He puts his hands on my upper arms, and I dip my chin, scorched by the caring and concern in his eyes.

"Yeah." I chuckle bitterly. "I'm sure those paparazzi will just love that."

"Have Chris come pick you up."

Chris is my sponsor, who I doubt will want to land in the center of media (not to mention police) attention right now, or ever, on my account. So I tell Milton that.

"Then I'll drive you. If that's what it takes."

In this moment, it really hits me. He thinks—he actually believes—that we will be getting back together at some point. My heart crumbles inward on itself like an eggshell being crushed. Just yesterday, a mere twenty-four hours ago, this would have been all I wanted. Maybe it would have been difficult, after everything, but I would have made it work. But now it's impossible. Everything I've built over the last fifteen years—as tenuous and shaky as it may have been—is about to come tumbling down, and again, I have my brother to thank.

I hastily gulp back the tears that have cropped up, but it's too late; they spill out, their wet tracks tracing the half-moon circles under my eyes. Milt reaches for my face in a clumsily tender gesture, with the intention of wiping them away, probably, but I turn my head at the last second.

"Milton, you need to leave."

He blinks, not yet comprehending.

"Now," I say, raising my voice. "I want you to go home."

"Why?"

"It doesn't matter why. Just leave, okay? Get out."

He looks hurt, confused. "No."

"No? Just who do you think you are?" I snap.

"Your fiancé." He holds my furious gaze in his, and it's almost too much. But I have to make him leave, for his own sake.

"Ex-fiancé. We're broken up, remember? Because I'm an alcoholic, addict, and thief." I spit every word at him, watching him flinch a little more with each one. "And you have nothing to do here. So go."

Any normal man would lose his temper by now, snap back at me, maybe even yell. Or slam his fist into the wall as close as possible to my head without actually grazing my hair, raising a small cloud of paint dust and making a dent in the drywall. Like my exes from a life before Milt would have done. I would have accepted it as normal, even as proof of love. But this is Milt, and instead of punching walls or yelling, he just shakes his head. "I only wanted to be there for you."

"Well, I don't need anyone to be there for me."

For a moment, just a moment, he looks like he might lose it and say something I most definitely deserve to hear. But he holds back. The look in his eyes is sadness.

"When you change your mind, you know where to find me," is all he says. He turns to leave, almost needing to duck when he passes through the low doorframe of my old room. I can't help it; I get up from the bed and follow him, hovering in the doorway as he descends the stairs. I hear him say a muffled goodbye to Cynthia and Jim, who sounds nonplussed. The front door closes and locks behind him, and still I stand there like an idiot, barely holding back tears.

I'm not the one who should be crying, I know. How could I ever have seriously thought I could have a normal life? How could I ever have—

"Wow, now that's what I call a scene. Addie, I nearly squeezed out a tear. What a performance."

The voice is a shock, like a handful of ice thrown down the back of my collar by a playground bully. I spin around so fast I nearly lose my footing, and still, I can hardly believe my eyes when I see my stepsister standing there at the end of the hall. How long has she been there? What has she seen and heard?

"What the fuck are you doing here?" I ask, furious at the hoarseness of tears in my voice. Cynthia hadn't said anything about my stepsister being here. Or maybe she had. I was so medicated and lost in my own thoughts that I could have easily forgotten.

And it makes no sense. There's no reason for her to

be here. She should be at her own fucking McMansion with her dentist husband. Sipping rosé with other suburban wives with too much time on their hands.

"I, unlike you, have a right to be here," she says. The longer I look at her, the more I notice things that are out of place. Her mascara is smudged, and there's a half inch of roots lurking underneath her tasteful caramel-blond dye job. She's had to fake it since she was fourteen or fifteen and her natural cherubic-white hair turned a more ordinary ash-blond. And she's wearing pink sweatpants. My steppie, wearing fleece that dates from 2004 and probably has something spelled in rhinestones across the ass. Her chipped toenails peek out from under the pants' worn hems. The queen of sky-high heels is wearing flip-flops.

I take a step toward her, and instinctively she recoils, her back against the door of her old room with her name spelled out on a baby-pink plaque in black princess cursive, a crown over the middle *a*.

After all these years, I still can't stand the sight of her.

# CHAPTER ELEVEN

*Eli Warren got away with what he'd done to his mother and stepfather. It sounds a little extreme, considering he will spend the next twelve years locked up—six in a juvenile psychiatric facility and six in adult prison. But when you consider the facts of the case, as I present them here, it becomes chilling to think that in a little over a decade, Eli Warren, then only twenty-four years old, will be walking the streets again. How much more damage will he do? Whose lives will he destroy? We have no way of knowing. But I can tell you, from my vast experience working with sociopaths, child and adult alike, when it happens again, it will be even more brutal.*

*—Into Ashes: The Shocking Double Murder in the Suburbs* by Jonathan Lamb, Eclipse Paperbacks, 2004, 1st ed.

### *FIFTEEN YEARS EARLIER: AFTER THE FIRE*

Andrea has lost track of the days she has spent here, and the burn ward smell that clings to the bedsheets has seeped into her pores until she's stopped noticing it. She slips from mind-dulling pain into fogginess whenever the nurse adds some painkiller to her IV. The bandages that cover her upper chest and back need to be changed daily, and another, older nurse comes in to do that.

Today, she stays a little longer, brushing Andrea's hair with a little comb and even helping her wash her face. While she tears the comb through Andrea's matted hair, she keeps chattering on and on about how beautiful it is, how lucky she is. Andrea doesn't protest, even though something in the woman's pleasant alto voice is strained today, unnatural. It's what you say to ugly girls, that they have great hair. That's what you say to girls who will never wear a low-cut prom dress or even a T-shirt without being stared at in the wrong way. Deep down, without even fully understanding it yet, she feels like she lost something she barely knew she had.

She can see it plainly on the other nurse's face, the younger one who doesn't hide her thoughts as well. When Andrea asked her about Eli, the woman stopped cold midway through changing the IV bag and the look in her eyes struck Andrea speechless. A moment later, she averted her eyes and pretended she hadn't heard.

Because everyone knows it now. When the older nurse

wheels her out into the yard, other patients stare and whisper—Andrea would like to believe it's just her imagination, but she knows it's not. She's now known as the girl whose brother killed her family and disfigured her for life.

And all the while, when the older nurse changes the bandages, when the pediatrician comes in and asks her how she's feeling, when the younger nurse brings her food even as her gaze avoids Andrea as if the blistering third-degree burns were contagious, something is brewing in the back of Andrea's mind. Something not quite strong enough to break through the surface but growing stronger every minute she spends in this place. Something like a silent scream that started sometime when she saw the flames race across the carpeting in the hall and hasn't died since.

The nurse, Belinda or Melinda or something like that, is plaiting her hair deftly, somehow managing not to pull or snag so much as a strand, and Andrea begins to understand. A sense of foreboding fills her long before the woman finally ties the end of the braid with an elastic band and says, with artlessly feigned casualness, "You have a special guest today."

The police again? Andrea wonders. Did she say something wrong? Or maybe it's the social worker, a young woman with bleached dreads and a tiny blue gem in her right nostril who came in to "evaluate" her—despite the sound of it, it came down to a few easy questions Andrea answered without hesitating.

She feels like she should ask who it is but she doesn't have time. They are all there at once: the social worker, in a stuffy skirt suit that clashes with the rest of her, one of her doctors, a tall woman with curly hair, the other nurse, who's wearing lipstick for the occasion. As soon as Andrea sees who's following her, her guts twist. It's not just one or two but a whole crew, with one of those giant fuzzy microphones and a massive camera, black and gleaming menacingly with its little red lights and lenses that look like gasoline spilled in a puddle. Another man, oblivious to Andrea and everyone around him, tests the flash of his Nikon. Another woman holds aloft an audio recorder. Andrea sees logos that are faintly familiar, local stations, a local paper.

But then some kind of commotion starts at the door, and they all part, as if on cue, cameras and lights and microphones all turned to the doorway like they're expecting the president. But instead, a familiar-looking man walks in, wearing a suit and tie, followed by a woman in a burgundy twinset, giant gold earrings gleaming beneath her bob hairdo. The woman, too, looks familiar, so familiar that Andrea forgets to breathe. The social worker steps forward. She looks uncomfortable, self-conscious, and stiff.

"Andrea," she says in a convivial tone Andrea hasn't heard her use before, "I'd like to introduce you to your new family."

Flashes go off, and all the cameras and devices swivel to her at once, their shiny black eyes devouring her.

But Andrea is looking past them, past the social worker, past the man and the woman who leans forward with an expectant smile. She's looking at the third person, the sullen girl standing behind them. She's wearing a navy dress with a Peter Pan collar, and it's so out of character that Andrea almost doesn't recognize her at first. The girl glowers at Andrea from behind the short curtain of angel-blond hair that barely reaches her chin.

That's when she knows she's been cheated. Like in one of those stories where the genie grants your wish word for word, but it isn't quite what you had in mind.

And in that moment, the scream that's been gathering in the back of Andrea's throat like a storm finally tears its way to the surface and breaks free.

# CHAPTER TWELVE

Leeanne regains her composure, the smirk returning as she plays with the ends of her hair.

"So," she says, "he cracked. Again."

"Shut the fuck up," I say under my breath.

"Or what? You're going to make me?" She smiles sweetly. It looks like she's let her lip injections lapse. Her whole face has a droopy, unhealthy look to it in spite of the uniform fake tan she's been applying since her teens. "The psycho sister of the psycho brother. That'll make a nice interview. I should go talk to some of those guys outside."

I advance toward her, fists clenches at my sides. Panic flits across her face, but she doesn't have time to react. I slam my palms down on the door, trapping her between my arms, and she lets out a shriek. Steps thunder behind me, and I turn around to see Cynthia racing toward us, barefoot, her shoes in her hand. "Stop it right now!" she bellows. I let my arms drop to my sides as Leeanne cowers by the door, hands covering her face.

"Why is she here?" I snarl. "Did you bring her on purpose? To gloat?"

"Fucking psycho," Leeanne murmurs behind me.

"Language," Cynthia snaps on autopilot, but there's no real energy behind it. "Jesus, Andrea. She's not here to gloat. Did you think that—"

"Then why doesn't she just go back to her mansion? She just wanted in on the action, is that it?"

"Fuck you, Andrea," Leeanne says, her voice tired. She slinks away from the door, past me, to stand near her mother, her arms crossed and her hands tucked under her armpits—the same pose she always took when she'd done something bad she was trying to hide. Her hair falls into her eyes, and she huffs. "I'm not here to gloat. Only you could think that, because you think everything revolves around you. If anything, you should be gloating."

"Leeanne," Cynthia whispers angrily. I look from one to the other, trying to puzzle out what's going on.

"Charles and I are separating," Leeanne says with a grimace. "I'm here to stay until we work out what to do with the house. And since the market for luxury housing isn't exactly booming in this economy, it could be a while."

My breath whooshes out of my lungs, and I slump like a deflated balloon. "Shit. I'm sorry."

"Like hell you are," Leeanne says with a shrug. "So for the time being, you'll have to put up with me. And if I were you, I'd take it down a notch, because I'm sure those vultures outside will be very interested in what I have to tell them. Not to mention that woman. What did she say her name was? Figueroa?"

Cynthia starts to say something, but I'm no longer listening. I storm past her, through the half-open door of my old room, letting the door bang against the wall as I push it aside. I grab my purse from the bed where it's sitting, sling it over my shoulder, and thunder down the stairs. Leeanne's mocking laugh reaches me from the second floor, followed closely by Cynthia calling my name imploringly. When I glance over my shoulder, she's coming down the stairs, shoes still clutched in her hand.

"Wait!" she calls out, an ugly, screechy edge to her voice. "What are you doing?"

"Going home," I say, to myself as much as to her. I look around: The key to her car hangs neatly from the hook by the front door. I grab it as I shove my feet into my sneakers. When she sees what I'm doing, she yells at me to stop, but she's too late—I'm already opening the front door.

I thought I was ready for the flashes exploding in my face, for the swarm of shouting people. Still, it takes the breath out of me in a way I didn't expect—memories come flooding back. Memories of another time, of the first time Eli ruined my life.

"This way, Andrea!" someone yells, and I instinctively look. He's a tall, scrawny guy, and all I can see of him is the man bun atop his head since his face is hidden behind a camera that snaps and snaps and snaps.

"Andrea! Did you see your brother? Did he call you? Did he come to your home?"

And in the meantime, the hipster keeps snapping away.

Well, they're about to find out I'm not a twelve-year-old girl anymore.

I raise my arm and slap the camera out of his hands. He didn't expect it, and the heavy thing draws a wide arc as it swings on the strap around his wrist. The strap slips. He tries to catch it and fails. Crash. Broken glass and plastic. Cursing, he dives to retrieve what's left of the camera while I look at the others, who have fallen into a kind of stupor I know won't last.

"No comment," I say, pressing the button on the fob. Cynthia's SUV beeps, and I climb into the driver's seat. I can only hope my license isn't suspended, although there's no reason it should be. I haven't done anything wrong, and as far as I know, I'm not suspected of DUI.

I turn the key in the ignition and then pull out of the driveway and onto the street. The SUV is the kind of heavy, clunky gas-guzzler only someone like Cynthia would drive but right now it works in my favor. None of them dare throw themselves in front of the vehicle and try to play chicken.

Still, I zigzag around familiar streets of the neighborhood for ten or fifteen minutes until my hands are no longer shaking and I feel confident that no one is tailing me. Only then do I direct the car to the highway.

I'm going back to the town house. To the only place I can still call home.

\*     \*     \*

To my surprise, when I pull into my driveway, I don't see any journalists lying in wait. At least as far as I can tell. It could be that they decided I wasn't interesting enough or realized I had nothing new to tell them. Or it could mean something else has happened to draw them away. Some new lead or new development. I try not to think about it too much.

The town house is the last in a row of four, the corner unit that cost fifty grand more than one sandwiched between two identical ones—all for a couple of windows and a couple of hours of natural light daily, since that side faces north. But to Milt, the price difference wasn't an issue. The whole street is like that, identical blocks of four identical houses, in that modern cube-like shape, burnt-orange brick and black trim and shiny thermal windows for Denver winters. A garage and a patio in the back. The embodiment of middle class, whatever that means anymore.

I normally never use the garage, parking instead in the vast driveway that fits my prehistoric car and Milton's Prius just fine. But today I go the extra mile—key in the combination, climb back behind the wheel as the garage door slides up, and then pull in next to the boxes of books I never unpacked and Milton's old road bike hanging on the wall.

But if I'd been hoping I'd feel safer or more comfortable here, among all the things we picked out and arranged ourselves, I was wrong. The house is Milt's, and he bought the lion's share of all the furniture—since, of course, all I could afford on my own, with my social worker salary, was Ikea. Once again, I find myself feeling like the charity case, slack-jawed with awe at someone else's house where I'm now supposed to live.

He never reproached me for any of that. He even gave me the room with the biggest window to use as my office, which I rarely used—whenever I had work to finish at home, I'd just huddle on the living room couch next to him, my Mac balanced on my lap.

Ever since he moved out, I've fallen behind on cleaning. On my way to the coffee machine, I step over a clear bag of recycling I never took to the curb. I take a look at the counter and groan. Coffee cups sit haphazardly all over the place, their varying levels of cold coffee leaving rings on the ceramic. I push them to the side and start the espresso machine, which whirs to life at the push of a button. I can instantly smell the coffee beans being ground up somewhere deep in its chrome core, and it covers the stale smell of the dishes and discarded takeout containers.

While I wait for the coffee, I run upstairs and get the phone charger from where I usually leave it plugged in, next to the bed. I come back down and plug the phone into the socket by the kitchen counter, thumb the power button, and hold my breath. My relief hardly bears description when the empty-battery icon appears. So the phone's not dead—just the battery.

While the phone charges, I busy myself emptying the coffee cups and washing one of the mugs for myself. My head throbs. A Tylenol would be nice. Sadly, in the medicine cabinet in the downstairs bathroom, I'm greeted by a row of empty bottles I never got around to throwing out. I rattle them one after another, but all I have are expired allergy pills and a blister pack of sore-throat candies. I gather up the empties and toss them in the trash. Through the hollow clatter, I hear something, and my head snaps up, a jolt of panic racing up my spine.

My phone. It's ringing.

I race back to the kitchen where the phone skitters across the counter as it buzzes and rings. Milt has a special tone, so does Cynthia. It's neither of them. I trip over the recycling bag, curse, narrowly avoid clipping my forehead on the counter, and recover myself just in time for the phone to go silent again. I reach it in a final bound and pick it up—one missed call, unknown number. No voicemail—yet.

My skin prickles. The curtains are closed, and the only source of light in the entire open-concept space is the large spherical lamp over the kitchen counter, its orange glow soft and diffuse.

Figueroa's words come back to me, and their full weight hits me. He followed me. He knows where I work and probably knows where I live.

My phone buzzes and elicits a piercing chime that makes me jump.

You have one new voicemail.

# CHAPTER THIRTEEN

*The trial had drawn national attention and was extensively covered by news outlets. What's more, the case was among the first to become viral on social media. Speculation ran rampant on message boards and blogging platforms such as Blogger and LiveJournal, where several blogs devoted to Eli Warren sprang up overnight.*

*The fascinating and conflicting details of this case also captivated the attention of the masses, beyond the run-of-the-mill conspiracy theorists and true-crime junkies. And it's hardly surprising. Like Columbine and other similar tragedies, it falls frighteningly within the realm of the possible.*

*How well do you know your own child? Could a charming demeanor and good-looking exterior be hiding something sinister? If this precious boy, the*

*beautiful son, the golden child, could turn out to be a*
*monster . . . who can be trusted?*
           *—Into Ashes: The Shocking Double Murder in the*
           *Suburbs* by Jonathan Lamb, Eclipse Paperbacks,
                                            2004, 1st ed.

*FIFTEEN YEARS EARLIER: BEFORE THE FIRE*

Ever since she ran from the counselor's office, Andrea's been waiting for something vague and nefarious to happen, for someone to come drag her right out of class or for someone to show up knocking at the door on Sunday night when she's eating dinner with Eli, their mom, and Sergio. But it's been two weeks and nothing has happened. No one has come to see her.

And as for the bauble she grabbed from the bowl on the counselor's desk, either he didn't notice or he never knew it was her. Andrea knows she should hide it someplace safe—maybe their hiding place, the one that Mom and Sergio don't know about. There's a loose tile in the bathroom, right by the cabinet below the sink. That's where they hide things no one else is supposed to see.

She found out the little bauble was a lighter by accident. It's made so that the little hinges of the lid are hidden, and she only noticed that the lid could be opened when the edge of her fingernail caught underneath. She pried it apart, and the lid popped open, revealing the little wheel and button. She clicked it, and a smooth, neat flame shot out with a hiss. She marveled at it for a few seconds before shutting the lid again, pressing down extra hard to make sure it closed properly. She could have the lighter with her at all times, at school, at dinner, out on the playground, and no one would ever see anything but a cute keychain or pendant. It could be her secret, finally something she had only to herself.

She can't stand the thought of someone taking it away.

She knows she should wait until she's alone, until her mom is at the other end of the house so she can't overhear the clattering of the tiles by accident. But she's impatient. The lighter is heavy in her pocket, tugging it down like it's made of lead.

So while her mom makes dinner, Andrea sneaks off to the bathroom, locking the door behind her. Just to be on the safe side, she turns on the tap, both the hot water and the cold, on full blast. Still, she keeps checking the door, looking over her shoulder as she eases the tile out and reaches into the hiding place beneath.

Confusion paralyzes her. She slowly pulls her hand out and puts the lighter back in her pocket. Then she reaches back in, palm empty this time, grasping, fingertips feeling around the edges of something smooth and angular and finally—sharp. With a gasp, she pulls out her hand and examines the paper cut on the knuckle of her index finger. As microscopic droplets of blood form along the edges, she peers into the hiding place and the realization hits her: There's money in there. Not just a few dollar bills, crumpled and used up and soft as suede. A handful of crisp, new twenties, their edges so sharp they'd sliced her skin open like a razor blade.

She inspects them with a kind of reverent awe just as her mother knocks on the door.

"Addie? Are you all right in there? Dinner's ready."

"Coming!" she yells out, but her voice comes out wrong, so wrong, brimming with falseness. She's a bad liar, always has been, not at all like her brother, who could make anyone believe anything.

"Is everything okay?" her mother asks through the door. And then the unthinkable happens. The doorknob rattles as she turns it, and the latch comes loose. The door opens, startling them both.

She only sees her mother's eyes, round like coins, dark, and her firmly set lips.

"Andrea," she says, tilting her head in that way she does when you're about to be in trouble.

Andrea's face scrunches up in spite of herself. And everything unravels.

# CHAPTER FOURTEEN

I can't grab for the phone fast enough, my heart hammering in the back of my throat. My hands become so damp that the touch screen won't work, and I have to wipe the screen on my shirt before I can unlock the phone. I press it to my ear.

You have one new message, the recorded voice informs me with canned warmth. The message clicks on without being prompted, some static, some noise, and then a sharp intake of breath.

"Hey," says a young female voice, and my knees buckle with sheer relief. "Ms. Boudreaux...I mean, Andrea." I finally exhale and close my eyes. Sunny. If the girl were here, I'd hug her. "I'm sorry to bug you, but you said to call if things got bad."

I said to call 911, not my personal cell. But she did have the number. I know it's because she doesn't want to get the authorities involved. And that, in turn, is because she's on the run, for the umpteenth time, from the umpteenth foster home, and her next brush with the system might involve juvenile detention. Not trusting the police isn't exactly uncommon among the people I work with—and our shelter is supposed to be a safe zone.

"Well, I think Shawn found me again. I saw one of his...one of his girls, and I know she saw me, and now she's going to tell him where I am. I'm in the bathroom in a McDonald's by the highway, and I don't know where to—"

I don't have time to finish listening to her rambling, shaky-voiced message when the phone beeps, announcing that I have another call. Sure enough, it's the same unknown number. I curse under my breath, and for a moment, I consider just waiting it out. Maybe even turning off the phone. But what conscience I have left squeezes my rib cage like a vise, and, already cursing myself out for my own stupidity, I answer.

She sounds like she's crying, and I grimace, glad she can't see me through the phone. At the same time, my mind is racing, working out connections, untangling the threads. I see an opportunity, and as heartless as it makes me, I can't let it go so easily.

"Ms. Boudreaux," she says in a loud, hoarse whisper, forgetting to call me Andrea again. Then again, she's sixteen, give or take a couple of years, and to her, I might as well be a dinosaur at twenty-seven.

"Sunny," I say. We require ID at the shelter, and if hers is fake, it's a really good one. That, or her parents were hippies, although judging by her age, it's the wrong generation. "What's going on? Where are you?"

Whimpering, she tells me she's still at the McDonald's but she can't stay much longer, and Shawn might already be waiting for her outside.

I debate calling 911 myself and letting Sunny Jones, if that is her real name, become someone else's problem. The thought only lingers for half a second.

I sigh and grit my teeth. "Okay," I say. "I'll come get you."

She bursts into expressions of gratitude amid sniffles and sobs. I hang up and get the key to Cynthia's car, trying not to think of what will happen if any journalists decide to follow me.

In the garage, it's so much colder than in the house that I huddle in my light jacket as I make a beeline for the car. The street looks empty, no journalists—or anyone else. I pull out of the driveway while cranking up the heater to full capacity; the fans roar as hot air whirs through the car. But the cold seems to penetrate to my core, and it lies in wait there, curled up around my heart.

Pretty soon the sleepy residential streets give way to a well-lit commercial artery where life bustles on, in spite of the chill. The postapocalyptic hideousness of Denver in the early spring has been patched up and decorated with pretty streetlamps, garlands, and brightly lit store and restaurant windows. There are even a few hipster types lining up in front of some trendy eatery, hands shoved into pockets and feet stomping to work up heat. To wait in line in front of a place when the street is teeming with half-empty restaurants to suit any taste—I'll never understand it. When I was a kid, a fancy meal was Red Lobster.

Sweat breaks out along my spine when it occurs to me.

Hesitant, I reach for the knob of the radio but pull my hand away. I hit an infuriating string of one red light after another, and it feels like an eternity until I'm finally out on the highway, without all these traffic signs and cars and people to pay attention to. Alone with my thoughts.

Taking a deep breath, I finally turn on the radio, searching until I find a newscast. But they're blabbing on about something unrelated, and after a couple of minutes, I zone out.

I struggle to remember what date it is, until I glance at the dashboard. Cynthia always keeps her car clock up to date. April 10.

In two weeks' time, to the day, my brother set fire to our house. I always made a conscious effort not to mark the date in any way. At first, Cynthia insisted that we honor my mother's memory, and she'd make us all go to visit her grave. I don't know who paid for the tombstone—maybe Cynthia's husband did, like he paid for my hospital bills and my laser treatments. Somebody always pays for everything, as he used to say.

What's left of Cassandra Warren Bianchi is in a discreet grave tucked into the corner of a cemetery on the outskirts of town. A flat tombstone reads *Cassandra Bianchi*, with her birth and death dates underneath. When we'd come to visit her, I'd stand over it, clutching an overwrought bouquet of roses in my hands while Cynthia led a "minute of silent prayer." Although nobody was actually praying, I'm sure. The very first year, a couple of photographers came with us to shoot pictures for an upcoming short piece in a local paper. My burns itched beneath the black wool dress Cynthia made me wear, which covered me from neck to midcalf. I squeezed the roses' prickly stems through the crinkly plastic and wondered where they buried Sergio.

Maybe his family took care of it. Or maybe there wasn't enough left to bury.

Then I left Cynthia's house, and that put an end to the visits. The day Eli murdered my life became just another day in late April.

"...announced a press conference later tonight about the ongoing manhunt for Eli Michael Warren, wanted for the gruesome murder of a young woman in northeast Denver that occurred sometime last night. Authorities continue to warn the public to be careful and not engage with the suspect, who is considered highly dangerous and possibly armed. Warren first came to notoriety in 2002 when he was convicted of arson and the first-degree murder of—"

I can't listen for another second. I thumb the button and flip through one station after another—commercial, classical, hip-hop, techno. The upbeat new hit of the latest pop wonder of the week fills the car with its generic electronic beats, her auto-tuned voice caterwauling in the speakers. It's as catchy as it is forgettable, and for a moment or two, it succeeds at knocking all the thoughts out of my head. I crank up the volume and turn onto the exit ramp, toward the cluster of fast-food restaurants around the gas station.

This particular spot is well-known in my line of work. The neighborhood is a small tangle of crooked streets, locked in from all sides by the multilane highway, which makes it unappealing for condo builders and other attempts at gentrification. It remains a mix of boxlike houses from the 1920s and square, squat apartment blocks from which satellite dishes spring up like mushrooms, where you can rent a roach-infested one- or two-bedroom for a couple hundred dollars cheaper than anywhere else. If you don't mind the incessant roaring of cars right outside your window or constantly inhaling pollution. Or if you don't have anywhere else to go.

I avoid looking at the buildings looming to my right as I pull up to the McDonald's. Never mind that I told Sunny to avoid the area where Shawn, her former boyfriend/pimp, runs his business. I didn't think she'd listen to me anyway. Where else can she go in a cold, unwelcoming city, except the one place she knows—the place she calls home, as close to a home as she's ever had?

Inside the McDonald's, I make a beeline for the bathrooms. Sunny is sitting near the sink, feet in ridiculous high-heeled fur boots, and she's tapping happily away at her phone like she forgot she called me at all and that her life is supposedly in danger.

She looks up, and the goofy grin slides from her face. "Hi, Ms. Boudreaux," she chirps, forgetting—again—to call me Andrea. Sunny refuses to see the shelter's visiting psychiatrist so I can only guess at the nature of the disorder that makes Sunny act the way she does. Maybe it's just aftereffects of extreme neglect. But her particular combination of childlike naïveté and fearlessness, bordering on stupidity, never fails to attract the wrong sort of people.

"Come on," I say.

"Is he out there?"

*He* being Shawn, presumably. "No. I didn't see him. Even if he is, you're with me." Truth is, I'm not so sure I can be much help against the six-foot-four Shawn with the scalp tattoo, but it seems to reassure her.

We go to the car, Sunny sauntering behind me. She oohs and aahs when she sees Cynthia's Cadillac—only someone like Sunny can be impressed by this mastodon. She appreciatively bounces on the soft leather seat.

"I'll drive you to the shelter," I say, to bring her back to earth.

She stops bouncing as if on command. "No." She gives a vigorous shake of her head, her ratty ponytail whipping her face.

"What do you mean 'no'?" She's already gotten thrown out once for smuggling in a bottle of bourbon, which is against our rules. But she's been behaving since.

"Another one of his girls told him I go there. So I can't stay there anymore."

"You have nothing to worry about. We'll never let him in."

"But he'll be waiting for me outside." Her face, still pretty and somehow managing to retain its childlike charm, crumples in an instant. Her eyes become shiny, her eyelids red and puffy, forehead creased. "I can't go. He can't find me again, okay? He'll beat my face in."

Genuine tears stream down her cheeks. In the years I've worked at the shelter, I've seen so many Sunnys I've lost count; there are only so many ways this story can end. I picture this baby-faced girl, whose rough living hasn't caught up with her looks or health yet. Picture her dead of an overdose in some crummy motel, left to convulse and choke on her vomit by some john only interested in saving his ass from a criminal charge. Picture her bleeding out in an alley after a Shawn or someone similar hits her too hard too many times. Picture her turned away at even the last, rock-bottom shelter because she's high, drunk, strung out—left to go back into the icy night, straight to her death.

There's a reason I went into social work. I wasn't going to go to college at all—would have dropped out of school had Cynthia let me. But since I had to do something, I figured I might as well try to make a difference. To atone for my brother. For what I saw and hadn't seen happening before my very eyes, for months or years.

"Okay." *This is a bad idea*, my rational mind screams at me. *A terrible idea.* I squeeze my temples. "We're going to my place. And tomorrow I'll find you another shelter. Out of town. I'll call, make arrangements, get you a bus ticket."

She looks doubtful but hides it with an eager smile. And I understand, in the back of my mind, that it will be a waste of time and money. That she'll be back on the Denver streets within the week, make up with Shawn, and resume her march toward the end.

So be it, then. If I can delay it for a week only, that's what I'll do.

As I drive, she settles in, relaxing into her seat. She cranes her neck to look out the window and, disappointed, starts to play with the radio stations. Before I can tell her to knock it off, she lands on the news station.

"...have established the identity of the victim in the shocking northeast Denver murder. A press conference is scheduled for later tonight. Stay tuned."

# CHAPTER FIFTEEN

*The details of that night remain uncertain. The facts known to the investigation are that, around midnight on April 24, Warren doused the floor in the upstairs hallway with nail polish remover he had taken from the bathroom cabinet. Then he set it on fire—with a lighter that could never be found, despite a most thorough search of the scene.*

*Eli's sister, Andrea, later told the police that Eli Warren repeatedly said he wanted their parents, especially their stepfather, Sergio, to die. I want them to burn, she quoted him saying. When she woke up and smelled the smoke, she noted that Eli wasn't in his bed in the room they shared, down the hall from their parents. Nor did she see him when, panicked, she rushed to wake her mother and stepfather to get them out of the house.*

*By then, the police already had their suspicions.*

*Traces of the accelerant were found on the remains of the floor upstairs, and forensic experts excluded the possibility of an electrical fire or any other malfunction.*

*Perhaps this had been a petty act of destruction, not uncommon in children with behavioral problems. But this particular tantrum turned out to be a perfect storm. The smoke alarms in the house hadn't been maintained since the house was originally built in 1976 and were not functional. The windows of the master bedroom had been sealed for winter and didn't open properly. The Bianchis succumbed to smoke inhalation fairly quickly.*

*Seeing how far the situation had spun out of his control, Eli Warren had to cover his tracks. The prosecution suggested he had gotten rid of the lighter before going back to the house for his sister. What can that tell us about Eli Warren's intentions? He had planned to get away with it. Until he was cornered, with his sister's testimony and evidence mounting against him, he believed he would get away with murdering his parents.*

*One thing is certain: This was the work of a clear, methodical, and thoroughly sociopathic mind.*

*—Into Ashes: The Shocking Double Murder in the Suburbs* by Jonathan Lamb, Eclipse Paperbacks, 2004, 1st ed.

*FIFTEEN YEARS EARLIER: BEFORE THE FIRE*

Her rumbling stomach takes her by surprise as she creeps upstairs to her room. In all the commotion, everyone forgot that she hadn't had dinner. Forgot about her altogether. Hell, she forgot about it herself. As if she temporarily ceased to exist, melting into the wallpaper.

Their mother and Sergio aren't home. They left less than an hour ago. Andrea didn't dare ask where they were going. Their faces were grim, and she thought she was better off staying out of their way. They didn't say when they were coming back, and they dressed like they would for a meeting with the principal or something equally ominous—her mother in a skirt and twinset, Sergio in dress trousers and a button-down shirt.

They forbade Eli to leave the room he shared with Andrea until they came back. She never thought he'd obey. Normally, he'd be out and about the second their parents left, disappearing behind the shut door of the rec room to get on the computer, again, or lounging on the couch in front of the TV, smirking at her—*What are you going to do? Tell on me?* She wouldn't, and he knew it.

But to her surprise, he hasn't moved from the room.

Although she's almost at the top of the stairs, she changes her mind and turns back, tiptoeing all the way down and then right past the open doorway to the living room, to the kitchen.

A quick foray into the pantry yields a handful of granola

bars that her mom bought to replace cookies—for Andrea only, since everyone else chowed down on double chocolate chip as usual. But her mom was concerned with Andrea putting on two clothing sizes in the last three months so it was decided to "cut back on the junk food." The cookies now sit on the top shelf she can't reach without pulling up a chair.

Besides, if her mom notices missing cookies, in the mood she's in, Andrea will get in trouble too. As if taking a cookie were as bad as taking a hundred dollars from Sergio's wallet.

Andrea stuffs the bars into her pocket and creeps upstairs. The door of their shared room creaks softly when she slips in.

She fully expects to see Eli up and about. But he's so still and silent, with the blanket and comforter pulled over his head, that for a fleeting second she thinks he may have snuck out. Without thinking, she pokes the shapeless lump of blanket.

He turns over so fast she has no time to jump back, only to bat the comforter away with her outstretched arms.

"What the hell do you want?"

Despite the darkness—the only light comes from the lantern on the patio outside, filtering through the blinds—the fury of his glare scorches her. Guilt turns sour in her stomach. They had a rule about not getting into the hiding place when anyone was home. If she hadn't broken it, if she'd been more careful, if she didn't immediately dump all the blame on him, none of this would be happening.

No matter that it was, really, all his fault. Nothing in that hiding place was hers. Certainly not the money.

Her brother sighs and sits up on his bed. The Star Wars logo on his T-shirt stands out starkly in the semidarkness.

"I just want to know," she says softly. She can't see his face clearly, but she knows he's grimacing.

"Yeah, yeah. Whatever."

"Why did you do it?"

"What the fuck do you care?"

The first answer that springs to her mind is *I'll tell Mom you were swearing*. She bites it back, ashamed of herself.

"I needed it, all right?"

All that money? But he couldn't spend that much on anything without their parents noticing anyway. "What for?"

"Oh God." He shakes his head, and his derisive laugh is quiet in the dark. "You're my twin. How are you this stupid?"

"Don't say that!" she retorts, but her voice comes out whiny, juvenile. "I'll—"

"Tell Mom?" he mocks in a falsetto. "Go ahead—you're good at that, aren't you?"

She draws a sharp breath, insulted. "When have I ever ratted on you?"

"Seriously? What about earlier?"

"I didn't!" she snaps back, indignant. "Everything in there was yours. And I didn't take that money."

"But it was your sticky hands in there when you got caught."

"So?"

"So, you were only too happy to go and pin everything on me, like a coward."

"What was I supposed to do?"

He shrugs and leans back on the bed, putting his feet up. "Share the blame."

No, she thinks angrily. He can't say that; he can't ask me for that—it's not fair. He was the one who stole; he was the one who started the hiding place. It wasn't her fault. Why was she supposed to take the blame? The injustice of it makes her choke with tears. She gulps heavily but she still can't speak.

"I would have done it for you," he says, and she feels worse. "What did you want in there, anyway?"

"Nothing," she mutters.

He only gives a soft, skeptical *uh-huh* in response.

# CHAPTER SIXTEEN

We get to the town house when it's already getting dark. Sunny stares out the window like a bewildered child, face pressed to the glass. The place must be akin to a zoo to her.

My inner voice, which I've managed to ignore up to now, is pretty much shrieking. Sure, let the homeless girl into the house that doesn't really belong to you. Just don't leave her alone for more than a minute and then remember to check your valuables.

While I drive into the garage and wait for the door to slide closed behind us, Sunny prattles on: *Thank you so much, Ms. Boudreaux-I-mean-Andrea, I'll be good, you won't regret it, I promise.*

All the curtains are drawn, as I left them, and when I flip the light switch, the glow of lamps fills the space, warm and cozy. Naturally, the moment she's inside, Sunny drops the bubbly-little-girl act like the proverbial hot rock. She slouches into the living room, shrewd eyes taking every-thing in.

"Shoes," I call after her, trying to imbue my voice with some semblance of authority. She rolls her eyes, thinking I don't notice, but kicks off her ridiculous boots without needing to be told twice. She already left tracks on the hardwood floor, but I decide to let it go.

"Not bad," she says after a cursory examination of the living room. "That gig of yours must pay a ton."

"It's not—" I start, intending to tell her the house is ac-tually my fiancé's. Ex-fiancé's. But I catch myself in time. I should not be justifying myself to this girl. Apprehension and, yes, regret, settle in with each passing second. I never should have brought her here. *Addie. You're too soft. Too trusting. That's why you let them do this to you...*

Fuck you, Eli, I think, surprised at the intensity of emo-tion that twists my gut.

"Think you can order a pizza?" Sunny asks nonchalantly, settling in on the couch. "Pepperoni. Or bacon and sausage. Just no mushrooms. I hate mushrooms."

No *please*, no *thank you*. I bristle, but the truth is, I'd have to order pizza or something similar anyway because there was no food in the fridge when I left yesterday, and I doubt it magically appeared there in the time I was gone. My stomach betrays me by letting out a gurgle I'm sure she can hear.

"Vegetarian," I say through my teeth, remembering be-latedly that I don't do the vegetarian thing anymore—that was Milton. "But no mushrooms."

She grimaces but then shrugs. "Your call. You're the boss!"

While I get the takeout brochures from a drawer—Milton didn't like them pinned to the fridge door with magnets—Sunny saunters up to the fridge and throws open the doors.

"Whoa. Got anything to drink in here?"

I give her an icy look, and she shakes her ponytail. "Kidding, kidding. Going to be a good, proper guest, yeah?"

Is that a question? I wonder sourly. "Pinelli's okay?" I ask, finally retrieving the brochure I need.

She answers with a grunt and a grimace. "I want Pizza Hut."

"Well, Pizza Hut doesn't deliver all the way here. I'd have to go and pick it up." And I don't want to leave the house if I don't absolutely have to, especially with her here.

She makes a noise meant to convey disappointment. But within five minutes, the pizza is ordered, and I find Sunny back in the living room, cross-legged on the couch, remote in hand as she flips through the channels on mute.

My heart leaps, and my mouth forms a silent no. *Please please please, stop on some lame reality show or something.* But it's too late. She stops on the twenty-four-hour news channel.

"Oh, hey," she says, bouncing excitedly as she thumbs the Mute button. The sound comes back, so loud it makes me jump. "I've been keeping track of this. So fucked up, huh?"

I keep a neutral face but my mind is threading together a million connections per second. A thousand motivations, reasons she called me, tonight of all evenings. Everything takes on a sinister cast. I want to storm over, pick her up from my couch, and shake the answers out of her.

But all I say is, "Yeah."

Sunny gives me a strange look, her eyebrows rising, and I'm sure that any second I'll be unmasked. But the anchor's voice, melodic and well poised, cuts through the tension.

"Denver police are holding a press conference right now regarding the identity of the murder victim. The victim's name is Adele Schultz, age twenty-two."

I'm light-headed from holding my breath as the image cuts to the press conference. There's Figueroa, her clean-cut partner next to her. She's standing right in the spotlight, but I can tell that she handles it with comfortable ease, like a Hollywood star. She hasn't changed her clothes, or maybe all her outfits are identical, and she still has those flyaways around her head. It looks like she put on some lip balm though. She gazes into the camera with unnerving calmness, and I'm consumed with the feeling that she can see me right through this screen.

"We assure you, we are doing everything we can to track Eli Warren down. The brutal murder of this young woman will not go unpunished."

A little to her right, I can see the photo of the victim mounted on an easel, grainy looking from being blown up to poster size. I tilt my head to see better—which turns out to be unnecessary because the photo fills the whole screen a moment later.

I take a good, long look at the girl my brother murdered—allegedly. She's smiling, her face is plump, she wears hoop earrings, and her mascara is clumpy and dramatic.

"Looks a little bit like you," Sunny says, and sucks her

teeth. For a split second, I had managed to forget she was there.

Figueroa is on the screen again.

"We are still establishing the connection between the victim and Eli Warren but right now we're leaning toward the theory that they were romantically involved."

"Sure," Sunny says, too loudly, and clicks her tongue. "He killed his parents, and now he killed his girl. Shocker."

She doesn't turn to look at me as I hover behind the couch, and I wonder, for real this time, whether she made the connection—Andrea Warren, the girl orphaned by a fire her brother started, and Andrea Boudreaux, her social worker. I always wear shirts with collars that go up to my chin and long sleeves to work. She's never caught a single glimpse of my burn scars.

Disinterested now, her curiosity satisfied in the most morbid way, she picks up the remote and is about to click away from the news channel. But she hesitates, her hand hovering, when Adele Schultz's face fills the screen once again.

"Hey," she says, pensive, "I think—"

Sunny turns to look at me over her shoulder, her face lighting up with a grin of almost childish excitement—glee at being privy to a secret she can't wait to share.

"Haven't I seen her around the shelter before?"

# CHAPTER SEVENTEEN

*Once Eli Warren found himself facing the consequences of his actions, he resorted to the tactic sociopaths typically fall back on. He cast blame. He made ludicrous accusations of abuse: against teachers, a school counselor, and most importantly, his stepfather. The stories he told were positively lurid with detail, something out of a tabloid. Unfortunately for Warren, these same details worked against him: Medical expertise proved that the assaults of which he accused his stepfather simply never happened. When he heard the recording of his sister's testimony (Andrea Warren was at the burn ward at the time, recovering from injuries she sustained when she tried to get to her mother, who was trapped in the master*

*bedroom), he reacted with an outburst of pure rage.*
*The house of cards came tumbling down around him.*
        *—Into Ashes: The Shocking Double Murder in the*
     *Suburbs* by Jonathan Lamb, Eclipse Paperbacks,
                                                  2004, 1st ed.


### FIFTEEN YEARS EARLIER: BEFORE THE FIRE

It's been a few days since the hiding place incident, and on the surface, everything seems to be going back to normal. At least Eli seems to. He no longer complains about being deprived of TV and computer time, no longer sulks or picks at his food at dinnertime. As far as Andrea can tell, he has reverted to his usual self.

Afterward, Andrea couldn't remember exactly how they came to be at Sergio's furniture store on that Thursday afternoon. Their mother wasn't home when they got back from school. Her car was gone, but there was no note. Andrea wasn't alarmed by it—Cassie did this more and more lately. She seemed to think the twins were old enough to take care of themselves.

She was certainly right.

Sergio wasn't due to come back until well past nine, and one of them—it must have been Eli; it had to have been, but she couldn't remember for sure—suggested going over to the store to say hi. She had no idea why he would have suggested it. Eli hated the store. When they were younger and had to stay there while Cassie finished her shift, he always whined and complained about how dusty and boring it was. They weren't allowed to jump on the beds or even sit on the couches. They were supposed to sit in the staff room the whole time, a little windowless room where everything smelled like microwaved lunches, and do their homework.

As soon as they walk in through the big sliding doors, she can see the store is almost empty. Halogen lights hum over the showroom, which sprawls across the entire floor. It's not much of a showroom—rows of desks, rows of beds, rows of couches. A middle-aged couple is wandering amid the couches without much enthusiasm. The woman picks up a price tag, looks at it, and lets it drop back half a second later.

Andrea wants to wave to the cashiers, but Eli determinedly grabs her hand and pulls her along in the opposite direction. "We should find Sergio," he says.

"What's the hurry?"

"I have something to say to him," Eli replies after a pause that lasts less than a heartbeat. But it's enough to plant the seed of anxiety in Andrea's mind.

"Eli, what—"

"I want to apologize," he says. He stops abruptly, without warning, so she walks into him and stumbles. He grips her wrist hard before letting go. "Be careful."

"Apologize?" she says in disbelief.

"Yeah. I'm sick of being grounded. C'mon—I can charm him into forgiving me. I can tell him I'll work off the money at the store, or something, and in exchange he'll tell Mom to back off."

Andrea is doubtful. "Do you think it'll work?"

"Oh yeah," he says with a dismissive eye roll. "She'll do what he tells her. She doesn't want him on her back right now—trust me."

"Why would Sergio even listen to you?" Andrea grumbles, but he turns and resumes walking without acknowledging her. He pushes his way past a door that reads STAFF ONLY. Andrea follows him, realizing too late that they're in the wrong place.

This isn't the workers' lounge or the office—this is storage. It's freezing cold. She huddles in her coat, her hands in her pockets.

"Why are we here?"

"He's always here at the end of the day," Eli says, annoyed, like it's supposed to be obvious. "Doing inventory. Don't you remember?"

She doesn't, but she also doesn't want to admit it.

"I'll go look for him," Eli says. "You could help, if you want."

She shakes her head. She doesn't like it here. Narrow rows of shelves on all sides, all the way to the sixteen-foot ceiling, all piled with heavy brown boxes plastered with warning signs.

"Climb on the thing," her brother says, pointing at a mobile ladder near one of the shelves. "You'll be able to see the whole place."

"No way." Since they were little, they were forbidden to go anywhere near the ladder. There's even a chain with a warning sign in place, but it can be easily stepped over.

Eli sighs and rolls his eyes. "Come on," he says, and

pushes her out of the way. He puts his foot on the first step. Brings the other one next to it. Swings his leg over the chain. "See? Not too hard."

"We're not supposed to."

"Whatever. No one can see us."

"You'll get in trouble."

"Oh yeah? You'll tell on me?" His tone is humorous, but she can hear the barbs underneath. Her face flares hot. And when he motions impatiently for her to join him, she obeys.

One step, two, four. He's always a step above her, goading her onward. Six, seven, eight steps—and he's reached the platform. Above it, the three remaining rungs are painted orange, because you're not supposed to stand on them.

"This isn't so bad," he's saying. "Look. You can see everything."

Instinctively, she turns to look. She isn't sure what comes next. Did he push her? Did she make a misstep? Did she get dizzy? The next thing she knows, everything is sideways. Her stomach flips, and the rush of air fills her ears, the floor grows closer and closer, and then nothing.

# CHAPTER EIGHTEEN

I wake up feeling like I drank three bottles of tequila the day before, or got hit by a truck head-on, or maybe both. Sitting up with a groan, I realize I've passed out on the love seat, my spine curved in an S shape and stuck that way.

On the couch, I find the pillow and blanket I got for Sunny. Sunny herself is nowhere to be seen, naturally. That's why I fell asleep here instead of my comfy bed. I didn't want to let her out of my sight, at least not until I was sure she'd passed out cold.

So far, it looks like she beat me at my own game. A cursory check confirms that Sunny is no longer in the house, and neither are the change and crumpled ones and fives in the bowl near the entrance. Or the tiny gold earrings I left by the sink.

I guess I should feel lucky she didn't call up Shawn or someone like him to clean out the electronics.

All my careful prodding and questioning didn't get me any closer to figuring out whether Sunny really saw this Adele at the shelter or if it was just wishful thinking of a girl badly in need of attention. Although I'm not worried. I highly doubt Sunny will be calling up the police to share her theories.

With my joints and spine cracking like I'm eighty, I plod to the upstairs bathroom. Sure enough, Sunny also swiped some makeup from the cabinet. I sigh, unable to muster any anger, and then ditch my clothes and climb into the shower.

It's earlier than I thought, around the same time I'd get up for the day shift at the shelter, when I did those. And my next step forms in my mind as I let scalding water run over my head, my hair slicked to my neck and shoulders. When Milt lived here, he never once complained about having to take a barely warm shower after I'd used up the hot water in the tank.

Once I've dried my hair and put on clean clothes, not to mention a layer or five of deodorant, I feel like myself again. The sight of Cynthia's car makes me wince, a sharp reminder of the day before, but I get behind the wheel anyway.

As I get closer to my destination, there's no police tape on the spot where I crashed. I almost miss it. I slow down on purpose when I drive by, wrestling with the temptation to stop, to put on the hazard lights. To leave the car, to wade into the bleak grass, letting it whip my shins. To walk as far as the horizon, peering at the ground at my feet. Looking.

But I don't stop. Instead, I keep going until I get to the shelter, which sticks out of the concrete and flat grassland like a gray pimple. Cynthia's car looks out of place in the parking lot next to the handful of sensible Hondas and the lone electric car that belongs to my supervisor, Marla Etan.

In the much less forgiving light of day, everything looks completely different. Last year we all got together to re-paint the walls, with paint and supplies bought with our own money because our funding was as miserly as ever. We picked an assortment of purples, soothing greens and blues, cheery yellow—all meant to put the shelter's resi-dents in a better, healthier, can-do mind-set. But the result looks like a children's jail with posters of missing teenagers next to guidelines for safe sex and safer drug injections.

The social worker on front-desk duty still sits behind bulletproof glass. She salutes me, not without a shade of hesitation. I scan my pass, and the door unlocks with a beep, a green light flashing above it. I'm now in the com-mon room / cafeteria, with the dormitory and shower stalls to my right and the offices to my left. The offices are for those seeking counsel who might want some privacy.

A few teenagers are spread throughout the common room—a small group cross-legged on the floor and a cou-ple of rough-looking girls nearly passed out on the shabby couch. In the corner, a drip coffee maker hums, spewing horrible coffee into a pitcher stained with brown sediment rings. Next to it is a stack of miniboxes of cereal no one shows any interest in. The smell of the place—a pecu-liar mix of tobacco, burned coffee, and chemical lemon cleaner—assaults the nostrils the moment you walk in, but you stop noticing it within minutes. Today I can't get used to it. Instead, I become hyperaware, like a scent hound, detecting all the undercurrent smells: sweat, pot, despair.

"Hey," I say as I approach the teens sitting on the floor. The nearest one lifts her head, and I only now realize it's a girl, shaved hair and all. She has those stretching hoops in her earlobes. The one next to her, a guy hunched over his phone, dreadlocks obscuring his face, hardly stirs at all.

The girl looks at me questioningly. I decide to just jump in because otherwise I'll never work up the courage.

"I need to know if you've seen her around before," I ask, holding out my phone. On the screen, a picture of Adele Schultz. The one everyone has seen, the picture everyone will know her by from here on out. From the news.

Interest flashes briefly through her watery gray eyes but gives way to indifference. "Nope."

The guy looks up, at last, craning his neck to see the photo.

"Please," I say hoarsely.

The buzz-headed girl pulls unsubtly on the guy's sleeve. "Don't talk to her," she whispers loudly, and then turns to me. "Are you police?"

"No, Cass. Come on. She works here," chimes in the third one, a girl with short hair dyed Kool-Aid green. I've seen her around before, often. I usually remember all their names but not today.

The one she called Cass—same name as my mother's—measures me with an icy look, clearly not eager to put her trust in me, police or not. I'm authority, which to her is all the same.

"Andrea," calls a voice from my left-hand side. My head snaps up. The tone is that of cheerful surprise but I can read the notes it conceals. Marla is standing at the door of her office. "I didn't think you'd come in today at all. A word?"

I follow her to the office. She lets me in first and then gently shuts the door behind me—exactly the same as she does with the teenagers she counsels. Especially when the news is not so good.

Marla's office is the only one that's personalized: a framed picture of her husband and adult daughter on her desk, a Monet print on the wall flanked by two motivational posters, a bowl on the edge of the desk filled with those little caramels from the dollar store.

"Look, Andrea, I'll have to level with you," she says, folding her hands with their pointy manicure. "I think you should take a break."

I can't say it's a total shock. But I can still muster a certain amount of indignation. Plus, she's looking at me as if she expects me to be surprised.

"I don't need to take a break," I say. "I'm fine."

Marla heaves a patient sigh. I study her—pixie cut, rectangular glasses with a bright-purple plastic frame, pursed lips. She reminds me of Cynthia in more than a few ways, except Marla chose to channel her relentless will into something slightly less shallow.

Just like Cynthia though, she can't stand to be disobeyed. "This whole thing with your brother," she says, and doesn't continue. Just lets the phrase hang there. *This whole thing with your brother*, as if it's self-explanatory.

"What does that have to do with me? With my work?"

She leans in closer. "One of our charges saw you on the news. And you know how they talk. Before long, they'll be making up all kinds of stories, and that...that just undermines their confidence in this place. It's supposed to be a...a safe haven—do you know what I mean?"

"How is it any less of a—" I cut myself off, shaking my head as if trying to get rid of a bad dream. "So what? That means I don't need a job? An income?"

"No one is firing you," she says firmly, more and more reminiscent of Cynthia. And just like with Cynthia, I know by the tone of her voice she won't budge. "I am talking about a temporary leave of absence. Once all this is sorted, you can come back."

"Paid leave?" I ask pointedly.

She looks away.

"Andrea, please. Work with me here. This is a touchy situation. We could get our funding cut any day as it is. And you...Well, you have your fiancé, don't you?"

I stare at her, astounded, not quite believing what just came out of her mouth. I don't even correct her, remind her that he's my ex-fiancé. And after all, I still live in his house, don't I?

"Who was it?" I ask dryly.

"Pardon?"

"That saw me on TV." And is now running her big mouth. I know the answer without her needing to say it. Sunny.

Marla's lips, already thin and shapeless, press together until they almost vanish. "I don't think you get it. You brought him here." She puts her hand down on the desk, her rings clacking loudly. "Understand? You brought him. I know you didn't do it on purpose but does it matter? He was out there watching you. You and the vulnerable girls coming and going at all hours, with nowhere else to go. How does it make us look, do you think?"

*This whole thing isn't what it seems*, I want to say. But understanding hits, along with a pang of betrayal. Figueroa already spoke to her—probably bled her for every detail about me, my work hours, which coworkers I don't get along with, how I take my coffee. And then she probably made a few subtle or not-so-subtle threats. And Marla, who cares about the shelter above all, sold me out.

Not a single word leaves my lips. Marla gives a subtle nod, but I don't need to be told. I turn around and leave, storming through the common room. Someone in the corner gives a wolf whistle when I'm almost at the door.

Without giving it a moment's thought, I flip him off before slamming the door behind me.

The second I step toward Cynthia's car, I stop, overcome with a feeling of wrongness that seems to rise from the very bottom of my soul. It knots in my gut, instinctive.

On the back window of the SUV, in the layer of tiny splatters of dirt, someone drew a heart.

# CHAPTER NINETEEN

ADDIE, it reads in crooked letters inside the heart.

Frantic, I look around. The air is chilly and crystal clear, but in all that bright sun, the shadows are darker and deeper than ever. I draw in an icy breath as I fumble for my car keys, feeling like a character in a bad horror movie. My hands are clumsy, shaking, and I manage to drop the keys to the ground. I crouch, pick them up, and get up so fast my head spins.

"Eli?" I call out, fully aware of how crazy I must look. My heart thunders but no answer comes. He wouldn't show up here now, I try to reassure myself. It's too big of a risk. He wouldn't dare.

But these are all solid, rational things, and they fail to calm me.

"Where are you?" I yell out. My voice rolls across the open lot, uncomfortably loud. In that moment, I could swear something moves in my peripheral vision.

Primal fear fills me. In a panic, I thumb the car key, and Cynthia's SUV responds with a reassuring beep. I clamber inside, slam the door shut, and engage all the locks. My hands on the steering wheel, I pant, not daring to look anywhere but right in front of me.

The car, with its hulking, solid weight, is a comfort. I start the engine and begin to maneuver out of the parking spot but as soon as I turn the car around, he appears as if by magic, out of thin air.

A tall, dark shape, in the shadow of the building, right at the edge of the lot.

I slam on the brakes, then change my mind, shift gears, and hit the gas pedal. In that moment, I'm 100 percent certain I'm about to mow my brother down with my car.

*Like you should have.*

But as the SUV roars toward the building, I blink, and the figure is gone, like it was never there.

I swerve at the last second and screech onto the road leading out of the parking lot. Sweat pours down my back as the SUV steadies its speed, careening away, away, away from the shelter.

Away from him.

Only when I'm at a safe distance do I pull over by the side of the road. Forgetting the hazard lights, I stop the car, drop my forehead on the steering wheel, and burst into tears.

I sob out my helplessness to the purr of the Cadillac's engine, grateful for once for Cynthia's predilection toward tinted windows—the affectation of the politician's wife who never was.

I paw my way through the glove compartment (in this monster of a car it could fit a small suitcase): hand lotion, Tylenol, those clip-on sunglasses Cynthia uses, and, finally, tissues. I gut the little plastic pouch and use a whole handful of them to blow my nose and wipe my eyes. Still sniffling, I pop a Tylenol and flip open the visor to reveal the backlit mirror there.

I'm a horror show—red nose, swollen eyelids. It looks like my eyelashes disappeared altogether. I'm not, and never was, one of those girls who look pretty when they cry. I've never been able to pull off that thing so many girls have down to an art form, making people feel bad for me by releasing one or two artfully placed fake tears. And real tears aren't pretty; real tears strip away all the prettiness, leaving you raw and vulnerable like a newborn. That's why tabloids love pictures of famous women bawling their eyes out, almost as much as they love those no-makeup shots.

There's a photo in the center insert of that god-awful true crime book, a photo of my brother pretrial. He's wearing the requisite jumpsuit and handcuffs, and his expression is that of mournful resolve, his eyes shiny. A child in a situation no child should have to face.

In that book, the caption reads, *The only tears Eli Warren ever spilled were for himself.*

Instead of hitting the gas pedal and getting out of here— Where would I go, anyway?—I check my phone, and my heart jumps when I see the sheer number of notifications. Texts and voicemails to boot. My hands sweaty with foreboding, I unlock the phone and scroll.

The texts are mostly from Chris, my sponsor at AA.

Just checking to see if youre ok. Followed by, A, get in touch. I want to know how youre doing. **Chris doesn't like apostrophes and isn't friends with Autocorrect.** I better see you at the meeting tonight. **Chris isn't dumb.** It's obvious to anyone that no way am I showing my face there, or anywhere, tonight. Or tomorrow night, or the night after that, or any night for the next year. Or five. Or however long it takes for this thing to resolve. For the police to find my brother, arrest him, and then the trial, the appeals—because I know there will be appeals, that he'll insist he's innocent until the very end.

My mind fills with the two images of Adele, side by side. The smiling picture from the news and the one Figueroa showed me. Could he have done it? Truth is, I don't know. And that's not the question anyway.

There's also a text from Milton, asking me to please call him, and all the missed calls are from a certain familiar number so the voicemails must be from Cynthia. I'm about to listen to them—or delete them without listening—but another text pops up silently on the screen. Chris: Answer my texts A. I know youve seen them.

Maybe it's that vulnerable feeling that has had me by the throat since earlier, but instead of answering Milton, instead of driving home, I thumb Chris's name in my contact list.

The phone barely has time to ring before my sponsor picks up. "Andrea," Chris says in a level voice, "how are you doing?"

I'm about to answer before I realize I haven't thought of what I'm going to say. On the other end, Chris jumps to conclusions. "Please tell me you're not drunk."

"I'm not drunk," I say, grateful for the out. And it's an easy one. "I promise."

"You're coming to the meeting tonight." It doesn't sound like a question.

"Don't you think it's not the best idea right now?"

"I think it's *the* best idea," Chris says firmly. "More than ever, actually."

"I'm not going to fall off the wagon," I say.

"In times of crisis, that's when we need friends the most." This worries me—Chris has never been one for platitudes, and something about the words rings with a tension that wasn't there before, a falseness. The idea of Chris judging me hurts way more than I expected.

"We'll see," I say, and before the inevitable protests can start, I hang up and hit the gas pedal.

I drive home and spend the afternoon watching the news on TV while also keeping an eye on what's being posted online.

There's a lot about Adele Schultz. Not all of it good— more of it bad, truth be told. After that first smiling, beatific picture, more crop up online: wild, blurry party pics and what looks like a mug shot—which shouldn't be possible because she would have been a juvenile and that record should be sealed. Yet there she is, looking strung out as hell, premature hollows under her eyes, sullen expression, and a bruise on her cheek. Adele had problems with drugs, run-ins with the police, and a long history of unsuitable men. Of which my brother, supposedly, was the last and worst.

But no matter how hard I search and scour every online

source, I can't seem to find any up-to-date info. It would seem that Adele fell off the radar for the last couple of years, or at least cleaned up enough to keep out of trouble.

I click the search windows closed and turn my attention to the TV, where Adele's mother, Colleen, is giving a press conference. Well, the police are—I can see Figueroa's shoulder and half her face at the edge of the screen, looking on with an expression somewhere between motherly and squeamish.

"This man is a monster." Colleen is sobbing. She's a wreck—I know they played it up on purpose to pull at viewers' heartstrings and drive their hatred of the suspect to a boiling point, but she just looks like she partied too hard, for far too long, and didn't notice her best years were behind her. Her dry, black-dyed hair has six solid inches of salt-and-pepper roots, and her eyebrows are tattooed on—badly. Her face is the color and texture of a leather purse.

"He killed my baby girl. He killed her. I can't even have a last look at her pretty face. My baby girl was everything to me." She smears tears with the heel of her hand, and my mouth twists in a grimace. As far as I know, her "baby girl" barely registered on her radar for most of her life. The internet wasted no time turning up the sordid facts either. Colleen's home in northeast Denver, a dilapidated little bungalow, had seen its share of interventions by child protection services. Adele did dismally at school and spent several months at a time in foster homes while her mother cleaned up her act. Colleen was never outright abusive—she was one of those who actually do love their children, in their own way; they just can't bring themselves to make any sacrifices to show it. Such as getting out of bed earlier to make them breakfast and taking them to school. Or doing homework with them instead of going out to get drunk at a dive bar with a new boyfriend. I've seen my share of those parents—it's heartbreaking.

"Please help us find him. He has to pay for what he's done." Colleen breaks out in ugly sobs. Figueroa takes her place, doing a poor job of hiding her victorious grin. My brother is easily the most hated person in the country right now.

Next, the screen cuts to an "expert in child psychology." A blond journalist speaks to him and the camera at the same time: "But do you think this is somehow connected with the crime he committed back in 2002?"

The man looks vaguely familiar. I glance at his name as it scrolls at the bottom of the screen, and it's terribly familiar too, in that can't-quite-grasp-it kind of way. He looks straight at the camera as he talks.

"What you have to understand is that Eli Warren should have been locked up for life. He never should have been allowed to walk the streets as a free man. Eli Warren is a psychopath of the most dangerous variety, someone with no remorse or conscience. He's done this once before, and now he did it again. And like last time—"

Unable to stomach any more, I turn off the TV. Once my rage has cooled to a manageable point, I pick up my phone. For a moment, I contemplate calling Milton but my throat squeezes, and I'm not sure I could muster so much as a word.

I check the time. The AA meeting starts in a half hour,

which means I have just enough time to drive there but not to change or make myself look decent. It's hard to believe I last showered this morning. It feels (and looks and smells) like it's been a year. My shirt has sweaty crescents under the armpits, and since it's pale-gray cotton, they're extra obvious. My face has a mirrorlike oily sheen, especially around the nose and forehead, the circles under my eyes a deep blue.

I splash water on my face and then use more water to slick down the flyaways sticking out to and fro from my ponytail. They'll go back to the way they were before I get to the meeting. But I think Sunny also helped herself to my tube of hair gel, because it's nowhere to be seen. Ditto my only belt, so my jeans, which have gotten saggy around the waist and hips over the last day and a half, shall remain saggy. I put on another shirt, a black T-shirt I fish out of the hamper that looks clean. Then, just as I pull it over my head and realize it's way too big, I notice it's one of Milton's. With that stupid Lacoste crocodile over my heart.

My eyes start to burn. If I'd still been hesitating, my mind is now made up. I just need to do something with myself so I don't dwell on everything I've lost.

Or everything I might still lose.

# CHAPTER TWENTY

*Much was made by the defense of the fact that Eli Warren pulled his sister out of the fire. Surely, if Warren had no remorse and no compassion, he would have let her burn?*

*But after assessing Eli Warren, I could only come to one conclusion. He rescued his sister because he was hoping she would take his side and help him lie that the fire was accidental. When she finally told the investigators what she had seen and heard the night of the fire, he realized that his pawn had disobeyed and turned on him. Eli Warren saw that as betrayal of the highest order.*

*—Into Ashes: The Shocking Double Murder in the Suburbs* by Jonathan Lamb, Eclipse Paperbacks, 2004, 1st ed.

*FIFTEEN YEARS EARLIER: BEFORE THE FIRE*

"What were you even doing there? Why?"

Andrea leans her forehead against the car window. She's nauseous and exhausted. Her puffy coat had saved her from a broken arm, the ER doctor said, and instead she merely bruised her shoulder. She did, however, have a concussion.

She doesn't remember getting to the ER. She doesn't know how long it was before someone found her or before she regained consciousness. She only knows that Eli was nowhere around.

"Why did you go there all by yourself? I told you—"

I wasn't by myself, Andrea wants to say but doesn't. There's no point. "Where's Eli?" she asks instead.

In the rearview mirror, her mother's face creases with concern. But her expression is clueless, and Andrea figures out what happened before her mother has a chance to answer.

"He's at home. You scared me to death! I get home from my shopping, and he tells me you took off to the furniture store. By yourself! What on earth were you thinking?"

"I'm sorry, Mom," she whispers, but it's too soft, and her mother, annoyed, asks her to repeat it.

"I'm sorry, Mom." There's no point in defending herself, she knows. She really should have seen this coming. Eli isn't the forgiving-and-forgetting type.

"I can't have you running around by yourself at all hours of the day," Cassie says.

Andrea isn't listening. Something preoccupies her, something her mother said. Nothing seems to add up. Maybe it all broke into pieces when her head hit the cold concrete floor but she can't make the pieces fit back together.

She asks a question but Cassie is distracted. She repeats. "What did you buy?"

"What?"

"When you went shopping."

"Nothing!" Cassie's face flares in anger, hot and unexpected. "What the hell does it matter, anyway? We're talking about you here!"

She goes on. Andrea lets the words flow through her aching head. She pictures them dissolving like ice crystals and evaporating. She cracks the window open to let them out, rests her head on the back of the seat, and closes her eyes.

\*     \*     \*

Andrea wakes with a sudden jolt. She lies there, disoriented, trying to remember when she managed to fall asleep. She's sprawled on top of her bedcover, fully dressed, a puddle of drool drying beneath her cheek. On the bed across, she can make out Eli's prone form under the blankets.

Then she hears noises downstairs and understands what woke her up. Alarmed, she sits up. The digital clock says it's past midnight. If her mom walks in and sees her, still not in bed, she'll be mad.

But for some reason, instead of hastily undressing and

diving under the covers, she stays still, listening. They're arguing in hushed but angry voices. Andrea hears the tension in them, humming like a power line.

She gets up, trying to be as quiet as possible, and creeps toward the door. She opens it just enough to slip through and emerges into the hall.

It's dark out here. All the lights are out except for one downstairs. She hides around the corner at the top of the staircase.

"...don't defend him. I can't believe—"

"Cass, calm down. There's a way out of this."

"Really?" Her mother's voice is a low hiss, and Andrea has to strain to make out what she's saying. "Have you been paying any attention? What if they decide to go through with it?"

"They won't go through with anything," Sergio rumbles, but he doesn't sound as confident as usual. "Think about it. If they sue us, the whole thing will get out into the open. And they don't want that right now. Can you imagine what a circus the press will start when they find out that—"

"Whether he did or didn't do it is irrelevant. We could be in a shit-ton of trouble regardless. Do we even have money for legal fees?"

"We'll come up with something."

"*We'll come up with something!*" she mocks. "It's not the nineties anymore, Sergio. The store barely stays afloat. Another year like this, and you can only cut your losses and close. Nobody wants overpriced clunky crap from Italy when you have Ikea around the corner. We're broke. And this thing could be the final straw after which we end up living on the street. Then what?"

Andrea shrinks back. Her bare feet are freezing on the floor, and it feels like her teeth are about to start chattering.

Her stepfather mutters something under his breath.

"What did you say?" Her mother's shrill voice cuts through the silence.

"You heard me. Sorry you couldn't do better but you know how it is."

The silence lingers, leaden. Andrea doesn't dare breathe.

"Oh, really?" her mother says softly but her words have an unmistakable edge. "Is that what you think? That you're so irreplaceable?"

Sergio gives a short, bitter laugh. "Building yourself a life raft already. How like you. I should have known from the start."

"Fuck you," her mother says calmly. Steps thunder closer, and Andrea knows she must move, quickly. She retreats, making for the door of her room, and closes it behind her just as her mother climbs the stairs.

Andrea's heartbeat is frantic, her back sweaty. Halfway between the door and her bed, she freezes and listens. The steps stop in the hall outside. For the next few seconds, the only sounds are her own heartbeat and the soft creak of the floorboards.

Then the steps grow farther and farther away.

She looks in the direction of her brother. His face is smooth, pale, and calm in the dim light filtering in from outside. He's sound asleep. Or at least faking it really well.

# CHAPTER TWENTY-ONE

*I'm going to my meeting,* I text Milt as I'm maneuvering the Cadillac SUV out of the town house's driveway. Then I think of him chiding me for texting while behind the wheel and set the phone down in the cup holder. I keep glancing at it, nearly missing a stop sign. Bad Andrea. But no answer arrives.

I don't know what I've been hoping for, what the reason was for this childish display. Did I expect him to pat me on the head? To tell me he's madly in love with me and we're getting back together? He may be in denial but I sure am not. All the meetings in the world aren't going to fix what's wrong with me.

I can't stomach the radio so I hit Play on the CD player out of sheer habit. My old car, may it rest in peace, only had a CD and cassette deck. This one is equipped with an iPhone jack but Cynthia never mastered it. Or maybe it's just another facet of her obstinate clinging to the past. But there turns out to be a CD in the player. Only instead of music, words pour out of the speaker. It's an audiobook on CD. I always wondered who still bought those, when you can get them right on your phone.

" . . . so you might ask yourself, is this normal behavior? Should I be worried? And that's normal and a perfectly natural thing to wonder about. And of course, we know how children and teenagers can seem like alien creatures sometimes. But some things are a part of normal development, learning to empathize with other human beings, learning to form bonds, learning to fit into the world."

I frown, eyeing the CD player. Children? Teenagers? Did I miss something?

"Some children, however, never manage this process. The sociopathic child sees no problem with lying and deceiving. He feels no guilt or remorse. In this chapter, I will present to you the proof, provided by the people who knew the subject, that Eli Warren is a sociopathic individual and has been that way from a young age."

I reach for the Eject button so fast that the car does a little zigzag on the road. Gripping the steering wheel, I straighten the SUV, ignoring the angry honks behind me. A Honda passes me, the driver flipping me off through the window.

The CD pops out of the player without a sound. I hold it up with my fingertips. INTO ASHES BY JONATHAN LAMB, it reads in red font, like an old Stephen King novel. The moment I lay eyes on it, nausea sweeps through me, and I set it down on the passenger seat.

I've never read that thing—it's more than I could stomach. But I did look at it once, at a big-box store when I was a teenager. Cynthia was hunting down bargains a few aisles over, and there it was, sitting next to the Harlequin romances and mass-market John Grishams. I thumbed through it, stopping only when I hit the glossy photo insert.

Photos of the house, photos of Cassie, of Sergio. Photos of our school. Lots and lots of photos of my brother. But really, I had to admit to myself, as I scanned each shiny page, I was looking to see if I was in there somewhere too. I wasn't. All that was left of me was my arm, in one of the cropped family pictures. Eli Warren's sister reduced to a dimpled elbow and plump, freckled shoulder poking out of a tank top. In the shuffle, everyone seems to have forgotten I existed at all.

I still wonder if it was intentional—if it's exactly what he wanted.

And then, like any lazy teenager skimming her reading assignments, I peeked at the ending. Wished I hadn't. I still remember that paragraph of the epilogue, pretty much word for word.

*But the question the justice system found itself facing—the question that haunts us all, without a doubt—was, What do you do with a manipulative sociopath and cold-blooded murderer who's only twelve years old? Do you gamble on the chance this is just a macabre phase, a flaw that can be fixed with time and the right treatment? Or do you think,*

*instead, of the people he has hurt and of the people he*
*may still hurt if he's allowed to walk free?*

I grip the steering wheel and focus on the road unfolding in front of me in an endless stream of taillights. I'm
entering evening traffic, denser than usual tonight. Stuck in
a car, alone with my thoughts and with Jonathan Lamb's
magnum opus. Great.

This is the man I saw on TV earlier, I think suddenly, the
realization going off in the complete vacuum of my mind.
Jonathan Lamb—that's why the name seemed so familiar.

It's as if floodgates open in my mind, and irrational,
burning, violent hatred for the man rushes in. My fingernails sink into the cushioned steering wheel cover. And
since he's not here, the natural impulse is to take my rage
out on the next closest thing. I glower at the CD, wondering if I should snap it into little pieces or throw it out the
window.

But I don't do that. Slowly, as if it might bite, I slide the
CD back into the player.

RESUME flashes in pale-blue letters on the CD player.
Okay, then. Resume.

" . . . was the principal of George Washington School from
1997 to 2003. She agreed to speak with me at her home in
Wellshire."

I thumb Fast-Forward.

" . . . seemed like a normal thing—a typical adjustment
period when a new student tries to make friends and forge
deeper connections. You see, at our school, most of the students have been together since elementary school. We're

a very tight-knit community, the students and the parents. Everyone knows each other. It can be hard for a newcomer to carve out a place for himself. But this is what I, and his teachers, noticed. He seemed to become friends with everyone, everywhere he went. Immediately, he had this large group of . . . I wouldn't say friends. It wasn't so much friendship as a kind of . . . awe. They were followers. That's the word I'm looking for."

"Was he particularly close to anyone?"

"That's just it. In spite of that whole herd of followers, he didn't have any real friends. He seemed to cast them off with remarkable ease, as soon as they stopped being convenient."

"Did Eli Warren have problems with other students?"

"If you're talking about bullying, the school has a zero-tolerance policy."

I only snap out of my weird trancelike state when I pull into a parking spot. I turn off the engine. The CD player dies with it, and I sink into the quiet, the hum of the city locked outside the SUV.

In retrospect, listening to that wasn't the ideal way to put myself in the AA mind-set. But what's done is done. I flip the visor down, inspect myself in the mirror, and practice my facial expression. I used to do that before school, when I went back six months after the fire. Arranging my features into the look everyone was expecting to see. Grieving, but not totally crushed. Human, but never vulnerable. Sad eyes and a knowing half smirk, half smile.

But I'd worried in vain. No one bullied me, or picked on me, or tried to victimize me. In fact, people avoided me like

I was poison or like I had a contagious disease they didn't want to catch. Leeanne and her friends were the first to act like I didn't even exist. Everyone else just took their cue.

Now I make myself smile. Not too wide, no teeth. I tug my cheeks up with my fingertips, seeing if it makes the hollows under my eyes disappear. It doesn't. The smile props up my cheekbones just enough so they don't look sunken. It'll have to do.

There's still five minutes until the meeting starts. Everyone must still be hanging out in front of the coffee machine, swilling horrible filter decaf because it's nine and some of them have to go to bed right after, to get up early in the morning for their jobs. This is the scene I desperately want to avoid so I trudge across the lot as slowly as I can.

The meetings take place in a church basement, even though, technically, this particular chapter is the secular AA, which was part of the reason I chose it. Having to pretend to be remorseful is bad enough without dragging Jesus into it. When I first started, they were in a gymnasium of a community center. But then the gymnasium started evening Zumba classes or something like that, and the meetings had to be moved.

I take out my phone and text Chris. Just got here. On my way. But the text remains unread as I turn off my phone and push past the door.

It doesn't look like a church. No religious doodads, no icons, only one cross, discreet, on the wall above the foldout table with the coffee and prepackaged baked goods, oatmeal cookies that taste like shortening, and oily muffins.

I bet the religious AAs have home-baked stuff, courtesy of some soccer mom who once leaned too hard on the chardonnay.

I just start thinking about how I wouldn't mind a horrible decaf coffee and a Twinkie when I walk into the room, and it hits me what a bad idea this was. No one has noticed me yet and already the armpits of Milt's T-shirt are turning damp. Ironically, I find myself craving a glass of wine.

"Andrea!" Before I know it, Chris appears out of my blind spot and encases me in a hug. Which is alarming in itself, since Chris isn't the hugging type normally. I remain awkwardly straight backed as she murmurs in my ear, "I told Gordon about the situation. Hopefully he can keep it under control."

Situation? Control? What the hell is happening? I extricate myself from her hug.

"No one will quiz you. Unless you want to share."

"I don't," I say, maintaining my mouth in that careful close-lipped smile.

Chris shakes her head. "I'm really sorry. A couple people...were talking. Maybe..." She trails off, and her gaze darts away.

"Maybe what? I shouldn't have come after all?"

Chris grimaces. Her usually glossy chestnut hair looks unwashed. She fiddles with her keychain, its three-year badge glinting dully, and turns it around and around like a lucky rabbit's foot.

When I first started going to meetings—after Cynthia pretty much forced me to, under threat of pressing charges about the money I'd been stealing from her for months—I didn't have a plan. I wasn't sure how to play it so I decided to try to get away with the bare minimum: I stole money and jewelry from my adoptive family. I pawned my engagement ring. I'm out of control, and I'm very sorry, and so on—that sort of thing. I wasn't going to talk about Eli. I didn't want to be That Guy's Sister yet again.

But despite my obligation to go under threat of prosecution, I found myself strangely drawn in. There was something about this circle of people, complete strangers to each other, opening up with their innermost secrets, sharing their most painful, low moments.

And they weren't happy with my basic, rudimentary facts, delivered in choppy, simple sentences. In Gordon's words, I was holding back, which showed my lack of remorse. No, they needed all the juicy details, and I obliged. I spoke vividly about drunken benders, passing out in strange men's apartments. Of cheating on my fiancé with a stranger for some cocaine and ending up pregnant, not realizing it until I had a miscarriage at a gas station. It was oddly liberating, and after a while, I started looking forward to the meetings.

When Chris offered to be my sponsor when the time came, I jumped at the chance because, among other things, she didn't seem to get quite so much morbid enjoyment out of hearing me or others recount the horrors of our existence. I figured she wouldn't try to get more out of me or grill me about what I told her. At five foot two, she's shorter than me and looks younger than her forty-three years. Chris was once married to a lawyer and had the dream life: handsome husband, big house, five-star vacations. Enter fertility problems, four rounds of failed IVF, two trips down into the wine cellar per day, and eventually the hormone shots gave way to Vicodin. Then, I'm not entirely clear on the exact circumstances, but she crashed her car into the Mercedes her husband gifted to his mistress. The husband and then mistress have twins now. Chris lives in a rented apartment on the outskirts of downtown.

I knew going in that she (or Gordon or anyone else there) would never become a friend, let alone a confidant, but I have to admit that I grew to enjoy her company.

"Chris," I hiss, catching her sleeve, "what do you mean you told Gordon? I thought the whole point was—"

"That it's supposed to be anonymous, yeah," she answers. "But I think it's too late for that. Someone saw you on TV."

Great.

Everyone moves to take their seats. We don't really sit in a circle—the room isn't big enough for that. It's rows of those desks with the chairs attached, like a classroom, because the rest of the week there are drawing classes here, a poetry workshop, and some kind of Bible study group. Gordon sits in front of us, like a teacher facing a class. Whenever someone gets up to talk, everyone else turns. It doesn't sound too bad but try doing that thirty times in an hour. My neck always hurts after these meetings.

Today, though, I can feel the unease. You'd think I were a black hole that would suck them in if they so much as glance at me. Others are noticing the tension too.

Oddly, a part of me is relieved that this is an excuse to

stop going to these things. But another part of me will miss them.

Gordon starts to talk. Maybe I watched too much TV but before I started the meetings, I'd pictured our addict patron saint as the rangy, mottled type with a beard and faded Metallica T-shirt circa 1989. Gordon couldn't be any further from that. He looks like a Sunday school teacher, and I've never seen him with so much as a five o'clock shadow on his still-handsome face. If he hadn't stood right in front of us and told us, I never would have begun to guess at the sordid story behind the clean-cut façade. Under the sleeves of his sensible, well-pressed dress shirt, his arms are so gouged with injection scars that their surface looks like gnarled tree bark.

He's a compelling speaker. Once upon a time, he sold stocks or bonds or what have you. Now he sells sobriety to people who, for the most part, don't have the insurance to get into rehab. It's working, mostly. Since I started going, no one has yet to leave the group; on the contrary, three or four new faces have appeared in the crowd. There's something karmic about the whole thing. I thought the place would be a giant self-pity circle jerk where we'd take turns blaming unhappy childhoods, abusive spouses, bad genes, chemtrails, whatever for our failings while everyone else nods and dabs their eyes with tissues—kind of like the support group Cynthia signed me up for postfire. But the first thing he told us was to stop feeling sorry for ourselves. That only by taking responsibility for our past actions can we take back control of our lives. If group therapy had been anything like that, maybe it would have actually worked.

I may not belong here, not in any true sense, but I was always oddly transfixed by his speeches. Except today I can't focus on anything.

When I glance around, I notice I'm not the only one. I feel people's eyes on me. I can't remember anything like it. I never attended Eli's trial, since I was in the burn ward until long after it was over.

I force myself to focus on what Gordon's saying. He's talking about things that can make us fall off the wagon. *Stresses*, someone pipes up. *That's right, Diane, stresses.*

"Like somebody from our past," drawls a woman's voice behind me. Chairs and necks creak in unison as everyone turns. "Coming back into our lives."

I don't remember the woman's name. She has red hair and a redder face, rosacea exacerbated by years of drinking, most likely. She has her sticker name tag on her sweater but I can't read it because her handwriting is so smudged. I think the first letter is a *w*. Wanda? Wendy? Wilma?

"Somebody from our past coming back," echoes Gordon behind me, his voice tense as he tries to take back control of the room. Wendy-Wanda isn't looking right at me—she's looking at the spot right above my head. But nobody is fooled. "Enablers," Gordon says. "People who encourage you to do things you'll later regret."

"I mean, that should definitely be something you share with the group," Wanda-Wilma says pointedly. "Right?"

"If it was relevant to the situation, sure."

My gaze darts from Gordon back to W, and this time it lands on hers like a fly in a flytrap. I'd expect her to look away, embarrassed, but she doesn't. She looks quite triumphant.

In a split second, I decide I'm not going to let this continue. I stand up with a clatter of my chair-desk contraption.

"Hey, Whitney." It's Whitney, of course—I remember now. Amphetamines Whitney who punched out a coworker's teeth during a psychotic episode induced by too much meth in her morning coffee. She has to attend court-mandated meetings. "Since we know what you're talking about anyway, maybe we should go outside, and there, you can ask me all your pressing questions."

"I just find it interesting, is all. That you never brought it up once." The room starts to murmur. "I mean, we heard about you throwing up at your job interview and that miscarriage story. But you never mentioned—"

"Whitney," Gordon pipes up, but it's too late. She's too far gone—we both are. I hear Chris whispering my name but ignore it.

"Why does it interest you so much anyhow? You worried I'll go crazy too?"

"Stop it," Chris speaks up.

"Or is it envy? Because I definitely won your bullshit little misery contest now."

The shocked look on Whitney's face is worth it. To hell with this. Cynthia can press charges now if she wants. I'm out of here.

I storm past the other desks, kicking someone's purse out of the way, and throw my weight against the exit door.

"Andrea!" Chris yells after me but I don't stop. I feel bad for letting her down, and I wish I could tell her I hadn't meant to deceive her the way I have. And that I'm sorry, deep down, for lying to all of them from the start.

But of all things I have to feel bad for, frankly, it's not the worst by a long shot.

I narrowly avoid clipping another car as I pull the Cadillac out of the narrow parking spot. This gas-guzzler brings me nothing but problems, and I should probably give it back before Cynthia decides to report it stolen—I wouldn't put it past her.

So I stop, look up a car rental place close to Cynthia's, and then call and reserve myself a nice, unremarkable Ford coupe. Then I drive the Cadillac back and leave it in the driveway. After an agonizing moment's thought, I get back into the car, eject the CD, and take it with me.

I can see even through the tightly closed curtains that the lights are on. I briefly contemplate ringing the doorbell—just to let her know I brought the car back. But Leeanne's car is parked by the sidewalk in front, so I stop, hesitate, weigh the pros and cons—I'm not so sure I can handle Leeanne right now without doing something I'll regret—and then turn around and start to walk away.

Halfway to the sidewalk, the unmistakable sound of the front door opening makes me wince. No sneaking away now. The lantern next to the door flickers on, and my shadow falls, tall and misshapen, on the path ahead. I've been seen after all. The sound of Cynthia's voice makes me stop.

"You might as well come in," she says. She sounds alarmingly hoarse. When I turn around, all I can see is the silhouette against that blinding porch light. She's wearing a bathrobe, her hair piled up messily on top of her head.

"You need to pick up your phone. Or at least check your messages."

My heart jumps into high gear. Oh God, what now? Eli—

"Jim had a heart attack. He died this afternoon."

# CHAPTER TWENTY-TWO

*When I spoke to Warren after his sentencing, the whole experience struck me as profoundly bizarre. Even dressed in a faded mint-green jumpsuit and paper flip-flops, Eli Warren was still every bit the golden boy, the most popular kid in his class. His hair flopped carelessly over his blue eyes, like some singer from a boy band, and his white grin let you know that he knew full well the effect he still had on people. Fortunately, the staff at the facility are well trained to handle even such skilled emotional manipulators as Warren. But looking at him, lounging in that plastic chair like a rock star, was unsettling. In a macabre sense, he is a sort of star, subject of notoriety in certain obscure online forums, a cautionary tale in classrooms. And he seemed to be enjoying every minute of it.*

*—Into Ashes: The Shocking Double Murder in the Suburbs* by Jonathan Lamb, Eclipse Paperbacks, 2004, 1st ed.

### FIFTEEN YEARS EARLIER: BEFORE THE FIRE

When it comes to the world of adults, Andrea knows next to nothing. She thinks she understands some things but others remain hopelessly out of reach. Is it a thing that comes naturally with age, she wonders, or will someone eventually have to explain the rules to her? Right now, it's frustrating, like trying to read a book in a foreign language. You recognize the letters, but the words make no sense. *Sorry you couldn't do better.*

And if she doesn't ever get it, who will explain it to her? Not her brother, that's for sure.

More and more often lately, she finds herself panic-stricken. It's a physical feeling that overwhelms her. The first couple of times it happened, she thought she must have been dying. It was like all the air had been sucked out of the room. She'd struggle to breathe, but no matter how many deep breaths she pulled into her aching lungs, she couldn't shake the feeling she was suffocating.

She feels like everything is breaking apart and she's being left behind. It's bad enough that her mom has been angry and distant lately, always distracted. The other night, she left a pot on the stove, and no one noticed until the smell of acrid smoke penetrated all the way to the second floor. The bottom of the pot was scorched and deformed, and the pot had to be thrown out.

Her parents had a huge fight that night. The Sergio she knew would have laughed it off and then poked fun at her mom for weeks about being forgetful. But instead, he blew up at her. *What were you thinking? Are you trying to burn the house down?* And she yelled right back, *You could have installed the new smoke detectors like I asked you a million times.* This went on for what felt like hours, until Andrea crept to her room and pressed a pillow over her head. Still, she could hear their voices from downstairs, right through the thin walls. And the smell—the nauseating smell wafted in the air for days after, a foul reminder that nothing was the same.

Eli does his best to stay out of the way lately. Makes himself a ghost, slinking around corners, not appearing at meals, and the strange thing is, no one seems to notice, let alone care.

The one upside seems to be that everyone also pays less and less attention to her. She glimpses things, over-hears things that a month ago she never would have. Sergio has begun to smoke more and more openly and unapologetically. Her mom talks on the phone for hours, sniping about him to some friend of hers and not caring that Andrea is within earshot. And her brother—well, he does stuff that disgusts her and seems amused when she walks in on him. She thinks he sometimes leaves the bath-room door unlocked on purpose so she'll stumble in.

She's wary of this new role, of being the invisible eyes and ears of the house. One day, she suspects, she will see or hear something she won't be able to ignore.

That night, she's doing homework. This activity she once loathed has become a welcome respite from the silent tension that fills the house. A distraction. She's alone in her room, with only the cozy glow of the orange desk lamp for company, and it's strangely serene. Her brother is somewhere else in the house. Come to think of it, she hasn't seen him do his homework in days. She can't say she misses his company.

The last assignment is finished. Andrea closes her notebooks, puts away her books, rearranges her gel pens, until finally there's nothing left to do. She wishes she had a book to read other than the old textbooks and children's books that gather dust on the lone shelf over the desk. Or better yet, a TV right here in her room that she could watch. She's been meaning to ask for one for her birthday. But now she knows they have no money, so . . .

She takes the lighter out of her pocket. She hasn't parted with it since the incident with the hiding place, transferring it from one pair of pants to another or hiding it in the inside pocket of her backpack if she has to. She flicks it open, and with a satisfying click and a hissing sound, the flame shoots out, the size of the fingernail on her pinky and so pale blue it's almost transparent. For that reason, it seems extra hot, more than the typical orange flames of candles and matches. She could look at it forever, utterly fascinated.

A noise from downstairs takes her by surprise. Her hand

falters, the flame flickering, and she narrowly avoids dropping the lighter right onto the rug by her feet. She flicks it closed and puts it back in her pocket, her heart hammering. On shaky legs, she gets up and creeps to the door and then peers out into the hallway.

Empty. The door of her parents' bedroom is closed, and there's no light under it. Her mom isn't home—Andrea has no idea where she is because her mom no longer feels the need to tell her where she's going or when she'll be coming back. Andrea supposes she's old enough to be left alone, and anyway, she *isn't* alone. Her brother is home too.

When she makes her way down the stairs, she sees a pair of work boots by the door and understands. Sergio is home. But she didn't hear him come in, and he didn't yell hello up the stairs like he normally does.

There's clanging in the kitchen. He's probably making some food. Andrea feels bad; she could have made sure something was ready, even if it was just a frozen pizza she could have popped into the oven. Too late now. She should go say hi but something stops her.

It's not one set of footsteps she hears. There are other, lighter steps dancing around the heavy ones that belong to her stepfather.

She advances cautiously toward the doorway to the kitchen until she hears her brother's voice, lost among the clanging of dishes. She can't quite make out what he says. She holds her breath.

" . . . if I tell?"

"Keep your mouth shut," grumbles Sergio. Andrea feels

a chill. She has never heard him use that tone with anyone. Not even with her mom when they're fighting. It's low and filled with simmering anger.

She considers going back to her room but she doesn't trust herself to step quietly. They will hear the slap of her bare feet on the floor, and it'll only be worse.

She doesn't know what drives her but she takes a small step forward. Then another. Then another.

She can see through the doorway now, at least partially. Her brother comes into her line of sight. His back is turned to her; he can't see her. Any moment now, he will sense her gaze with the back of his head, turn around, and then...

But he doesn't. He remains oblivious.

Sergio's steps thunder closer. A few more inches, and she'll be able to see him too.

"This is all because of you," he says, again in the same frightening tone. "You little piece of shit."

And before Andrea can back away or lunge forward or stop him or even scream, Sergio backhands her brother across the face so hard that he falls over.

# CHAPTER TWENTY-THREE

I'm still dazed when I get to the car rental place. The shaky giggle I've been holding back for Cynthia's sake finally escapes. That bastard, I think, and shake my head. He sure knew his timing. Opportunist to the end. Holding on to his secrets, big and small, to the last.

Cynthia told me he had made arrangements in case of his sudden death, with instructions to carry them out as soon as possible. There would be a reading of the will later, although I know he had little to leave to anyone.

The car keys and my credit card change hands, and minutes later, I'm at the wheel of my not-so-new vehicle. Sure, compared to my old car, this is near luxury. I try not to notice the holes in the seat with the filling spilling out or the fact that the whole car smells suspiciously of smoke in defiance of the red NO SMOKING sign dangling from the mirror.

At least I can be reasonably sure that, unlike the trendy new startups that let you rent cute little electric Smart cars and drop them off wherever, this place doesn't put GPS trackers in their vehicles.

I don't know the exact address but I have a pretty good idea where I'm going. I've done my share of house visits in this neighborhood when I was starting out in social work. I'd seen the picture of the house on the internet, which, along with the leaked details of the woman's run-ins with social services, had no business being there. But people can be heartless when a story is deemed interesting enough. I should know.

It's not a short drive from Cynthia's neighborhood, even this late when there's practically no traffic. I look up the best route on the map on my phone but do my best to memorize it instead of using the GPS. I don't know why I'm taking the precaution—I'm not doing anything criminal.

As I drive onto the highway, I pop the audiobook CD into the player, bracing myself. The CD starts playing from the beginning, the solemn voice reciting the author's name, publisher, and cover credits. Cursing, I mash the buttons, but I have no idea where it left off so I stop at random in the middle and let it play.

"Chapter Ten. I spoke with Gregory Ainsworth at the school where he works as a counselor, providing support for students under duress, be it academic problems or social difficulties or, often, troublesome situations at home."

A memory scratches like a cat in the back of my mind. I eye the CD player, wary. What did he say the name was?

"We met at his office after hours, after all the students and most of the teachers have gone home. The school gives off an uncanny vibe, hallways quiet and lights dimmed. Every once in a while, we're interrupted by the bell, set to ring at regular intervals, bellowing to no one. Mr. Ainsworth's office is a quiet, serene place with the cozy air of someone's personal library or study. I can imagine students feeling safe here, comfortable to confide in this soft-spoken man. The following is the transcript of our interview.

"Mr. Ainsworth, throughout your career, you've often dealt with students who are victims of abuse at home."

"That's correct. It's an unfortunate reality, and in defiance to any preconceived ideas people might have, it occurs regardless of status or social class. No one is safe. Truth is, we never know what goes on behind closed doors in a family, no matter what the outright appearances may be. However, there are signs one can observe when a child is a victim of emotional, physical, or sexual abuse."

Ainsworth's voice is different from the other narrator's, but it doesn't resonate with me. It's not his. This one is well-spoken and borderline effeminate, all traces of regional accent scrubbed from it. The real Ainsworth, I remember now, sounded like a smoker, and there was a pronounced Minnesota drawl to his vowels. Which, ironically, came across as a lot more trustworthy and pleasant. Once I remember the voice, the rest of the picture reappears in my mind, building up like pixels until it comes into full focus. The knitted sweater, the muted scent of tobacco.

I can't help but feel betrayed that he spoke to this quack.

"Can you tell us how these signs typically present?"

"Well, the most immediately obvious one is a significant change in behavior. A child becomes withdrawn; his or her grades drop. This is something teachers most frequently observe, which is the catalyst for a more thorough investigation into the student's home life."

"And did Eli Warren present any signs?"

"See, Jonathan, the fact is, I only got to talk to Eli Warren once, in the winter of 2002."

I frown. Eli never told me this.

"Before that, I observed him, in the same general way I observed others. He was generally popular and well liked. Contrary to his sister—"

A small tremor runs up my spine and into my hands. But "Ainsworth" goes on, moving away from this line of thought without missing a beat.

"But he fit right in. He seemed to make a lot of friends rather quickly."

"Did he exhibit any signs of abuse then?"

"Not as far as I could tell."

"What did you talk about in the winter of 2002? Did he come to see you on his own or . . . ?"

"No. He did not. His teacher sent him."

I have to pause the CD because I need to concentrate on driving. The tangle of streets makes no sense: one-ways that go around and around like a maze, a cul-de-sac without a warning sign. I drive past rows and rows of those little duplexes that make up most of former working-class neighborhoods that have now been appropriated by hipsters willing to pay a grand a month for a studio with a kitchenette.

Every once in a while, I pass a gaping hole in the wall of buildings, like a missing tooth, where one has been demolished by a development company. Placards advertise the condos to come, glossy digital images of a marketing agency's idea of a perfect life. Much like my town house. In some spots, those condos are already built, and not a single one I pass remains uninhabited. Their geometrical façades look bewildered, out of place, like they just got teleported here from some parallel world.

Soon enough, I leave the condos behind, and the farther they recede in the rearview mirror, the more everything looks dusty and muddy, semiabandoned. This part of the neighborhood didn't get the treatment. Yet I find myself feeling more at home here, where the sprawl hasn't yet reached. It's more honest.

At last, I find the house I saw in the pictures online. When I see it, I understand why no one's thought to sell it to the developers—and no one likely will. It's nestled right below the viaduct, the last house tacked on at the end of its street. Grime coats the windows and once-white door. I don't blame Adele's mother for giving up on washing them. I'd get tired of the losing battle too. Which is a shame because up close, out of the blurry photos, it's one of those 1920s buildings that attempts coquettishness. The façade is brick, not cheap vinyl, and there are stylish patterns around the windows and doorway. I feel sad for it.

I have my pick of parking spots on the empty street. I look around but there doesn't seem to be any press nearby—no doubt that'll change once they catch my brother, I find myself thinking. And then the trial and sentencing and the whole circus. No doubt Jonathan Lamb is already accosting the poor woman for an interview for the sequel to his true crime book.

When I come up to the door, however, I notice that the doorbell has been ripped out, dangling on exposed blue wires. Anticipating the worst, I knock.

After no answer comes within a couple of minutes, I circle the house, which takes a few strides—it's a simple cube that must feel claustrophobic, especially when you're hounded by press. Behind it, where other buildings on the street have a tiny backyard, this one has a paved-over lot in which an early-nineties car is rusting amid weeds that sprout up from the cracks in the asphalt. There's a small patio with a plastic chair, its grooves holding water from the last rainfall. Through the curtained window of the patio door, I see a dim glimmer of light.

I admit, in that moment, common human decency almost makes me turn back and leave this woman alone. I consider just getting back in my car, doing a U-turn, and going after someone less vulnerable, someone who could actually help me. Instead, I maneuver my way past the puddles on the pavement, onto the patio, and up to the door. Before I raise my hand to knock, the curtain moves aside, startling me.

The face I'd seen on TV doesn't look nearly as bad in real life; I blame societal expectations of what women are worthy of gracing a screen. She's been crying, clearly, but there's no makeup to run and bleed into every crevice in her skin. She considers me with surprising shrewdness. Then I hear latches turning, and the door opens a crack. With a clink, the chain holding it in place tightens.

The woman evaluates me with a quick once-over. Her gaze lingers on my neck, and my hand shoots self-consciously to cover the waxy pink-white flesh there.

"I know who you are," she barks hoarsely. "Come in."

# CHAPTER TWENTY-FOUR

"How did you find the address?"

"Online," I say. Beyond the door, I find myself standing in a tiny kitchen space. It surprises me with its cleanness: no pile of dishes, no empty pizza boxes or beer bottles. Maybe I've misjudged her. Then again, my work experience suggests that such people rarely change before it's too late, and once the irrevocable has happened, the change doesn't last because whatever they had to lose, they already lost.

"My neighbors," she says dryly, by way of explanation, as she follows my gaze. "Helped me clean up. Ana from two houses down brought me groceries and wouldn't take any money when I offered. Beer?"

Bringing beer to a grieving mother seems dubious to me. So she's well enough to hit the liquor store, at least. But after the AA meeting, I'm a bundle of nerves so I agree.

She fetches two bottles of cheap lager from the fridge and opens them by wrapping her hand in the hem of her wrinkled pink top and twisting the caps. That isn't enough to deter me; I take a sip. It's weak and watery and tastes like stale bread.

"How do you know who I am?" I try cautiously.

"Your neck." She nods at it. "We're in the same boat, you and me. He killed your mom and dad, right?"

"Stepdad," I correct, more out of reflex than anything. And I realize with growing incredulity why she thinks I'm here, the only reason she opened her door to me. Unwisely.

For her, I decide I'm willing to play the part. "I don't know what to say. You must be devastated."

She heaves a sigh and takes a long swig from the beer bottle. "Look, the things I said on TV—you did see that, didn't you?"

I nod.

"They're things they told me to say. That woman, Figueroa." The mention of her name makes me suppress a tiny shudder. "But that doesn't mean I didn't mean them, right?"

"I'm sure you meant every word."

"But let me tell you, she's a horrible woman. A bad person." She lingers on the last two words, the hoarseness of her voice deepening as if for emphasis. "She has no compassion. Treated me like garbage. I could tell she didn't believe me, even when I said the exact words she told me to say. Can you imagine having such a cold heart? I did love my girl. I did." She nods her head to punctuate each word. "I wasn't always perfect, but who is? Your mom, the one who died. She can't have been perfect either, not all the time."

She stares me straight in the eye as she says that, her gaze suddenly clear and sober. Her eyes are a wishy-washy light brown, as if they couldn't decide what color they wanted to be.

I try to think of my mother but all I can conjure up is that grave, the flat tombstone and dying flowers. I try to remember her face. She was young—only in her early thirties, although at twelve, that seemed old to me. Her chestnut mane was beginning to sprout gray hairs ahead of its time but she covered them obstinately with hair dye. She was reasonably pretty in a practical way; the only makeup she troubled with was mascara and lipstick. But the specifics, the features, are lost to me. Hopelessly blurred. I realize I don't remember our last conversation, the last words she ever said to me.

"You weren't a bad mother, Colleen," I say, even though it's not true. And since I can't have her continue with the self-reflection much longer, I decide to jump in. "Did Adele live here? With you?"

Colleen nods absentmindedly. "Over there. Her room. The police went over every inch though, messed it up. Me and Ana put it back together."

"May I?" But she's glassy-eyed, staring off into space at the area just above the kitchen sink, like she forgot I was there. I move across the room, into the short hallway with two doors.

It's going to be useless at this point, I think. If, like she says, the police combed through everything...

The room is tiny, like I expected, but neater than I thought. Probably thanks to this Ana person. Maybe because of that it looks impersonal, unlived-in. Like it was just a place to crash for a night, not the room of a girl in her early twenties. There are clothes folded on top of a shabby dresser. A beaded curtain serves as a closet door, violent pink, the only splash of color. When I pull it aside with a soft clinking sound, I see a couple of stray hangers, no clothes, and old shoes piled up on the floor. Mostly empty tubes of makeup sit lined up on the bedside table.

Colleen has followed me and is standing in the empty doorway. I ask whether the cops took the door off its hinges.

She shrugs. "No. Never had a door when we moved in."

"When did she leave?" I ask.

"She's always been coming and going but the last time she left was 'bout six months ago. It's not like what they're thinking." Colleen doesn't specify who but I understand, from experience. People like me, social services, police. "I didn't throw her out. She was always welcome here. She could keep living with me till she was forty—I wouldn't've minded. It's like when she was a kid, even if I brought a boyfriend home, I'd always tell her in advance, you know? And we didn't have a fight or anything. She came to visit once in a while."

"Did she tell you why she left? Did she find a new place to live?"

Colleen's look speaks of utter powerlessness and despair. She can only shrug. "I asked but she wouldn't tell me. I figured it was with that boyfriend of hers." Her face contorts with grief and horror that she can no longer struggle against. She clasps her hand over her mouth. Boyfriend? She must mean Eli.

I can't resist. "Did the police find anything?"

Colleen shakes her head. "I don't know. I wasn't here. They told me to leave so I was over at Ana's."

"That must have been hard for you."

"You have no idea." She takes another sip—more like a gulp—of her beer. "They're horrible people. Horrible."

"I know." I can't imagine there's any love lost between this woman and the forces of the law.

"No empathy. At all. Heartless. You think I don't know what they were doing here? Did they think I'm dumb?" She's becoming agitated, her words slurred. "When it's clear as day that he did it. That he killed her. Why search her room? They think I'm too stupid to figure it out."

"What do you mean?" A little icy shiver races up my spine. I pretend to turn my attention to the makeup tubes on the bedside table.

"They think they'll find something to make it all look like it was her fault," Colleen says, her voice quavering. "You know, they find things, and I've seen other murdered girls in the news, and—" She cuts herself off and takes a deep breath. "I thought—if they find drugs or something like that—they'll just say it was a gang thing and won't look for him. The person who did it."

My heart starts to beat awfully fast.

"That's all they need," I say in agreement. "An excuse. Nobody wants to bother. To do their job."

"Yeah." She nods eagerly. Her face is turning red, from agitation or alcohol or both. "Because we're not rich, and she was— She had problems...It's like her life don't matter, you know?"

"I know."

"Are you going to try to defend him? Because let me tell you, there's not a thing on earth that—"

"No. Why would I defend him, of all people? Think about it, Colleen." I compose my face into a softer, mournful look that's supposed to be relatable and trustworthy. "He killed my family. I haven't even spoken to him in fifteen years."

That's because he was not allowed to contact me under any circumstances. But she doesn't need to know that.

Looking lost, she drains the last of the beer and sets the bottle down on top of the dresser. I wonder how many beers preceded it before I got here.

She sighs. "They found money," she says, hanging her head, her gaze straying from mine like a guilty dog's. "The police. Lots of it, hidden all around the room. I have no idea how she got it."

I nod encouragingly, my mournful smile stiff on my lips. I have a pretty good guess how she got it.

Her look is pleading, almost desperate. "It wasn't anything—anything *bad*, you know what I'm saying?"

"I'm sure it wasn't. She was probably just saving up," I assure her.

She continues rambling, without missing a beat. "And

they took it. They took it all. Can you imagine? Heartless people. It was her money, which means it was mine too. I could have used it around here." Her gaze unfocuses. "For the funeral, of course."

"Of course," I say. Of course.

# CHAPTER TWENTY-FIVE

*I thought Eli would initially refuse to talk. But on the contrary, he seemed enthused—especially when he found out I was writing a book. Sure enough, any attention-loving, narcissistic person would be elated to be the subject of a book. I don't suppose it made a difference to him that the book was not exactly portraying him in the most positive light.*

*One of the first things he did when I told him was ask, petulantly,* Will my sister be in it too?

*I asked him how he felt about his estranged sibling. Eli Warren looked at me with surprise, which I suppose was feigned.*

*"How am I supposed to feel about her? We're twins. We have the same thoughts."*

*He didn't elaborate further, only to say,* I just hope she reads your book once it comes out. She's a very bookish person, you know. I'm sure she'll love it.

—*Into Ashes: The Shocking Double Murder in the Suburbs* by Jonathan Lamb, Eclipse Paperbacks, 2004, 1st ed.

## FIFTEEN YEARS EARLIER: BEFORE THE FIRE

*What did I see?*

Andrea asks herself that question over and over. *Was this because of the stolen money? Did Sergio hit my brother? Or did Eli fall over somehow? Did he trip? Did he drop something heavy? Did I fall asleep at my desk and imagine the whole thing?*

She hasn't asked Sergio. The thought never crossed her mind. Not so much because she was afraid but because no matter how she'd phrase the question, it would come across as an accusation.

Eli had made her angry. When she asked him, head on, he just shrugged. Then he told her, in his most condescending tone, to go do homework or something. The next morning, he wore his hat pulled low over his face, and if he had a bruise, she couldn't see. That afternoon the bruise was there though. At least, *a* bruise. She tried to figure out if it was on the right side, tried to remember where exactly Sergio hit him, if he did hit him. She couldn't.

Eli shrugged again and gave a lopsided grin. "If Mom asks me, I'll say I got into a fight at school."

He didn't address another word to her all day. When they got home, their mother saw the bruise. She gave her son a look Andrea couldn't read. There was no sympathy in it, only what looked like anger, with a hefty dose of fear. And doubt.

Andrea didn't dare say a thing.

# CHAPTER TWENTY-SIX

I drive straight home, taking the long route to steady my nerves. I'm halfway home when I remember about the CD. Irritated, I stab my fingertip onto the Play button. It picks up right where it left off.

"Eli's teacher sent him to your office?"

"Yes. The seventh-grade gym teacher. There had been an incident involving another student."

"Can you tell me about it?"

"For confidentiality reasons, I can't mention any names."

"Understandable."

I grind my teeth. How am I hearing about this for the first time just now? I try to remember. I was too absorbed in my petty twelve-year-old problems back then: not having the right clothes to fit in, not wearing a bra when other girls did, not having the courage to shoplift that lip gloss I wanted. It was long before I noticed anything weird about the way Eli acted. Did something happen that winter? Did I hear anything through the middle school rumor mill? Not that anyone was in a rush to pass on the latest juicy gossip to me, the girl no one liked.

"In gym class, there was an altercation between Eli and another student."

I note the careful, deliberately vague choice of words. It tells me absolutely nothing, and I understand that's the intention.

"The other child wasn't hurt, thankfully, so the school decided not to get the parents involved. The teacher and the principal sent Eli to my office. The intent wasn't so much for me to evaluate him or determine whether he presented a danger to anyone else at the school but for me to give him a lecture. That's not what I was told to do directly but it was understood."

"Did you evaluate him nonetheless?"

"I had a conversation with him. Not a long one. But it was enough for me to get a glimpse beneath the surface, Jonathan."

"The surface?"

"Yes. Clinical sociopaths—they're cunning, even as children. You know this, I am sure. But for the readers, I'll reiterate: The face the sociopath presents to the world is not his true face. Underneath the charm and easygoing likability lurks a whole other being, devoid of remorse or empathy. The sociopath's victims will eventually see this other face, and the change is quite drastic. It can be extremely unsettling to see that mask drop, and at first, people are reluctant to believe it. They make up all kinds of excuses, try to explain away what they had seen."

"You make him sound like some kind of werewolf or vampire."

"That's what a sociopath is, in all senses but the literal. It is that bad. And whenever the sociopath is forced to reveal his true self, when he loses control of his public perception, that's when he can become extremely dangerous."

"Do you believe that's what happened with Eli Warren?"

"I did not evaluate Eli Warren after the fire. But that day in my office, I saw the true face of Eli Warren, the one his peers or other teachers did not see."

I realize I'm clenching my jaw to keep my teeth from chattering and busy myself with turning up the heat in the car. But cold isn't the problem. The fans begin to whir—more like howl—and hot air fills the car, too much too fast. Within moments, I'm sweating and have to crack open a window.

"Can you tell me about this conversation?"

"I can tell you the main points. My approach, in those kinds of cases, is usually not to threaten the child, be it with punishment, suspension, telling the parents—you get the idea. First, I ask for their side of the story and try to figure out the motivations behind what they did. And then I go from there. To be honest, in this case, it was difficult to imagine. But still. I wanted to give him a chance to explain himself.

"Eli sat there, across my desk, and his body language didn't signal any kind of distress. No nervousness. No remorse that I could see. He was relaxed, looking around.

As I asked him questions about what had happened, he'd shrug and then casually try to shift the conversation. This went on for maybe fifteen minutes, and then...Well, it's hard to describe. I guess the best explanation is that he just got fed up. In answer to my next carefully worded question, he just shrugged and told me exactly what it was he did. He sounded annoyed more than anything else."

I find myself thinking that it does sound like Eli.

"I asked him why he did it. To my dismay, he smiled, this big, sincere grin of a twelve-year-old child. He leaned over the desk and said, and I'm paraphrasing but the meaning is essentially the same, *Listen, Mr. Ainsworth, you're going to go to the principal and tell her it was a misunderstanding and I'm a good boy. Or else I'll go home to my stepdad and tell him you touched me. And then I'll show him where and how.* Naturally, I was shocked."

"I can only imagine."

I pause the CD and focus on the roar of the wind in the car window. It's cold and humid and smells like exhaust but I let it whip my hair out of my ponytail and around my head. I take a deep breath, clench then unclench my hands on the steering wheel, and—oh, what the heck—close my eyes. I picture my car's wheels loosening on the damp asphalt, the car going gradually, gracefully off track, across the yellow line, right up until the moment it collides with the concrete barrier. I can almost taste the metallic blood in my mouth, feel the shattered glass and twisted metal, smell the fire. It'd be like yesterday but times a hundred, and faster, I hope. It's so easy.

Then a long, hysterical honk snaps me out of it. My eyes fly open. The first millisecond is a moment of mad terror, like waking up from a nightmare and not knowing where I am. But reflex overrides my deer-in-headlights brain, thank God—or my imagined scenario would have been a real one. I grip the steering wheel firmly, turn, and swerve back into my lane. The other car gives another honk as it passes me. My skin tingles in an almost erotic feeling. Inches from death.

I glance at the display on the CD player that reads PAUSED, my mind teeming with scenarios, some of which venture uncomfortably close to conspiracy theory territory. I remember Ainsworth's curious but kind gaze. That's why he left the room that time, I think, confused. Because it wasn't anyone else—it was Eli I was talking about. And there had been a precedent.

Now I realize there was more to it than I ever knew. The knowledge fills me with an uneasy feeling. With resolve, I press Play.

"As shocking as it was, I managed to regain my composure. I asked him whether he knew what harm such a false accusation could do to someone. He just smirked at me—like he knew and he didn't care. I have seen my share of problem children but I'd never seen anything like this."

"Later, he made the same accusation about his stepfather, Sergio Bianchi. But the investigation concluded that there was no basis for that accusation."

"As I'm aware."

"While in custody, he also attempted to make a similar accusation about you, Mr. Ainsworth."

"Yes. Officers came to my home to interview me about the matter."

It's one of those moments that make me remember I'm not listening to the real interview—just a transcript. Because the actor's voice is too smooth; it doesn't miss a beat, doesn't pause for shock the way Ainsworth would have. The way any sane person would.

"What do you think Eli Warren's motivations were in doing what he did?"

"It's hard to say, Jonathan. I wish I'd had a chance to talk to Eli again. But what is certain, even at his tender age, is that he is a danger to himself and others—mostly others. Who can tell what he'll turn into as an adult?"

"What do you think of the sentence?"

"I do not think it's sufficient. Not by a long shot."

The neutral voice on the recording announces the start of the next chapter. I don't have it in me to listen anymore so I spend the rest of the drive home listening to random pop songs on the radio.

The town house greets me with stillness. The air is stale but I don't want to open the windows. I go get my laptop and take a seat at the dining room table and then get up again to pace. I peer into the fridge, take out the two leftover slices of pizza from last night, and throw them in the microwave. While they're reheating, I check my phone: a bunch of irate texts from Chris, which I delete—can't face them for now—and a terse voicemail from Cynthia letting me know the funeral is tomorrow and I'm expected to come say my goodbyes at eleven thirty sharp.

I start to compose a text to Milt but then let it go and erase everything. If I told him what I was doing, he'd only try to talk me out of it, as any sane, logical person would.

I sit down, open my laptop, and enter Ainsworth's name into the search field.

# CHAPTER TWENTY-SEVEN

The next morning, I park by the funeral home a little past noon, about half an hour late. Yet my car is one of only four in the entire parking lot. This is not off to a great start.

And now I have to get through the whole thing without even a glass of wine to take the edge off. I'm edgy, too full of coffee and running on not nearly enough sleep. I should be somewhere else right now, I find myself thinking pettily. I should be stalking Ainsworth, shaking answers out of him. I should be looking for my brother. Should, should, should.

Instead, I'm here, at a funeral home that smells like jasmine air freshener. I should be up for some kind of record. I must bring my stepfathers bad luck.

There are more people inside than I expected. They must have parked elsewhere. I have no idea who they are. Most of Jim's connections (I'm not sure the Boudreaux family ever had genuine friends) were the result of Cynthia's relentless networking. And she then networked her way to a more-than-profitable divorce. Too bad the splitting up of assets coincided with the 2007 financial crisis, and the fancy house and cars suddenly turned out to be worth a lot less.

I see her now, making excruciating small talk with a tall, bony woman in a skirt suit. Cynthia is put together as usual, not a trace of the disheveled wreck from last night. But under her makeup, she looks gray somehow, lifeless, extinguished, and for the first time it occurs to me to wonder why she's the one organizing her ex-husband's funeral. Did she ever think they'd get back together? Did she hope until the end?

That would be the stupidest thing to hope for, and Cynthia has never been stupid.

I can tell the conversation between Cynthia and the woman in the suit has come to an uncomfortable lull so I decide to move in to the rescue. My stepmother looks away from the woman and at me with the same listless gaze. "Andrea," she says. I can feel the woman's curious gaze inspecting me, from my frumpy, hastily put together outfit of black trousers and sweater to my face, lingering a touch too long on the scar tissue visible on my neck. I bristle but ignore her. Instead, I take Cynthia's arm and lead her away, with only a brief apologetic look at the woman.

I want to ask her if she's all right but the look she gives me makes me reconsider. It's leaden, unwavering. "Thank you for coming," she says neutrally.

"Who was that?"

She shakes her head dismissively. "Someone from...back in the day." When they still had high-society friends and hangers-on. She must understand what it is I'm really asking, because she adds, "No, he wasn't seeing anyone. Or if he was, I don't know about it."

A heavy silence hangs between us, punctuated with the soft plinking of the sad classical music pouring from the hidden speakers. Their divorce, over a decade ago now, came out of the blue. One day we came back from school and Jim Boudreaux had moved out. Next thing I knew, there was a FOR SALE sign sticking out of the acid-green front lawn, and it just snowballed from there. We weren't given an explanation. Or at least I wasn't. Did he leave her for another woman, now that the political career wasn't happening for sure and there was no need to maintain the family-man front? Did Cynthia find out about some fling on the side and kick him out? Neither of these would be terribly surprising.

Cynthia reaches and grips my arm above the elbow with unexpected strength. She pulls me closer and then makes a motion like she's drawing me in for a hug. That's when I smell the whiskey. Masked carefully by some violently minty mouthwash but apparent all the same.

"Men like Jim can't be expected to be loyal," she says in a quiet, steady tone. "I know that. A truly wise woman won't make an unnecessary fuss over such trivialities. Remember this, Andrea. It'll serve you."

She's nuts, I find myself thinking, incredulous. Cynthia never struck me as the type to forgive cheating. But then again, I'm one to talk. Or to judge. Especially her. The one person who deserves contempt here is lying in a nice, glossy coffin, cold and dead and safe from any unfortunate consequences of his choices.

I try to extricate myself from Cynthia's viselike hug and feel a rush of intense anger. My fists clench, and I all but shove my stepmother away. She regains composure in a heartbeat. A couple of people give me looks, and suddenly I feel like I can't breathe in here, in the air freshener and heavy smell of morbid-looking lilies that sit on every surface.

"When you get older, Andrea," Cynthia says, "you'll learn. Try to be more understanding with people. Appearances aren't always real. Not everything is the way it looks."

She manages to be both smug and condescending in spite of her advanced state of inebriation. Oh, the things I could tell you, I think, and clench my fists harder. All your understanding, all your retrograde bullshit would go right the fuck out the window. You'd be flipping tables of canapés and smashing those flower vases.

I flee to the back of the funeral home before I give in to the temptation to say something. As I slip out through the back exit, it occurs to me that I haven't seen Leeanne yet. And sure enough, she's perched on a narrow ledge by the exit door. She's smoking a joint that sends me into a violent fit of coughs.

"And here I hoped you weren't coming," Leeanne says.

"Same."

She chuckles and holds out the joint. I make a grimace that must speak volumes, because she sneers and shakes her head in mock dismay. "What, it's not good enough for you? And I thought—"

"Where the hell did you even get this stuff?" I say. "From a tenth grader?"

"If you have anything better, feel free to share."

I wonder just how bad it would be to sneak around the building to my car. And then to just drive off without a goodbye.

"By the way," I say instead, "your mom is completely shit-faced in there. You might want to go check up on her."

"That's rich, coming from you. At least she didn't pawn anyone's jewelry, did she?"

I groan inwardly for the hundredth time in the last twenty minutes. "I keep forgetting about that."

"If anything, you're the one who should be getting shit-faced. It is all your fault, after all."

"You're crazy," I say, hoping my tone conveys contempt and nothing else.

Instead, she drops the joint, gets up, and crushes it into the ground with the toe of her shoe. She's not wearing sweats today but her nice clothes, which seem to fit poorly over the ten or so pounds she's gained. She jabs her fingertip at me, her gaze sharp and accusatory and not at all stoned. "You," she says with another jab of her chewed-up fingernail. "Because of you he left. And because of you, he's dead now. Happy? You always hated us. You hated our house, you hated me, you hated my family. It's all ruined now, for good. Happy? You and your fucking brother."

"What does he have to do with any of this?" I hiss.

"You two destroy everything you touch. Your whole

family is like…like poison. You're a disease, Andrea. My dad took you in like a stray dog. And you've never even spoken to him since he left. Oh, I remember. You were so happy he was finally gone. That you finally wrecked the family you loathed so much."

That's not entirely true. I did speak to him. On the phone. Once. Three years ago, right after my brother got out of prison. But I can't really tell her that.

Leeanne plunks back down on the ledge and buries her face in her hands. "Why don't you just fuck off," she says without looking up, her voice muffled. "You think you know everything but you don't know shit. So please, just go."

A mean, angry retort dances on the tip of my tongue but I bite it back, thinking about everything I learned in the last few days. I'm overcome with a strange feeling. I feel like crossing the distance between us, grabbing her by the shoulders, and shaking the truth out of her. You think I don't know anything, you hypocritical, deceitful bitch. If you only knew…

"You have no right to even be here," Leeanne yells after me when I turn to walk away. Her voice cracks, hoarse and ugly. I realize at last that she really is stoned, and not just on cheap weed. I shut the door behind me and let the stifling semiquiet of the funeral home engulf me. There's a photo on the big TV above the refreshment table, a family photo of Cynthia, Jim, and Leeanne from happier times. Leeanne is about twelve. She's wearing this powder-blue twinset thing with rhinestones, one I remember well from school picture days.

I think I hear Cynthia calling my name, or maybe it's someone else. Ignoring it, I make for the exit, walking as fast as basic politeness will allow. I need to get out of here.

As I turn around one last time, I see that the picture on the TV has changed to a portrait of Jim alone, from the same era—probably a professional photo for his doomed campaign. He somehow managed it, I find myself thinking. Managed to sneak away just in time to avoid answering for his actions. How very like him.

I wonder what all these respectful, black-clad guests would say if I told them what Jim and I talked about three years ago, when I called to let him know Eli had been released. When I asked him what I should do now.

He hung up on me.

# CHAPTER TWENTY-EIGHT

"Hello, I'm a former student, and I'd like to contact some-one who used to work here around the two thousands."

I hope I sound normal. And not like a journalist. I imag-ine they've had their share of media attention in the last couple of days.

"A teacher?"

"No. A counselor. Mr. Ainsworth."

A moment's hesitation. "I'm sorry. I can't give out confi-dential information."

"I just need to contact Mr. Ainsworth. I could use an email address, anything."

"Who may I ask is speaking?"

I draw a breath. "Andrea Warren."

It hasn't been Warren for a while, but the sound of the name has the intended effect. I hear a sharp intake of breath on the other end. The woman hesitates, clearly un-sure how to react.

"Ms. Warren," she finally says, her voice wavering between coldness and a clumsy attempt at kindness.

"Andrea," I say, giving her a reprieve from having to utter the cursed name again. "It's very important that I contact Mr. Ainsworth."

After some more sighing and awkward attempts to stall, she ends up giving me the phone number. "I'm not sure the number is up to date," she says apologetically. "Mr. Ainsworth hasn't worked with us in over a decade."

This much I gathered from the interview I just heard. I can't help but wonder whether he quit because of what happened.

"That's all right. Thank you."

I expect her to say her polite goodbyes as quickly as she can, but instead, she hems and haws.

"Thank you," I say again, prompting.

"Excuse me, Ms. . . . Andrea?"

"Yes?"

"Could you not tell him you got his number here?"

I start saying yes, of course, no problem. I'm not going to even think of asking why. But she supplies the answer of her own volition.

"I'm not sure he would want to talk to you."

*   *   *

It's early in the morning after another mostly sleepless night. The house is new construction so there aren't creaky floorboards or an old roof to blame for any noise I heard or imagined in the dark. I made sure every window was closed, the door bolted, every curtain and blind closed tight. But still, I couldn't shake the eerie feeling I had the other night before Sunny called, the feeling that I was being watched. I only nodded off once I turned on the bedside lamp on Milton's side. Then I could tell myself he was right here, reading some paperback next to me while I drifted off to sleep, like he had done so often when we were together.

After a too-long shower and a too-large coffee, I made the first phone call. Now I sit and stare at my phone, wondering whether I can really go through with this. That secretary was right—I'm probably the last person he wants to hear from right now.

But I need to know. I need an explanation. The truth— as if the truth has ever done anyone any good.

I dial the number quickly before I can change my mind.

It only rings once before someone picks up.

"Mr. Ainsworth?" I say awkwardly into the silence.

"Andrea," says the familiar voice. A heavy voice—the smoker's rasp grates more than I remember. "They told me you'd be getting in touch."

Really now, I think. So much for *I'm not sure the number is up to date*.

"I think I know what you're calling about. I've been expecting it. It took longer than I thought."

I'm not entirely sure what he means by the last phrase.

"The book, right?" he prompts. "The interview."

"Yes." I'm not sure if I should admit I hadn't read the interview until now.

He gives a gravelly chuckle. "I wouldn't have wanted to revisit it either. But now neither of us has a choice."

"I need to know what you were talking about," I say.

"I'm not going to tell you on the phone."

I barely have time to start composing a reply in my head, pleading and furious at the same time, when he adds, "We should meet. Do you mind coming here? I'm not very mobile these days."

Slightly dazed, I jot down the address.

*       *       *

I'm surprised and dismayed when I arrive at my destination. For some reason, I pictured a suburban house but one that kept some edge, had a high-powered barbecue on a vast terrace, a wine cellar. But Gregory Ainsworth lives in a rented apartment, in a building not quite nice enough to have been repurposed for yuppie condos. At least the elevator works. When I ring the bell, I wait for more than a couple of minutes until I hear shuffling behind the door. But when he unlocks it and lets me in, I begin to understand.

He's hooked up to an oxygen tank. Under his snug-fitting knitted cap, I suspect he's hiding a bare scalp. He looks thinner than I remember but not yet emaciated. Not like someone on the final stretch before losing the fight, but not like someone who's winning it either. I don't dare ask what he has, and he doesn't supply the information. He just gestures for me to follow him, and I do.

The furniture is minimal, but there's a couch and an armchair. He settles into the chair, and having no other options, I perch on the edge of the couch.

"So, he finally did it," Ainsworth says, wasting no time. "Killed someone else."

I must look taken aback, because he gives a grim smirk. "If there's anything this thing taught me"—he gestures around him, meaning the oxygen tank maybe, or the apartment, or me, or my brother, or the whole situation—"it's not to waste time pointlessly. He did kill someone again. Just like I thought he would."

"We don't know that for sure," I say, because it feels like I should. But it comes out uncertain, subdued.

"Please don't tell me that you of all people showed up here to take his side."

"I just—"

"Or else you would have been here much sooner. Before he bludgeoned some girl's head into a pulp. But it's too late now—he did, and everyone is losing their minds because it doesn't really play into the redemption narrative, does it?"

"Is that what you thought? Did you believe it?"

"Believe what?"

"What you said in the interview. That he should have gotten a harsher sentence."

He sighs, hovering on the edge of breaking into a fit of coughs. His eyes are watering but he speaks up, voice slightly strained. "What do you think?"

"The book was biased. If you said something else, then Jonathan Whoever wouldn't have included it."

He acquiesces with a nod. "True. And apart from the fact there were some things I couldn't divulge, not the entirety of that interview made it into the book. Because lawyers and...you can imagine." He waves his hand dismissively. "But I really did think it, for what it's worth."

I ignore the last remark. "That's why I'm here. I want to know the things that didn't make it into the book."

He examines me shrewdly. His eyes may be rheumy but his gaze is still sharp. "Really? You know, I could sell it to a journalist for a decent sum. Or even to that Lamb fellow. He called me, you know. Left a message. I could practically hear cash register sounds in his voice." He chuckles. "I didn't call back."

"But you answered my call."

"I did. Because there's a chance I might not have anything to lose, but the flip side is, I might not have much use for that money either."

I nod.

"And something tells me you, too, know more than you let on."

I contain a shiver. It takes some effort to look him straight in the eye.

"So let's call it an exchange of knowledge. Satisfy my curiosity before I pass, and I'll return the favor."

I stay silent.

"Well?"

"Okay."

"You first."

"That depends on what you want to know. I was a child then too." I don't like the way he's smirking.

"Okay, okay. Fair enough. You can ask me one thing. Then I'll ask you. Deal?"

I give a short nod and jump into it. "What were you talk-

ing about? What was the gym class incident? Did he get into
a fight?"

Ainsworth holds my gaze. "No. What really happened—
and you're not going to like this...The teacher caught
him before class. He was in the equipment room. He had
pinned a girl down on top of some mats and pulled down
her jeans."

He says it with perfect calm but it's enough to knock the
breath right out of me.

"You're saying that he—"

"He tried to. You understand now why it didn't make it
into the book? No one knew what to do. Only that it had
to be handled as quietly as possible. Can you imagine the
fallout if this had gotten out? For the girl, first and foremost. Think of the rumors that would have been started.
You know how people, especially preteens, can be to a
girl who was in that situation. But also for the school and
the girl's parents—there would have been utter chaos. And
nothing had actually happened, thank God—"

"So you covered it up."

"We handled it," he says firmly. "They sent your brother
to me to try to figure out what exactly happened and so
I could explain to him that what he'd done was unacceptable, and—"

"But he didn't actually face any consequences," I point
out.

"If we'd suspended him, your parents would have
wanted to know why, and so would the other kids. It
would have gotten out."

"Of course." I should be indignant, maybe even enraged,

but my mind is numb. I'm trying to piece it all together, figure out how what he just told me fits into the bigger picture, but I feel like too many pieces are still missing.

"And the way he reacted when I talked to him, well—you've read it. That's exactly how it happened. No embellishments." His calm is starting to fray at the edges. He suppresses a couple of coughs, badly. "He admitted that he tried to assault that girl, and I suspect he's done more than try with ... others."

I'm hovering on the edge of the couch, my every muscle taut with tension. "Others? Who?"

He finally succumbs and starts to cough. It goes on for a minute or two before he gets the coughing back under control. His lips look ashen.

"Listen, it's just ... It's what people like him do. It was obvious. Isn't that why you came into my office that day?"

I'm stricken. I don't know what to say. The numbness only grows deeper. He thought I was there to tell him my brother ... molested me? Abused me? Worse? I shut my eyes but it's not enough to shut out this room, reeking of medicine and a subtle undercurrent of decay. He *is* losing the battle, I realize with the same strange calm. He just doesn't quite look the part yet. But he's dying, and he knows it, deep down.

On the heels of that realization comes another. Should I tell him? Tell him the truth, as I know it? Not the whole truth—just about that day, the real reason I was there. That I came to tell him I thought someone abused Eli. That I was there to ask him what to do.

Ainsworth must notice my agitation, because he shifts

in his armchair and speaks up. "Look, you can tell me. I won't repeat it to anyone—don't worry. I have no one to tell at this point. I understand why you didn't want anyone to know." He nods sympathetically at my neck and arms. I haven't bothered to wear a turtleneck, and I'm wearing Milton's T-shirt again. The wider neckline shows more than usual.

Except this isn't about my burn scars; it's not even about my dead mother or the childhood I lost that day. My jaw grinds, and my eyes fill with tears. I don't have the where-withal to hide them, and he interprets them like I thought he would.

"I'm so sorry, Andrea. I'm sorry you had to go through all that. I wish you hadn't run out of the office while I was gone—I went to get the principal because after the incident that winter... You understand. And I'm sorry I was a coward when it mattered. I should have called you in and listened. I'm not saying I could have prevented what happened to your parents, but..."

I squeeze my eyes shut, and the tears run down my cheeks, leaving two cool trails. I sniffle and hastily wipe my nose with the back of my hand. He holds out a box of tissues. I don't take one.

"You couldn't have," I say. My voice wavers just enough. "Don't blame yourself."

He's too far to reach out and try to hold my hand. I stand up. "Thank you. Thank you for telling me the truth."

"There's nothing to thank me for." His voice drips with bitterness. His eyes are full of water again—oh God, is he crying too? The whole thing is grotesque in that Lifetime movie, Oprah way. But maybe it's for the best if I can exploit it.

"Just tell me one thing. I won't tell a soul—I promise. Who was the girl?"

He blinks, looks up at me, and I think that he finally saw through my game. That he's about to throw me out of his apartment without telling me a thing. But to my surprise and relief, he heaves a deep sigh that rattles in his lungs.

"I guess I might as well. I trust you'll respect her privacy."

I hold my breath.

"It was Leeanne," he says finally. "Leeanne Boudreaux."

# CHAPTER TWENTY-NINE

Leeanne Boudreaux, my stepsister.

Yeah, they covered it up out of concern for the girl. What utter bullshit. They covered it up out of concern for their own asses and for what would have happened if the school's greatest benefactor had learned that his daughter had been sexually assaulted by one of the students. I guess it was easy enough to talk Leeanne into keeping her mouth shut. Threaten with the stigma but also promise to boost her grades just a tiny bit. Piece of cake.

After all, nothing bad *really* happened, right?

It's the middle of the afternoon, I'm behind the wheel of my rented car, and I have no idea what to do with myself. Finally, I pull up to a Starbucks drive-through and get one of those giant coffees—full sugar and the whipped cream on top, please. In the parking lot, I try to hold back my nausea as I sip the concoction.

Should I call Leeanne, or something? And what— apologize?

At least now it's clear why she singled me out to make my life a living hell.

But at the same time, I can't stop thinking about my brother. The list of lies grows longer by one. He never told me—of course he didn't. I can't think of a way he could have made it sound like he was the victim.

What the hell did you do, Eli? What else did you lie to me about?

I can't think of many ways to find out.

From the start, I had been lying to myself that I wasn't going to do this, when I knew full well that I was. Isn't that why I rented the hard-to-track car? Or why I switched my phone off before I even pulled the unremarkable little Ford out of the parking lot, even though I told myself I was going home?

The drive to northeast Denver takes less than a half hour. The whole time, my preservation instinct and basic common sense are screaming at me in my head, making my hands tighten on the steering wheel, this close to just twisting it, making an illegal U-turn and going back. Going home. Maybe calling Milton—no, definitely calling Milton. Thank God my switched-off phone is in the glove compartment, and it's staying there.

I want no part in this. I shouldn't be involved. And if only I could, I'd—

I make the last turn and find myself on the street. I expected something more—police cars, or at least police tape. But there's nothing. I suppose forensics are done with it, having analyzed every inch of the place, every droplet of blood splatter, every piece of tooth and bone. Then Adele's body was taken to some lab so they could poke and prod at it some more, inspect the ridges of fractured bones and empty eye sockets, test the blood. Try to pry the answers from it.

I drive in front of the building slowly. It only has four apartments, four dirty-white doors, all of them anonymous and blank. It's the top one on the right. After I circle around, I leave the car two blocks away and walk through the alleys.

Although the sun is high over the horizon, here, in the damp shadow, it's colder—so cold that I find myself shivering. The backs of the buildings are even uglier than the fronts: no yards, just rusted emergency stairs and even more rusted balconies, trash cans and recycling bins. Graffiti everywhere.

Place must have seemed like quite a step up after prison.

I don't have to look very hard to find it because the back door is boarded up. Sloppily, which is lucky for me. I'm able to pry away the piece of plywood with ease. The glass had been shattered, only tiny shards of it remaining around the frame.

Did he do that in a fit of rage? Did she do it, in a last-ditch attempt to get help, to get away from him? I shake my head to chase away the thoughts. He didn't do it. He didn't.

I reach in, turn the lock on the other side, and go in.

I've been bracing myself for the sight and smell of gore, but what I'm greeted with is the antiseptic scent of cleaner and an expanse of grayed linoleum, not a droplet of blood anywhere. The place had been cleaned professionally. I guess whoever owns it wants its sordid history wiped away and forgotten as quickly as possible, to find new tenants and to move on.

If nothing else, it makes me feel reassured. They're really through with it now, I think. Figueroa and her crew aren't coming back here.

Still, I make sure not to touch anything. At home, I'd grabbed a pair of basic rubber gloves that I do dishes in, and now my hands are sweating inside them.

I don't have any illusions. I know that someone will notice that I broke in, that the plywood is missing, that there are steps echoing where there should be none. Every second I have is precious, yet still, I don't go straight where I intended. I can't help it—something pulls me, a magnetic compulsion. I want to see—no, I don't want to but I think I need to. I need to know how he lived for the last three years, while I was enjoying life in the town house with my blue-blooded fiancé.

The apartment is a small one-bedroom. That's a generous term because the bedroom itself isn't separated from the main space except by an open archway where a curtain used to hang. Now there's only an empty curtain rod with a couple of plastic rings still in the corner. Did it get taken away as evidence, to study the blood splatter? Did he try to wrap the body in it, try to dispose of it?

He didn't, I remind myself.

The small window is covered with yellowing blinds. Linoleum is ripped out in places. The kitchen isn't a kitchen but a corner of the main room: a stove, a sink, a squat little fridge that's not plugged in. The fumes of bleach burn the inside of my nose.

Hesitant, I push the bathroom door, which creaks as it swings open. At first, I wonder if all this is an exercise in futility. There's barely room to take a shower in here, much less hide something. Still, I kneel on the floor. What I first thought to be tiles aren't real tiles, just squares of vinyl made to look like ceramic. I try them with my fingertips—everything is solidly glued into place. All kinds of thoughts race through my head. If there was anything to find, they would have found it already, wouldn't they?

Except they wouldn't have known to look here. The only person who knows, besides my brother, is me.

The only person living, that is.

I try the second tile from the tub along the wall. It's as solid as the others, and my attempts to hook my rubber-covered fingernails under it to pry it loose are useless. I look around, and then, reluctantly, get up and go into the kitchen. A quick check of the drawers turns up a couple of mismatched forks and spoons. I take a fork, go back, and kneel again, sticking the edge of the handle under the tile, prod, push, prod.

Little by little, it starts to come loose. My heart is hammering, and despite the chill, my upper lip beads with sweat. Finally, the tile gives way and flies off so abruptly that I lose my balance and fall on my backside. The fork clatters next to me, scattering little bits of dried glue.

Beneath the tile, the opening is small and shallow, and right away I realize I found what I was looking for. There are layers of plastic so thick they're almost opaque, concealing something beneath them. The plastic rustles when I reach in and take the whole thing out into the light. It's surprisingly heavy, its weight in my hands alone filling me with dread I can't begin to articulate. When I peel away the last layer of plastic, they scatter on the floor in front of me—bundles. Rolled-up wads of cash.

It's like a nightmarish déjà vu. There must be thousands—tens of thousands—of dollars in here, tied with blue elastic bands. Like lettuce. I choke on a shaky laugh.

I don't know what to do with them all. I sweep them aside and peer into the hiding place—to my terror, there's more. Something white wrapped in a plastic grocery bag. I open it, not knowing what to expect and ready for anything.

Inside is an envelope. Not sealed, blank. In the envelope, a bunch of papers I can't make any sense of at first. And when I think that's all, I feel another shape stuck in the envelope's corner, a small card that I pull out gingerly.

My brother's face glares at me, same scowl as in the photo on TV, dark eyes and sunken cheeks. It's a driver's license, only the name on it isn't my brother's.

My head is spinning, and I have to close my eyes for a second. When I open them, the license is still there, as are the papers and the pile of rolled-up cash. And that means I have to start making sense of all this, soon. There's no way—no way in hell—I'm going to bring any of it with me. No, not a single bill or shred of paper leaves this place.

I ruffle through them—there's lots and lots of fine print, and some pages have a chicken-scrawl signature at the bottom that looks like he wrote it with his left hand. The name matches the one on the driver's license.

At the top of some of the pages, I see a logo. A company name. Access Research Center, it says in minimalist letters. The name and the logo are both vaguely familiar. That's because they advertise on buses and subway stops, things you don't really pay attention to unless you're absolutely desperate for money. They pay cash.

It hits me like a sledgehammer, the three pieces to the very obvious puzzle in my lap. Only then, slowly, the other pieces trickle in, and they don't add up as smoothly. Why live in this crappy apartment when he had a good fifteen grand stashed in the floor? Why hide it all? Why the same hiding place as back home?

Did he hide it from me—or for me?

I scoop up all the rolls of cash and start to frantically stuff them back into the hiding place: one, two, five, six. That's when I notice there's something else clinking around at the bottom.

Cold sweat breaks out all over my back, soaking through my shirt. The voice of reason that's been screaming at me in the back of my mind rises to a fever pitch: *I told you, I told you—this is a bad idea. You stupid, stupid girl.*

*You're too soft, Addie*, whispers Eli's voice in the back of my mind. *That's why everyone uses you and throws you away.*

I tear off one of the rubber gloves with my teeth because it's not important anymore. I reach in, and my fingertips brush against a surface so smooth and familiar it's like coming home. The cool of the enamel caresses the pads of my fingers as I pick it up. It rests so peacefully in the palm of my hand, and it feels like it weighs a fucking ton.

My little lighthouse. My keychain.

The last remaining piece of my life before the fire.

There's only one place he could have gotten it. From my crashed car, the night Adele was murdered.

# CHAPTER THIRTY

I'm sitting in my rented Ford, parked in the lot of a Dunkin'
Donuts, warming my hands on a Styrofoam cup of coffee I
have no intention of drinking. Only now, with my brother's
apartment and the crime scene safely miles behind me, I'm
starting to feel like myself again. The keychain is in my
pocket, and I check on it every five seconds, feeling its
familiar shape through the fabric. Still disbelieving that I
have it back.

They didn't find it in my coat or purse or in my old car.
Well, now we know why.

What the fuck did you do, Eli? What the fuck.

In a lucky twist, the car has a charger for an iPhone in
the glove box, and my phone is blinking at me from the
passenger seat as the battery fills up. I put the coffee in the
cup holder and pick up the phone.

A few taps on the screen and I'm on the Access Research

site, purified blue-and-white interface, minimalist and user-friendly. Just fill out our form and get paid!

As with most things, it's not really that easy.

Without letting myself hesitate, I thumb the phone number, and the screen switches to phone mode immediately. The line rings and then connects smoothly, with nary a click.

"Access Research Center, how may I help you?"

"H-hi," I say. Deep down, I didn't really think a real person would pick up.

"Hello," says the friendly, patient female voice. She waits for me to speak without urging or threatening to hang up, as I'm sure she's been instructed. I tell myself she was probably trained during a two-hour seminar and is paid ten bucks an hour. I can take her on.

"I was interested in one of your studies."

"Very well." She maintains the exact same intonation. "Age and sex, please?"

"Female. Twenty-seven."

"Where did you hear about us?"

"Er . . . your ad? On the subway."

"Wonderful." I don't see how it's wonderful but I find myself nodding along. "Any particular health conditions?"

"Like . . . what?"

"Diabetes, heart conditions, hepatitis B or C, HIV . . ."

"No."

"Fantastic! We currently have several studies that might interest you. Would you be willing to come in for a preliminary interview and information session?"

"Um, sure."

"Great. Would you prefer morning, afternoon, or evening?"

I hesitate.

"We seek to provide our participants with flexibility. A lot of them work full- or part-time or pursue their studies."

"Of course. Is anything available today?"

"We have a session starting at nine thirty. Should I pencil you in?"

"Yes."

"Terrific." Does she have a thesaurus laid out in front of her with all the synonyms for *fantastic* in a neat column? "Nine fifteen, come to the front desk. Do you have the address?"

"Yeah. Yes. I do, thank you."

"Great. See you later today, Ms. . . ."

I realize it's a prompt when the silence lingers. "Addison. DeVoort." I don't know why I give Milt's last name. Better than blurting out my own.

"See you later, Ms. DeVoort."

She hangs up. I put the phone back on the charger and start the engine.

Looks like I'll have to tough it out for a couple of hours. I take my hand off the steering wheel to reach into my pocket for the millionth time and let my fingertips brush against the cool enamel of the keychain. As always, its presence reassures me.

\*    \*    \*

I get to the Access Research Center jittery with a too-much-coffee, too-little-sleep buzz that makes everything look just one degree south of real. I drive past the place twice because it turns out it's housed on the third floor of an office building, no logo in sight. Only the list by the intercom indicates ARC, suite 300.

It looks like a dentist's office. A receptionist looks up from a Kindle long enough to point me to a windowless space that's a cross between a boardroom and a waiting room, where I take a seat at the long plastic table along with two others already waiting. One is an indifferent-looking Asian woman who's reading a newspaper in a foreign language, the other, a guy who can't be too long out of his teens. He looks as jittery as me but possibly not for the same reasons. Maybe it's the unflattering halogen lighting but the pocks that pepper his cheeks look too angry to be from regular acne, and his whole look has an air of unhealthiness. I bet he's going to get turned away, although who knows?

Then a woman with jowls and aggressively orange hair, clad in a white coat over her skirt and sweater, comes in and hands out pamphlets. I turn mine over: It's the list of their available studies. She goes on and on, chipper, about how we will all pass individual interviews to assess the state of our health and what study will be best suited for our unique selves. Those are the words she uses. She doesn't bat an eye when the guy asks how much and when we get paid. She tells him in the same polite, upbeat manner that it depends on the study, that all compensation is at the end of the trial, and that she has to inform us that due to a recent change in regulations, the compensation is no longer available in cash, only check or direct deposit.

He scoffs, scowls, and then, with a resigned air, asks what the best-paying study is. She repeats the line about our unique selves and our health conditions. He mutters something inappropriate under his breath, just loud enough for me to overhear, and slumps in his chair.

The orange-haired lady disappears, only to reappear minutes later and call the Asian woman into the office through the set of doors on the other end of the room. They're glass, but they're tinted white. Once they close, I can only see her silhouette behind them, growing blurrier and blurrier till she's gone.

It's me and the guy now. Can't say I'm supercomfortable with the setup, and the large and obvious surveillance camera in the opposite corner makes me even more edgy. The AC is invisible and silent, but it pumps arctic air into the room, so cold I half expect to see my breath condense. I wish I'd worn long sleeves. The guy is blatantly checking me out now. Not really checking me out, I realize after a sideways glance, as much as inspecting my bare arms and neck. Finally, after a few minutes of this, he speaks up.

"Is that, like, some kind of psoriasis or some shit?"

I turn to face him, tempted to tell him that no, it's a rare and highly contagious skin disease that's airborne. Instead, I press my lips together politely and shake my head. He informs me that "it looks really messed up," but before things can escalate, orange lady returns and calls him in.

Blissful loneliness. I let myself slouch, turning my attention to the brochure in front of me. I unfold it to see stock photos of smiling men and women of all ethnicities, with clean blue font describing available studies. I can't help but imagine my brother in this very room, waiting for his turn. Was this a last stop for him? Did he feel hopeless, resigned? He can't have had many other options. The court order forbade him from ever getting in touch with me, even after he got out of prison, with no one waiting for him, with no place to go. And I can't imagine the job offers were piling up for a convict with minimal education. He was smart at school, or at least smart enough to get away with cheating for better grades. Did he feel like his life had slipped away from him?

Or was taken from him.

I inspect the brochure, trying to figure out which study he would have chosen. Asthma. Migraines. There are two different studies for psoriasis treatment, and both pay quite well—not that it excuses the jerk for staring at me earlier. There's about fifteen total, but it's the last one that catches my eye.

*Males 18–30, with a history of psychosis, for trials of new medication.* There aren't any more details, just a short list of eligibility criteria.

My heart starts to beat faster. I look around but there's no one; the orange-haired lady and the other two candidates are still gone. I let myself imagine them being whisked away to some underground lab from which they'll never emerge, like something out of a B-grade sci-fi film.

I scan the brochure again, but the more I do, the more certain I become. I keep coming back to that one listing. It's not certainty—not with so little to go on—but it's also more than just a suspicion. Maybe a gut instinct. Or maybe... maybe I just know my brother well enough.

"DeVoort? Addison DeVoort?"

My head snaps up, and my spine tingles, like I got caught doing something bad. The orange-haired woman motions for me to come forward.

"Hold on." My voice has a tremor in it but I guess it's normal for first-time jitters. "What exactly are they going to do to me in there?" I smile nervously, trying to play it off as a joke.

"Just some health-related questions," she answers rather coldly. "But first, you're going to have to come with me, okay?"

"There's a study that interests me," I say.

"In due time. First, the evaluation," she drones.

"It's the last one. Males eighteen to thirty, psychosis medication."

Her brows knit. "Follow me, please."

I get up and make a step toward her. Then I realize she's not taking me through the white-glass doors but back the way I came, into the lobby.

"Miss," she says, a menacing edge to her voice, "come with me. Immediately."

"What medication is it?" I snap. "What do you give these people?"

She shakes her head, her lips pursed. In the same moment, two security guards shoulder their way past her into the room and walk toward me in a determined step.

"You have to leave now, ma'am," says the older (and taller) of the two.

"I'm not leaving."

"Yes, you are." He reaches to grab my arm but I pull away just in time. Only to realize the other one is behind me, and he seizes my other arm just below the shoulder. I weakly try to twist out of his grip.

"I don't know what you are, press, some kind of blogger..." The woman is practically spitting. "But you can't be here, or we're calling the police."

"I'm not a blogger," I snarl. "I'm—"

I cut myself off just in time. Outing myself is the last thing I need—I have to maintain plausible deniability to the last.

"Fine," I snap. "Fine. I'm leaving. You can let go of me now."

The security guard lets go but the two of them flank me all the way back to the lobby downstairs. After the doors close behind me, releasing me back into the cacophony of the evening traffic, they still stand there, behind glass. Watching me as I leave.

It takes me forever to get home. After working odd hours for so long, I forgot how trying Denver traffic can be. Plus, even once I white-knuckle through the worst of it, every light I hit seems to turn red right in my face. When I finally pull up to the town house, I'm exhausted and starving, shaking with hopelessness and anger.

I race up the steps, envisioning a long bath and maybe—

Why not?—ordering some takeout. I'm so absorbed in my
thoughts that I practically collide with the person waiting
for me at the front door.

I stumble back, cursing, but then she turns around.

"Andrea," Figueroa says, smiling. "I've been meaning to
talk to you. May I come in?"

# CHAPTER THIRTY-ONE

There are a million reasons I should know better. We used to instruct shelter kids about this all the time: You have rights, you don't have to consent to a search, you cannot be detained unless you are arrested. But the viper is right here on my porch, and incriminating evidence is in my pocket, and all that useful info evaporates from my head instantly.

"Come in," I say dumbly as I take the keys out of my pocket. Figueroa has to move aside in order to let me open the door, and she does, just barely. She stands there, in my personal bubble, as if she genuinely sees no problem with that. Like she's a close friend. I swear I can hear her breathe.

But she's nothing if not a gracious guest. She takes off her shoes without being prompted, and she compliments me on the house, the décor, the furniture. She doesn't point out I can't afford any of it on my own but I bet she already made that mental note and stashed it away deep in the whorls of that brain of hers.

"How have you been, Andrea?" she asks. She moves a crumpled blanket aside and takes a seat on the couch. My mind flies into panic mode as I assess the traces of Sunny's presence in the house: the blanket, yes, but also the pizza box, the two plates still sitting on the coffee table. Not that they stand out too much in the general mess but someone like Figueroa would notice.

"How do you think?" I retort, noting in my mind that it's the classic tactic of someone who's lying—answering a question with another. "My brother is wanted for murder, and now you show up at my house without warning."

"I didn't realize a warning was needed," she says.

"You call people up before you show up on their doorstep," I mutter. Although she's the exception, because she's police—showing up without warning is what she does.

"What can I say? You had a busy day." She's smiling. "Have a seat. Let's talk. Because right now, I have people going over every inch of that apartment, so whatever you found, they'll find it too."

I breathe in but there doesn't seem to be any room in my lungs. Of course. I shouldn't be surprised. I bet the place was under surveillance—in case he came back to it. Or I did.

"Anyway, if you had the idea to remove or tamper with the evidence, this is your chance to come forward."

"I didn't— I didn't remove anything."

"We'll see."

"I'm not what you think," I blurt.

"You can't make excuses for him forever, Andrea."

"I'm not making excuses!" My voice cracks. "I'm the same as you. I just want the truth."

"The truth is that your brother murdered this girl. We're going to catch him, and he's going to go to prison for it. The end. He won't bullshit his way out of it. No psychiatric facility this time. He's going back into a federal prison, and he's not coming out again."

She's looking me straight in the eye as she says it, taking pleasure in my reaction. Or is it something else? Is she waiting for me to slip up? Pushing me toward something?

"What do you want from me, then?" The words tumble out, out of my control. "You have the truth; you have proof of it. What did I ever do?"

"You're helping him. I don't know exactly how—yet. Or especially why. But you are."

*Wouldn't you, if it was your brother?* I don't say it. It's what she wants, what she expects, because it would be akin to an admission of guilt.

I open my mouth to deny everything—*I am not helping him, it was just morbid curiosity, he's a murderer but he's still family*, the usual set of retorts she's probably heard a million times. But then I close it, my teeth making a hollow clack.

I think about the money and the release forms. If I could read the fine print on them right now, I'd have a pretty good guess what it would say.

My brother tested some kind of medication for them.

While on that medication, he—allegedly—murdered a girl. Even this I can only speculate about. I can only imagine all the other layers of truths and half truths and outright lies my brother could spin around these two things.

In case I can't prove his innocence, these drug trials are Eli's get-out-of-prison-free card.

So why isn't he using it?

My gaze refocuses on Figueroa, who watches me with a pensive, calm air. Is she thinking the same thing? I'm more than certain someone already found the hiding place—I snapped the tile back into place, but it won't hold up to a police search. Someone already told her about the papers and the money. Someone is probably on the way to the research center right now, if they didn't already know about it.

"The girl. Adele," Figueroa says. Just hearing the name spoken out loud in my house is enough to rattle me. "We know she used to frequent your shelter. I have several witnesses who place her there . . . during hours when you were in charge."

I swallow. "I don't remember her. Lots of people pass through the shelter. Especially those in her circumstances."

She nods. "Here's the thing, Andrea, and perhaps this is what bothers me the most. You keep protecting him, when he just used you. You understand that, right?"

*You're too soft, Addie. That's why everyone—*

"He spied on you, probably for months, in defiance of the court order." She rattles off the words dryly. "He came to your work. He most likely got one of your charges to spy on you for him too." Her smile widens. "Ah. Now, there it is. The reaction I was hoping to see. Surprised now, aren't you?"

"That's insane," I say hoarsely. *How can she know? It's impossible, impossible—*

"There was a call from a cell phone to his own, made the night of the murder. The tower places it around the shelter. And another call, made to the same number later. She probably thought it wasn't trackable because it's a flip phone. But hers wasn't a pay-and-go. It was a regular phone, and she put her name on a contract."

I already know the answer but I still ask. "Who?"

"Elizabeth Jones. Known in your circle as Sunny."

# CHAPTER THIRTY-TWO

Rage crackles beneath my skin, my hands trembling as I climb into my rental car and slam the door. I don't know if I'm in any shape to drive. Not to mention that I have no idea where to look for Sunny. If she had half a brain, she'd be on the next bus to somewhere far away. But somehow, I doubt it. She doesn't know what she's dealing with. Like a lot of teenagers who grew up like she did, she lacks the life-saving preservation instinct that tells you when you're in a bad situation. Always trusting the wrong people for the wrong reasons.

To say she doesn't remind me of myself, once upon a time, would be a lie.

But the fact is, I let her into my house. Why? Because I felt guilty, felt like I owed her something. And now, as usual, I'm paying for it.

It felt like an eternity, waiting after Figueroa left, but

I had to be sure. I still can't be, not 100 percent sure, that she, or someone she sent, isn't watching me, ready to follow wherever I go. I take the most convoluted road possible, turning randomly again and again—but not one car seems to go out of its way to follow me.

This time, when I pass the place where I crashed, I barely notice. Just another stretch of a dark, empty, familiar road. Everything has been cleaned up by now, no more broken glass, no more caution tape.

The shelter's sign glows dimly, dwarfed by the two aggressive floodlights above the entrance. There are cameras watching the perimeter because Marla doesn't want people shooting up around the corner. I park the car and direct my steps to the main door, trying to remember who's on duty at this hour. Chrissy? Allan? Here's to hoping it's someone who doesn't hate me. With that, I push open the door.

I'm in luck: It's Allan, who's had a soft spot for me since forever. I always got the feeling that, if I didn't make sure to casually bring up the existence of my fiancé every time we spoke, he would have asked me out a long time ago. And perhaps he isn't too off base. We'd certainly make a more plausible couple than I ever made with Milton. Resolutely hippie Allan, with his round glasses and his hair either in dreadlocks or just unkempt, and me, freckles and no makeup—we'd look like one of those couples who go kayaking on the weekends. When all the shit went down months ago and suddenly everyone knew I was single again, he was this close, I could tell, but my murderous mood and shitty attitude must have kept him at bay.

I lean on the counter in front of the bulletproof glass. His expression changes when he sees me. His eyebrows crawl up his forehead, and I can't tell if he's glad to see me or just surprised. "Andrea," he says.

"Hi."

"I thought— Marla said—" He's visibly squirming.

"Yeah, I'm off work for a while." I try to make it sound as normal as possible. Although I'm convinced that, like pretty much everyone, he already knows the whole story. "Allan, I'm looking for Sunny. Has anyone seen her around?"

He hesitates, and I wonder if he knows but doesn't want to tell me or really has no idea.

"I think she might be in some kind of trouble," I add. "She called me the other day. That boyfriend of hers was stalking her again. She said she'd let me know she was okay but I haven't heard anything."

"Andrea..." He hems and haws, stalling for time. I glance at the locked door, expecting Marla to emerge any moment to shoo me away. But Marla has usually gone home by now.

"I know I'm not supposed to be here," I say, lowering my voice. "But I can't just let it go, can I? These kids don't get a week off, you know what I mean?"

Allan is one of those people who got into this job out of a desire to help and one of those even rarer people who has kept that desire, resisting the inevitable cynicism and pessimism that usually set in after about six months.

"I haven't seen Sunny, Andrea," he says. He looks uncomfortable but I don't think he's lying. "Your shirt is inside out. Are you okay?"

Distraught, I glance down at myself and realize he's right. I can't even tell how long it's been like that. Figueroa never said a word about it, but I'll bet she noticed. I'm coming apart at the seams. The situation that I thought was still in my grip is spinning out of control, fast.

"Yeah," I tell Allan. "I'm fucking peachy."

With that, I turn around and give a wink to the surveillance camera over my head. Behind me, I hear Allan nervously clear his throat and then gasp as I unselfconsciously pull the shirt over my head, clad only in my washed-out, once-white bra. My scarred skin glistens like pink wax in the unflattering overhead lights. I turn my shirt the right side out and put it back on. I can feel him staring, and when I turn around and give him a broad grin, his jaw is slack.

But I guess, as Sunny would have put it, I'm fresh out of fucks to give.

*　　*　　*

My phone rings as I'm walking to my car. When I take it out of my pocket, I see Chris's number and feel a short-lived pang of guilt when I hit Decline. I haven't answered any of her texts so she probably thinks I've fallen off the wagon. (Haven't I?)

But before I have a chance to put the phone back, it rings again. Groaning inwardly, I pick up. "Chris, I'm fine. I'm . . . sober. This isn't really a good time."

"I know you're sober," she says with strange calm, yet I can hear the anger behind the words. "I think we should talk."

"I can't right now. I have to do something important."

"It can wait."

"No, it can't," I snarl, unable to contain my irritation any longer. Just who does she think she is? Mother Teresa, Savior of Alcoholics? "There are worse things at stake here than me snapping and having a beer, okay?"

Her answer is silence. At first I think the call disconnected or she hung up. Then I hear her sigh. It becomes unnerving.

"Hello?"

Nothing.

"Chris, hey, listen—I'm sorry. I didn't mean to yell. I just—"

"I did some searching of my own," she says. I stop cold just a few feet away from my car, my phone frozen to my ear, my heart hammering.

"Researching you. You may have gotten carried away with your confidences. Too many details."

"What do you mean?" I feel like I'm speaking through a mouthful of chewing gum.

"I talked to some people who would know. And I don't think this is news to you, but your party years are basically a fabrication from beginning to end."

I don't move, my mind at a standstill.

"Now, the question on my mind is, Are you just making shit up to cover your real problems, or was the whole thing one big stunt for attention? Have you ever even done coke in your life?"

I say nothing.

"Andrea?"

I hang up the phone. Then, before she can call back, I block her number.

I drive straight to the place where I went to pick Sunny up a few days ago. The highway is roaring with cars, a mighty waterfall that swallows me up seamlessly without a splash. I take the exit to the little glowing island of twenty-four-hour civilization, if you can call it that. Half the pumps of the gas station are occupied, and more cars are parked in front of the neighboring fast-food joint.

The hot, greasy smell that envelops me the moment I get out of the car makes my stomach growl, despite the fact that my insides are still in knots—have been since Figueroa left. Still, before all else, I check the bathroom, as if Sunny might still be in there by some miracle. But I only find two unfamiliar teenage girls, who give me looks brimming with derision as they fix their heavy makeup.

So I go back out to the restaurant and get in line, ordering a double cheeseburger and large fries when my turn comes. My stomach growling has escalated, and I'm pretty sure the whole restaurant can hear it. I don't want company, least of all a dozen strangers watching me scarf down my heart attack on a plate under halogen lights so I bring my takeout bag to my car and devour the contents in minutes.

After all, they probably don't have double cheeseburgers in jail.

As if it can hear my thoughts, my phone chimes. The meal sitting like a brick at the bottom of my stomach does

a perilous jump but I pick up the phone and look. I think
I might throw up right on the rental's sensible navy seats
when I see the text.

You're close. You know where to find me.

Fuck fuck fuck fuck. What the hell is Eli doing? He can't
text me on this number, and he knows it.

*     *     *

Shit. I think of Figueroa tinkering with my phone, police
trailing me. Cell phone towers pinpointing my every move.
My first reaction is to switch it off but I realize it's probably
too late.

The realization comes to me suddenly, out of nowhere,
like it always does. Peering out the window, I see it, silhou-
etted against the dirty indigo sky: scattered rectangles of
windows glowing yellow, orange, and the occasional blue,
giant parasitic mushrooms of satellite dishes peppering the
rooftop. The apartment complex, the maze of four- and
five-story slum buildings from the seventies that were probably crummy even then. I search for the right one but I
can't see it from this angle—it's on the other end, farther
from the highway and the ramp.

Although we didn't see cars when we looked out of the
window, the distance wasn't enough to keep the endless
roar of the highway out of our apartment—it seeped in
even through tightly shut windows, night and day, summer and winter. We didn't notice it, just like we didn't

notice the diesel smell. After Mom married Sergio and we moved to the suburbs, I couldn't sleep for a while, deafened by the quiet that made my ears ring. I would lie awake in the room I shared with my brother and stare into the dark ceiling. The only sound was Eli's breathing, all the way across the room, and I wondered if all this was good or bad, and whether it even mattered, because just like with everything else, no one asked my opinion. They just made me confront the fact: This is how it's going to be from now on. And I'd float along, not trying to change or influence where I was going. All my attempts at self-determination were nipped in the bud from an early age. I learned to accept things as they were, try to find the positives, ignore the negatives, and move on.

*Pro: I kind of like my new stepdad. Or the fact that I have a stepdad at all.*

*Con: I have to go to the new school, and the other girls are always sneering at me, their faces like a language I don't speak.*

*Pro: I have a bigger, nicer room.*

*Con: My brother is starting to act weird.*

I make my way to the building on foot, after leaving my car at a safe distance. I don't need to check the rusted metal numbers over the lobby door—I know it's the right building the moment I see it. I'm overcome with a weird sense of calm, a kind of quiet despair, as if I already know things have spun way out of my control and there's little I can do. Floating. Again.

The lobby has a set of two doors, the first one without a lock, opening into a tiled area with mailboxes on the wall and a stand heaping with discount brochures from neighboring stores. Next to the second set of doors is a primitive, ancient intercom system, a list of apartments with little slots for papers with the tenant's name, next to a dialing pad and a speaker. It didn't work then, and I suspect that it doesn't work now. But before I try the door handle, something compels me to scan that list, my gaze straying way down before making its way back up, to the fourth and last floor where our apartment used to be. Since there's not an elevator, the top units were cheapest, and our sensible mother lugged groceries up four flights of stairs without complaint.

There it is. 417. My fingertip hovers over the little laminated paper the landlord has slid in next to the apartment number. I trace the letters, as if touching them will make them disintegrate, rearrange themselves into something—anything—else.

417. Andrea L. Warren.

Next thing I know, I'm swinging the door wide open, racing past it, letting it crash closed behind me. The inner lobby leading to the dank stairwell smells like stale cooking with a whiff of more-than-ripe garbage emanating from the giant black bins in the farthest corner; my stomach knots and I attempt to hold my breath—not a good idea, as racing up the first flight of stairs leaves me breathless, doubling over on the second floor's landing. I steady myself against the sticky pale-green wall and then yank my hand away from the rough surface as if it were white-hot—fingerprints. While I try to catch my breath, I use the hem of my shirt to clumsily wipe down the wall where I touched it. Oh shit, the door. I have to do the same to both door handles—although it's not as crucial, since the building houses over a hundred people who come and go at all hours, their tired, sweaty hands groping the handles, the oil on their palms obliterating any trace of mine.

My heart hammers from the effort as I make my way up one more floor. I remember trudging up those stairs after my mother, pawing at the splintery railing while she huffed and puffed ahead. *Exercise, Addie,* she used to say, with strained cheer through the breathlessness, *it's good for us!*

One more flight of stairs and I'm on the right floor, at last. I'm panting, and the fact that my heart is doing somersaults isn't helping. At the very end of the hall is 417. The carpeting muffles my steps—not that there's anyone obvious to hide from. The other doors stand still and mute, no shuffling steps, no locks clicking or curious faces peering out to see the intruder. Back then, everyone here minded their own business, and they still do.

I stand in front of the door to 417 for what feels like a long time. I could still leave, I think, knowing I won't. The doors were repainted not too long ago, sloppily—paint stains the apartment number. The locks look shiny and new. I glance around for a cursory check: The two closest apartments still have the old locks, which must be a pain to use by now. There's a doorbell, the old doorbell. I pull my sleeve over my hand and press it with my knuckle, but predictably, there's no sound behind the door. Paint job aside, the door is still flimsy, and I should be hearing everything as if I were standing in the middle of the living room. But nothing, and no one, moves.

I knock, also through my sleeve. Not that I expect an answer—I'm just delaying the inevitable. When I place my hand on the door knob, I feel like I leave a damp trace even through the fabric of my shirt. The doorknob turns without resistance, without so much as a squeak, and the door opens smoothly.

Beyond it is an empty apartment, nothing but dust and shadows. The lights are off, but the streetlights and the lights in the windows of the building across the street all add up to a flat, orangish glow that filters in stripes through the blinds. All these apartments come with blinds, I remember, grayed with time, sticky with dust.

"Eli," I whisper, and the echo picks up my voice, amplifying it into thunder that rolls through the whole apartment. There's no answer. "Eli?"

I feel like a fool. I'd kick something, if there were anything to kick except the walls. Of course he's not here. He's not an idiot—he's a lot of things but stupid was never one of them, and he was not going to wait for me here, in this apartment with my name on it. I thought he had no money, but now I know that's a lie—another one on top of many. Did he rent it to have an eventual hideout? Or did he do it just for the pleasure of messing with me? It sounds like Eli, but not like this, not without another, more concrete purpose.

And he would never wait for me here, where I would lead the cops right to him, to us both. He wouldn't bet his life on my ability to avoid being trailed. Hell, I know I wouldn't. I'm not a mastermind. I'm better at doing what I'm told. He'd be the first to remind me.

What I need to do is turn around and get the hell out of here. Wipe the door handles anyway, just in case. I need to go home, call Figueroa, and tell her everything. I think of the smug, self-satisfied look she had on TV, the look she will surely have again when she hears the whole story, and it's not even the worst thing I can imagine.

I use my scant legal knowledge to try to work out how much shit I'd be in: obstruction of justice, for sure, and what else?

The air in the apartment is still and stifling, with a sickening undercurrent of raw sewage, like a pipe had burst or something had overflowed. At first I hardly noticed it but now it seems to be thickening in the air. It's gag inducing. From where I'm standing in the middle of the room, I can see the alcove of the kitchen on one side and into the tiny bedroom on the other. There's no fridge or stove, and the bedroom is similarly bare. The bathroom door is the only one that's closed.

I take a step forward, aware of the squeak of my soles on the linoleum. He is in there, I think, and the fine down on my arms stands on end. I reach for the handle—unnecessarily, as it turns out, because the door opens without resistance, letting me tumble into the tiny room behind it. It's pitch black, and I feel along the wall for the light switch, find it, flick it, and, to my surprise, the ceiling light flickers on.

I stumble away, only instead of toppling out of the room,

I hit the door with my back and slam it shut, leaving me trapped, blindly pawing for the handle, unable to look away from the sight in front of me.

Sunny is in the tub, curled up in the fetal position. There's no gore, no blood, but it's impossible to mistake that empty shell of a person for being alive. I know she's gone even before I see her face. There's something, a stillness, about her that can only be final. Her ponytail hangs over the edge of the tub, its too-blond color dull beneath the single light of the bathroom. Next to the ponytail's ragged end, something else hangs, slim and black, like a snake.

I hear a little whimper, and for a split second, I rush forward with a flash of wild hope—Could she be alive after all?—but before my knees land with a thud on the bathroom tile, I already know the whimper came from me. Her face is bluish gray, eyes screwed shut—a small mercy: I don't know what I'd do if they were open, if they had been looking at me. Her hands, frozen into claws, are clutched to her chest. The smell of death is overbearing.

I catch myself before I can touch the edge of the tub with my bare hands. But not before I can see what killed her. What's wrapped around Sunny's neck still, glistening dully with that sheen of real leather. It's a belt. I recognize it because of the little silver studs: an expensive belt, one from my closet back home. One she stole before she left my place in the early hours of the morning.

Surprisingly, the first thoughts to rush through my mind are of a practical nature. How long before someone notices the smell, goes to investigate, and calls the police, if they haven't already? What else have I touched? Where have I left fibers of my clothing or lost a hair without realizing it? What can I do, and how can I cover my ass now that a teenage girl is dead, strangled? Because it won't bring her back, of course—nothing I do will. It never does.

Eli killed her, I realize with sudden clarity and calm. He killed her just like he killed the other one. He's not innocent. He never was, and now he played me again. Now I can't pretend none of this concerns me. I was naïve to ever think I could stay one step ahead of him.

I'm beyond worrying about clothing fibers and bits of DNA, because something tells me these things are about to be the least of my problems. And the worst part is, I should have known what this was about from the moment they identified Adele Schultz.

Fifteen years later, he managed to blow up my life all over again, and I never saw it coming.

He never wanted me to prove he was innocent. He wanted me to take the fall.

# CHAPTER THIRTY-THREE

*Eli Warren recounted proudly and in detail how he pulled his sister out of the fire. I let him go on, and the story, embellished with true imaginative flair and garnished with colorful details, took a little over forty-five minutes. When I subsequently turned the conversation to the fire itself, the gleam in his eyes seemed to flicker out for a moment.*

*"Oh yeah. They deserved it. But even if they didn't, what can I do, right? What's done is done."*

*He did not look or sound in any way remorseful.*

*Truth be told, my main emotion after my last conversation with Eli Warren was pity. Whatever way you spin it—and however he justifies it—he has done this to himself. He once had a family, a home, a*

*promising future. He threw it all away on a whim, in*
*a flash of anger.*

    —*Into Ashes: The Shocking Double Murder in the*
*Suburbs* by Jonathan Lamb, Eclipse Paperbacks,
2004, 1st ed.

## FIFTEEN YEARS EARLIER: AFTER THE FIRE

In the hospital, time stretches into infinity. It's not that Andrea doesn't have anything to do to pass the long hours. Since the fire made the news, maybe even national news, the gifts have been pouring in. They surround her from all sides now, piles and stacks of stuffed toys and books, and Andrea is hopelessly too old for all of them. But you can't really tell well-meaning women (it's mostly women, judging by the cards) from all over the state that a girl who's almost thirteen won't much care for Dr. Seuss.

She should probably have the books and toys donated to someone who has more use for them. She still might, when she can gather the courage to speak to someone. She's afraid the nurses might judge her, as if one wrong word, misunderstood or misinterpreted, will bring everything crashing down.

The visitor comes early in the morning. The only visitors she's had were police and social workers, because there's no one left to visit her. Her mom didn't have any family, and she isn't sure about Sergio, but why would his family visit her? She wasn't really his daughter. She wasn't even officially adopted. She remained a Warren, her father's last name.

The fire itself is still foggy. She did ask herself a couple of times where Eli was. She has never been away from her twin for longer than a few hours. Besides, she doesn't know what happens when your parents die. Do they put you in foster care right away or is there some kind of in-between limbo place where they keep you? Now she finds herself wondering. What will happen to her, after all? It seemed unimportant before but now, as the burns on her chest and neck get better, as the grafted skin heals, it has been monopolizing her thoughts.

When the visitor comes in, she wonders if she can ask him. He doesn't look like police. He's tall but portly, and old. He looks older than Sergio, in any event. He also looks vaguely familiar but she can't place him.

"Hi, Andrea," he says, and, without asking, takes a seat on the chair next to the bed. The chair is too small, and it groans under his weight.

"I'm here because there's something you have to do," he says, wasting no time on introductions. "I think you already know what that is, don't you?"

She shivers. She can't help herself, and she can't hide her visceral reaction. Not from him at least.

"They already suspect something, Andrea," the man says. He speaks in a measured, confident voice. It's meant to make people trust him, she thinks. But she, Andrea Warren, can't trust anyone. Not anymore. She will never be able to trust anyone again for as long as she lives. "Why do you think they haven't allowed Eli to see you?"

I should say something, Andrea thinks with a suffocating sense of urgency. I should stop him.

The man leans closer. "They're going to find out what really happened anyway," he says. "So you might as well tell them first."

Without warning, he gets up, as if to go, and Andrea betrays herself. She gives a start and reaches out to grab his arm, his sleeve, something—anything to stop him. His sharp gaze is on her in an instant, and she freezes. She lets her arm drop.

"I can count on you," he says, with an inflection that implies he already knows the answer. "And afterward, I'll make sure you're well taken care of. You can trust me on that."

Andrea gives a short nod. There's warmth in his words, reassurance—even though it all feels a little bit artificial, as clinical as the cheap art print on the wall above her bed. But she already decided. She knows what she's going to do.

It's only when the door closes behind him, leaving her alone with her thoughts, that she recognizes Leeanne Boudreaux's father.

# CHAPTER THIRTY-FOUR

APRIL 10, 3:22 A.M.

The headlights of the old Toyota seem to be the only lights in the whole universe. I slam the car door shut, and before I take another step toward the figure standing in the grass by the side of the road, I know that the red I see isn't just a trick of the light. Inwardly, I'm pleading, begging myself: Just get back in your car, drive away, never look back. Pack your things and move. To LA, New York, Australia. Put as much distance between us as you possibly can.

Get lost in a city of millions. Change your name. The last name already went, and now the first will go too. No more Addie Warren. Poof, gone.

But something in me already knows that it's too late. I can't get back in the car any more than I can raise our childhood home from the ashes.

In the back of my mind, I always knew this day would come.

"Why would you call me at work?" I snap. As if it even matters anymore. Eli is standing in the shadow of a tree, the only tree on this entire stretch of road. Its trunk isn't thick enough to hide behind, and my brother doesn't seem to realize it. When he moves and the headlights of my car hit his face, he looks dazed.

The blood splattered all over him gleams a deep, malignant cherry red. It makes his eyes look even bluer, their color as clean and vibrant as it was the last time I saw him. He always had all the beauty, and now he's lost it all. His eyes are the only things that are the same.

He holds up his hands.

"Are you crazy? I told you— Never—" I'm spewing words, making myself breathless. As if were I to stop talking, something irreparable will happen. "I'm the one who texts you. Never the other way around—never. You hear me?"

"Did you erase it?"

"You fucking bet I erased it. It's not my phone. What the hell were you thinking?"

He lets go of a shuddering breath. "Addie, you have to hear me out, okay?"

I feel like I'm about to have a panic attack.

"I came home, and she was there. Dead. That's all I know. I didn't do it, I swear to God."

"Who— What—"

"This girl. I picked her up at a dive bar, just fucked her once, nothing else. Didn't even get her name."

In spite of myself, I wince. "I don't need to know that."

"She was just there. On the floor. She didn't have a face anymore, Addie. This is so fucked. *I'm* so fucked."

"You have to call the police," I hear myself say and cringe. I sound like a social worker, a privileged little bitch who has no idea why the police are not an option. I close my eyes, exhale. "Okay. Where were you before? Were you alone?"

When no answer comes, I open my eyes again to see his face, disarmed, defenseless, desperate. "Fuck," I mutter. "Eli, just tell me: What do you want me to do?"

"I want you to help me, Addie. You know what's going to happen."

I catch myself grimacing every time he says the nickname. Why does he have to use it so much? It's just us here. It feels like it's just us in the whole damn world. I listen for any other cars, look out for headlights, but the asphalt beneath my feet is still, no vibration of faraway tires growing closer. We're alone.

"I'm going back to prison. They're not going to believe anything I say. Unless you help me."

I can't hold back a shiver and pull my jacket closed over my chest as if it could help.

"I can't help you anymore, Eli," I say, and we both know it's a lie. "We're not twelve years old. I have a job. I have a life—"

I cut myself off, wondering to what extent that's true anymore. I have no parents. Jim and Cynthia Boudreaux were never family except on paper, and because of that money I stole, they now think I'm some kind of alcoholic-junkie-thief and hate me even more. My relationship with Milton blew up.

The truth, no matter how deadening, is right in front

of me. The only family I have left is my brother, shivering in the headlights of my car, desperate and scared, covered in blood. He's the only one who was always on my side. Who would do anything for me. We're not just siblings; we're twins. We're supposed to have some special bond, right? We're supposed to read each other's thoughts.

To an extent, that's true. But it's always been very much one-sided.

"I tried to make something of myself," I say stiffly. "At least I tried." That has to be worth something.

"Let me remind you that I did not exactly have the same opportunities you had," he says. His voice changes, dripping with sarcasm and disdain.

"And whose fault is that?" I fire back.

"Really, Andrea? Really? We're going to go there?"

I hang my head.

"Because if we are, here's what I have to say: If I go to prison for this thing, I'm going to take you with me. You owe me. Don't forget that."

As if I ever, in a million years, could forget it.

"What do you want me to do?" The words come out flat as paper. I have no more fight in me.

"I'll have to leave town. I don't suppose you have any more money?"

I shake my head. "Not right now. Not...here."

"Just help me. Help me prove I didn't do it."

"I don't know how." I'm this close to crying, my voice thin and brittle.

"You're smarter than you give yourself credit for."

"No one can know that we spoke," I say hoarsely. "Let alone met."

"I know that. I'm going to leave now. I have to hurry before—" *Before someone finds her in your apartment*, I finish for him in my head. *And I will be left to clean up your mess.* "You took care of the phone?"

"Yeah. She has a burner, like all these kids. There will be no trace."

"The police—they're going to ask you questions about tonight. What are you going to tell them?"

"Let me take care of that. Just go."

I watch him as he turns around and runs off into the night. I don't dare look away for even a second. I don't dare blink, my gaze glued to the back of his jacket. My eyes are starting to burn when I can finally be sure he's vanished into the surrounding darkness.

I get back inside the car and check the time on the dashboard: 3:32 a.m. All this only took ten minutes, even though it felt like a lifetime.

And if I can't explain away these minutes, we're both screwed. Especially me.

*You'll go far for me, Addie, but you'll go even further to cover your own ass. You never changed.*

I give a violent shake of my head to get rid of him, and in that same moment, I know what to do. I start the engine, my foot resolutely poised to hit the gas pedal. My body feels floaty and light, disconnected from my mind, like half my blood's been drained.

I know exactly what I'm going to tell the police, the detectives, and everyone else.

Before I can change my mind, I put the car in reverse. The tires squeal, and my breath catches. I've watched enough crime shows to know how easy it is to read tire tracks. It's starting to rain; droplets bead on the windshield. The forecast said something about downpours late at night and in the early morning. Hopefully, that'll take care of it.

Hopefully, hopefully.

I'm far enough now. My foot trembles slightly but I steady it. I shift gears and slam my foot onto the gas pedal.

The sky, the road, the tree careen toward me.

Bang.

# CHAPTER THIRTY-FIVE

I should have known it was him the whole time. From the first time Adele Schultz showed up at the shelter and demanded I pay her off.

Pacing the tiny bathroom, trying to avoid looking in the direction of the bathtub—of Sunny—I agonize, painfully aware of the seconds ticking away. Each and every one of them could make the difference for me. Move ahead one square or go to prison? Should I take the belt, try to get rid of it somehow? I watch those documentary shows about catching criminals so I know it never works out. I can drown it in bleach, throw it into a sewer, and it will still turn up just in time to put the proverbial noose around my neck.

Then I think of the deep purple-black mark around Sunny's throat and can barely hold back gagging. If I touch that belt, I just know I'll throw up. That's DNA evidence, putting me squarely on the scene. I try to push it from my mind.

Focus, Andrea. I draw a deep breath. I need to get out of here—that's what I need to do.

And leave her? I make myself glance at the shape curled up in the tub. I've never seen a dead body up close, not when the house burned down, not later at the funeral, which I didn't attend because I was in the hospital. I've seen news footage of it—a three-second clip, just long enough to see that it was closed casket, of course. No bodies, only tacky flowers everywhere and the press, taking pictures.

Her face is chalky now, colorless, but it's still her face, the same girl I've spoken to dozens of times. Like she was only in there minutes ago. Like she could still be in there, trapped in all that still, dead flesh. My skin crawls just thinking about it.

I have no choice. Not like there's anything I can do for her. She's dead. Getting myself thrown into prison isn't going to undo that.

Yeah, whatever you need to tell yourself.

I exit the bathroom, leaving the door open. I want to close it but don't want to touch it even one more time than I have to, even through my sleeve. It takes seconds to cross the main room to the entrance but just as I reach for the front door, I freeze.

How long ago did she die?

I can't stop myself from shuddering as my gaze darts all over the apartment like a trapped sparrow. It lingers on the window, taking in the stripes of artificial orange light that fall through the blinds. In that moment, I get a distinct, spine-tingling feeling I can't mistake for anything: I am seen. He could be watching me right now, I catch myself thinking, and before common sense can get the better of me, I race to the window, part the blinds clumsily with my sleeves covering my fingers, and peer out.

But all I see is the building across the street, its windows a random pattern of darkness and light. Down below, I can see the empty sidewalk, a couple of cars parked here and there, and the corner of a playground.

I turn my attention back to the building across the street. Any one of those windows could be hiding him. I picture him watching me silently from across the street the whole time, making sure I came here and found the present he'd left me for my troubles.

God. All I did was ... all I did was use a girl's phone a couple of times. I've used other people's phones, too, and they didn't end up dead. *Because their phones were pay-and-go, untraceable.*

All Sunny did was wander into the shelter where the wrong person was working. All she did was find a safe place to sleep at night.

No matter how I twist and turn it around in my head, I can't find a version where her death isn't my fault. But it wasn't you who strangled her with a belt, I tell myself. It's the kind of thing Eli would say, without a doubt, and I continue the mental dialogue.

*Yeah, I'm sure it makes a huge difference to her.*

*But it makes a difference where the law is concerned—that's for damn sure,* he sneers. For some reason, his voice in my head doesn't sound like the man I met on a deserted road three days ago. It sounds like the twelve-year-old boy, already making that transition between boy and man.

I should leave. Right fucking now.

I let go of the blinds so abruptly that they jolt on their strings, raising a small cloud of dust, and I step back. I back out of the apartment, doing my best to stay focused and touch nothing with my bare hands, and quietly but firmly shut the door behind me.

When I next become self-aware, I'm on the highway, driving slightly above the speed limit. Disorientation gives way to confusion. I'm going the wrong way; this isn't the direction back home, to the town house. The lateral part of my mind that's been making decisions in my stead clearly chose to go someplace else. The exit I've taken numerous times before looms ahead, closer and closer. I can just go past and then take the next one, turn around.

But instead, I decide to listen to my subconscious and take the exit ramp that leads right into Cynthia's neighborhood.

Both cars are there, the SUV and Leeanne's sedan, taking up all the driveway space. I park by the sidewalk and go ring the doorbell, puzzled when pressing down on the button yields no result. Nothing resonates in the house beyond. Cynthia must have taken the batteries out.

Cursing, I knock, at first softly, and then pound on the door with my open palms, which finally gets her attention. There are hurried steps behind the door, and then her voice:

"If you're press, you're wasting your time. I'm not going to open this door if you pay me."

"It's me," I say. Her stunned silence is my answer. It occurs to me that she might not let me in. Why would she, after all? All I did was bring trouble to her door, time and time again.

But moments later, the locks click, and the door opens.

"Andrea," she says as she lets me past. The second I'm inside, she calmly shuts the door and turns all the locks.

"Well," she says, lips pursed. We inspect each other, mistrustful. She's without makeup, a sight I've seen only a handful of times in all the years I've lived with her, and now I'm shocked to realize how much older she looks underneath it all. She's dressed in slippers and that bathrobe she has that is more accurately described as a housecoat, a heavy, quilted, satin thing that has to be vintage and designer.

"Here you are," she says. "Finally."

"I just want to go to my room. Please. I'm tired, Cynthia."

"I imagine you must be. That your car out front?"

I nod.

"I'll have Leeanne take it back to the rental place."

I start to protest.

"Keys," she says, holding out her hand palm up. I can't argue. I take the car key out of my pocket and hand it over. It disappears in the pocket of her robe.

"The offer still stands, by the way," she says, looking at me pointedly. "That's why you're here, right?"

I look at her, slack-jawed, unsure what she's talking about.

"The lawyer," she explains. "I'll give him a call, and he'll be here in ten."

"No lawyer," I protest. At the same time, I'm wondering if she's right. Whether I did come here only for the sake of the comfort and protection that she and her family, and their money, always represented. Without even realizing it, I came running back to Mommy—or the closest thing I had to one—with my tail between my legs. It's not a comforting thought.

"Fine. Whenever you're ready. He's been warned of the situation. Told me to tell you not to talk to police or to that Figueroa woman—especially that Figueroa woman." My gaze flees from hers, and she groans under her breath. "You already did."

"I didn't tell her anything."

"Good. None of us will talk to her either. Go sleep, or whatever you need to do. And you have my word on this: No one will cross the threshold of this house without a pile of warrants signed by God himself."

I start toward the staircase leading to my old room but remember my manners and stop.

"Thank you," I say hoarsely.

Once I'm in the four familiar walls of my old room, I collapse facedown on my narrow bed and breathe in the smell of the bedspread, the harsh cleaning products Cynthia uses mixed with dust and the scent of disuse. The bedspread's generic pattern is the last thing I see before I close my eyes.

When I open them next, the ceiling light is off, and the room is dark. And there are voices downstairs.

# CHAPTER THIRTY-SIX

After the fire, after a trial that took three months—all of which I'd spent in the burn ward—my brother was sentenced to twelve years, half of them in a high-security psychiatric facility. Despite the outrage this caused in the media back in the day, the place was no different from any ordinary prison. I know this much because I looked the place up online. I went as far as finding an obscure forum with testimonials. Patients—inmates—aren't allowed to have shoes, pens or pencils, or belts, among other things. They're almost never left unsupervised. During mandatory classes, they write with soft-tip markers that are collected at the end of the class. Anyone who visits must have a special authorization and present two pieces of ID.

I could never go see him, for obvious reasons, even long after I moved out of Cynthia's house. And I'd be lying if

I said I was particularly eager to. All those twelve years, I lived in a fictional world, able to pretend that none of it ever happened. Even though my burn scars never allowed me to pretend there never was a fire, I was still able to explain it away, in my own imagination. In that parallel world inside my mind, Eli either died in the fire along with my mother and Sergio, or never existed at all. But like in one of those tales about people who make deals with the devil, I spent those twelve years living in dread and fear. Knowing that I might have been enjoying my freedom then but soon the day would arrive when the devil came to collect his dues.

If Eli were ever to contact me, I was supposed to report it to the authorities immediately. I still wonder what would have happened if I had. He would not have hesitated to tell them my secret—this much is certain. But would anyone have believed him, a convicted murderer, a known liar as far as everyone knew? And perhaps, had I been thinking rationally instead of being ruled by my fear, I would have taken advantage of that to cut my ties with my brother forever.

But after that first time, a day went by, then a week, then a month, and then I could no longer report him without raising questions. Then he contacted me again. And again.

*You owe me. If I go to prison, I'm taking you with me.*

We are bound by this secret, bound inescapably. Or rather, I am bound to him. He has nothing left to lose, and I have everything.

The night of April 10, when I crashed my car, just moments before it collided with the tree, a thought flashed through my mind: Please, let me crash too hard. Maybe if I'm dead or quadriplegic or whatever, I'll be no use to him anymore, and he'll leave me alone. And so I pressed my foot into the gas pedal, and I hoped.

I wondered fleetingly, like I had many times before, if it was all a big game to him. Keeping me tied to him forever. Tormenting me forever.

That's ridiculous, of course. He's the one who went to prison; he's the one whose life was ruined while I lived with my new adoptive family, the perfect family by all appearances. While I had every opportunity at my disposal. I should be ashamed for even thinking that—but funny how that works: Being ashamed never makes the thoughts go away. On the contrary.

Now I don't know what to think anymore.

The first time we met was two weeks after he got out. I was already dating Milton, and it was getting serious. I was working at the shelter, the day shifts—a lot less crowded and more manageable. It didn't take him longer than that to track me down and learn where I worked. I was there when he called me from a burner phone. I was in one of the little offices, busy with paperwork, and I swear, the moment my desk phone rang, I knew deep down in my bones that it was him.

"Meet me out back," was all he said the moment I picked up. I didn't have time to say anything, not even hello. Not that hello was worth much after more than a decade in prison for something he didn't do.

"There are cameras," I said in an even voice, quiet enough not to be overheard through the paper-thin walls.

"Out of range. No one will know."

I went. Of course I went. Not like I had a choice.

With every step I took away from the shelter, I felt like my skin was being stripped away stripe by stripe, leaving me a raw and vulnerable piece of meat and nerves.

He waited for me just off the parking lot behind the shelter, behind the trash cans and recycling containers. He looked relaxed, leaning on one of them, like we last saw each other yesterday.

"Hi, Addie," he said. "Looking good. How've you been?"

The sight of him knocked the breath out of me. I stood there, a few feet away from him, unable to move, my eyes swimming with tears. He was no longer beautiful—somehow, that was the first thing to register in my mind, not without an undercurrent of glee. He'd put on weight, his face was puffy, with bags under his eyes, and unhealthily pale, his hair greasy and flat.

"What? You don't have anything to say?"

The tears overflowed, and I choked out two miserable, little words. "I'm sorry."

He watched me cry, and a grin spread over his face, so familiar, like not a minute had passed since we were twelve.

"I'm not sorry at all," he said. "Look at you. You're doing something with your life. You're *helping* people!"

I wished he hadn't said that. Twelve years and still, I could never be sure if he meant it or if every word was sarcasm.

"All thanks to me. Right? Honestly, I half expected to find you strung out on Valium, seeing four shrinks a week. How is Leeanne?"

"You know about Leeanne?" I stammered.

"Yeah. You may never have come to visit but I did keep track of you. At least when you were on the news."

"You know I couldn't come to visit," I said through my teeth. "You shouldn't even be here now."

"What, you're telling me to leave? To get out? And we just reunited after so long."

"You weren't supposed to call me."

"No one's gonna know unless either of us tells them. You want me to just, what, disappear from your life—when I need you most?"

You don't need me, I almost said. You never did. "Do you—do you have a place to stay?"

"I'm at a halfway house. But I'll be out of there by the end of the month. Back in the real world, for good."

"For good," I echoed.

"You know what I've been dying to do? To get a cheese-burger. A double, and a milkshake, the works. Supersize fries and all."

I found myself fumbling for my wallet, handing over all the cash I had inside—sixty-odd dollars. I held it out to him in an almost supplicating gesture.

He looked at me, then at my outstretched arm, and then at the money. He had a look of pity on his face. "You think that's what it takes to make me leave?"

"Just take it. Please."

He did, his gaze never once leaving mine, like he was trying to hypnotize me. He took the bills from my hand and slowly, with deliberation, ripped them up, once, twice, three times, reducing them to green confetti.

"You should get a burner phone. We're going to need a way to communicate without anyone nosing around, aren't we?"

"No. Absolutely not." My voice trembled, and I willed it to steady. "You can never call me or text me."

"Texting. Yeah, that's a thing now, isn't it? I'm so out of touch with the times."

I continued. "I'll be getting in touch with you. Every month—"

"Every week."

I gulped. "Every other week. I'll text you. You'll come meet me out by the road."

"In the middle of the day, in full view of traffic?"

"You can't come here again," I said. "I'll...I'll change my hours. I'll work nights."

"That boyfriend of yours won't mind?"

He knows about Milt, I thought, a chill in my very bones. I didn't have time to question the why and the how. Only to deal with what was in front of me. "No."

Later that day, I went in to see Marla and changed my work hours to the night shift. None of the younger female employees wanted to do night shifts, not just because of frequent altercations with drunk or high homeless youths who could get angry when told we were out of beds for the night but because of the shelter's location in the middle of nowhere. Marla raised her eyebrows but didn't say anything.

Two weeks later, I took one of the flip phones our charges left in a special drawer per shelter regulations and used it to text my brother. I handed over a single day's ATM limit, three hundred dollars.

That night, I came home to Milt rattled. He wanted to know what happened, whether someone attacked me, or worse. I didn't tell him anything but I couldn't endure his presence next to me as I slept. I crept out of bed and spent a nearly sleepless night on the couch.

That night, I knew that Eli's sentence had ended, and mine was just beginning.

# CHAPTER THIRTY-SEVEN

Awake now, I lie still and listen.

"I hate to disappoint you but I don't know where Andrea is," I hear Cynthia say in her usual penetrating voice. "She isn't answering her phone, as I'm sure you've realized."

"It is absolutely imperative that I speak to her." Figueroa speaks more softly but her voice carries with the same intensity. And it's brimming with anger she barely holds back. "Do you have any idea where she might be?"

"No. And to be honest with you, we don't exactly have a loving and sharing kind of mother-daughter relationship. This is the last place she would come to stay. Have you spoken to Milton DeVoort?"

"I just sent someone to talk to Mr. DeVoort. Now I need to talk to Andrea."

My heart starts to thrum dully, the last wisps of sleep

torn asunder. Why would she send someone to talk to Milt in person?

"Well, unfortunately, I can't help you with that."

"I believe there was an incident involving your adoptive daughter and...an engagement ring? A family heirloom that—"

"Andrea's relationship with Mr. DeVoort is none of my business. They've called off their engagement, yes, but that's all I know."

Lying still on my stomach, I feel my blood turn cold, afraid to move so much as a finger.

"That's why I would have liked to meet with Andrea in person," Figueroa says. She clearly doesn't know Cynthia Boudreaux.

That's when I hear steps thundering down the hall and then down the stairs. Oh God. I forgot about Leeanne.

"Hi," she says in her best prom-queen voice. "You're Detective Figueroa, right?"

Figueroa must acquiesce with a nod, because Leeanne goes on.

"Listen, I understand that you're doing your job but Andrea isn't here. And even if she were, she doesn't have anything to tell you. The fact of the matter is, that man— her brother—is a monster. She suffered enough because of him, don't you think?"

"Ms. Boudreaux," Figueroa says, struggling to keep her voice amicable, "as much as I appreciate your input, I'm afraid this case has absolutely nothing to do with you."

"Nothing?" Leeanne retorts, barely missing a beat. "I went to school with him. And if you have a few minutes, one of these days, I can tell you what Eli Warren did to me, in detail. If it interests you, of course," she adds, her voice dripping with condescension.

I can't believe what I'm hearing.

"It very much does," Figueroa says levelly. "But that will have to wait for a better time. Right now, I must locate Andrea."

"If she shows up," Cynthia says, "we'll let you know."

"Please do."

The door closes, and I allow myself to breathe again. My vision is swimming; my armpits are damp. Minutes tick by in silence. Then, just as I'm summoning the courage to sit up, I hear soft steps behind the door, followed by an even softer knock.

"Come in." My voice is rough and hoarse from lack of use. I expect Cynthia to come in to check on me but when I turn my head, Leeanne is carefully closing the door behind her. Without further invitation, she comes over and sits on the edge of the bed, making the bedsprings creak. She reaches out and switches on the bedside lamp.

We stay silent for a few moments, each one expecting the other to speak first. Finally, she gives up.

"I took the car back, like Mom asked."

"Thank you." I'm more thankful than she'll ever know. "What am I going to do if I want to leave?"

"If you want to leave, you'll be in big trouble."

No arguing with that.

"I know," I say, and watch her back stiffen. "About the . . . assault."

She gives me an owl-eyed, blank look. Then, to my surprise, hangs her head. "Figures."

"Did he really..."

"For God's sake, Andrea," she says mockingly. "You're a social worker. Aren't you supposed to *believe* victims?"

"I...It's just..." My face grows hot. "He was twelve."

She shrugs. "That's what the newspapers would have said, if it got out. Depravity in our schools. *Y'all need Jesus.* Et cetera. And my daddy and his career, caught right in the middle of the scandal. Do you understand now?"

I'm starting to. I draw a breath sharply.

"Yeah, yeah. Republican politician's slutty thirteen-year-old daughter gets an abortion. It's such a stereotype. For all I know, I might have wanted to keep it." She gives a laugh.

"Was it really his? The—" I can't bring myself to say it. Baby, fetus, or whatever.

Leeanne holds my gaze for a long time. Then, infuriatingly, shrugs. "We'll never know now, will we?"

We sure won't.

"I had to tell my parents *something*," she says, desperation lurking beneath the smugness in her voice. "You must understand that. You work with *troubled teens*." Even as she says it, her nose wrinkles. Like it has nothing to do with her. "My parents would have killed me! And Eli did attack me. There were witnesses."

So this is it, I think, weirdly numb and light-headed. Jim Boudreaux simply used me to cover up his daughter's misstep. Our family drama must have been a godsend to him. And I went along with it because it was what I wanted. Because I was a coward and I saw a way out.

There was a fire, my parents died, my brother became infamous. I got my compensation—going to live with a rich family. Moving up in the world, as they say. And everyone else's lives went on as before.

"It's a shame Dad's political career went nowhere," Leeanne says. "He really could have been good at it."

I digest this silently. When I don't speak for a few minutes, she becomes increasingly ruffled. "Look, I know you think I'm the bad guy here but you have no idea what kind of person your brother really was. Is. Did you know that when middle school started, he went around telling people you were a hermaphrodite? That's why no one wanted to be friends with you." She shakes her head. "I know, I know. It was a different era. No unisex bathrooms back then. And I heard you used to wet the bed. Which I'm also guessing was his invention?"

"I know my brother," I say. I've never felt it to be more true.

Leanne grimaces and shrugs.

"Is that why you did it?" I ask. "Because you felt bad?"

Her eyes narrow, and her face rearranges itself in a familiar look of smug superiority. "Do what? The abortion? What kind of question is that?"

"No. You know what. Lie to the police for me just now."

She stops smirking and heaves a sigh. She raises her hand to rub her eyes but then she must remember she's wearing mascara, and she drops her hand back into her lap. "Because I feel sorry for you."

My breath catches. I push myself up to a sitting position.

"Look, I know what it feels like to make shitty

decisions," she says. The smirk creeps back onto her face. "I've had my share of fuckups, my failed marriage being but the latest. But at least I know I'm the one responsible, and only me. You, on the other hand, owe it all to your brother. And the worst thing about all this? If you'd just come forward back then, you could have avoided this whole circus. And you wouldn't still be on his leash."

# CHAPTER THIRTY-EIGHT

*Eli Warren had no visitors. Not from anyone he knew, not from his sister. Although the court did prohibit him from contacting her, I don't suppose she would want to make the first step either. So, for now and for the foreseeable future, there's no one to drop by during visiting hours. I asked him how it made him feel, seeing other patients get visits from their families and knowing he never would.*

*"It's a shame," he said with a shrug. He flipped his hair out of his face. "This guy, [name redacted for privacy reasons], got a supercool pair of sneakers from his mom. I wish I could have sneakers."*

—Into Ashes: The Shocking Double Murder in the Suburbs by Jonathan Lamb, Eclipse Paperbacks, 2004, 1st ed.

*FIFTEEN YEARS EARLIER: BEFORE THE FIRE*

Andrea is whiling away her lunch hour in a bathroom stall. It's pouring rain, so outside is not an option, but she found a way to reclaim the bathroom. She just locks herself in a stall and pulls her feet up onto the toilet lid. Voila. Invisible. If she's quiet enough, it's almost like she doesn't exist. And the best part is she gets to listen as other girls come and go and overhear all the gossip.

Except today the bathroom is empty because something is happening downstairs, a fund-raiser for the school dance that seventh graders are allowed to participate in for the first time ever. So all the girls are there, probably chattering excitedly about their dresses and what boys they wish would invite them.

Andrea knows she probably won't go—there's no point. There will be no boy and no dress. She's content to spend her lunch hour here, playing with the lighter.

Bringing it to school is playing with fire, literally, but she can't bring herself to leave it at home either, for fear of her mother or Sergio happening upon it, especially now that she and Eli have lost their hiding place. She's afraid to part with it, even for a minute. As a result, she keeps it in her pocket at all times, hoping that even if someone sees it, they won't know what it is. From the outside, it's just a cheap trinket from a souvenir shop, an enameled lighthouse.

She flicks it open, watches the flame for a few seconds,

and flicks it closed again. Counting the seconds it takes her to pull it out of her pocket, flip it open, and light it.

The bathroom door clangs open, putting an end to her calm solitude. She watches the girl's feet stomp over to the sink. A moment later, the water starts to run. Andrea freezes inside when she recognizes the trendy brand-name sneakers. She wonders what Leeanne is doing here alone, without her cronies.

The tap stops running, and Leeanne's feet storm to the stall next to Andrea's. Andrea forgets how to breathe. She listens to Leeanne fumbling. There's rustling, a wrapper being torn. Then Leeanne plunks down on the toilet seat, her jeans around her ankles. The seats are filthy—Andrea wouldn't be caught dead sitting on one.

Leeanne sighs deeply, curses under her breath, and finally, Andrea hears the soft trickle of urine that stops and then starts again. Leeanne draws another deep breath through her teeth and then chuckles nervously. She gets up from the toilet, turns around, and flushes with her foot. "Fuck," Andrea hears her mutter, and then something clatters to the floor right between the two stalls. It's so close she could grab it if she reached. Then, stupefied, she realizes what it is. She has time to glimpse the thin white stick and the pink stripes in the little window on its end.

Andrea has read about this stuff in the teen magazines she sometimes glances through at checkout at the grocery store. But that's for older girls—not middle school girls. She was sure that all the nasty rumors floating around about Leeanne and her friends were just that, rumors.

She dives for the stick at the same time Leeanne reaches

under the stall. She's faster, snatching the test away before Andrea can grab it. But it's too late. Andrea's feet are on the floor, and Leeanne sees them.

The stall door slams. "Warren!" Leeanne shrieks. "Come out here! You nosy little shit. Come out here so I can break your long fucking nose, you snitch."

She pulls on the door of Andrea's stall, yanking again and again. Andrea is paralyzed, watching powerlessly as the latch moves farther and farther to the left with each pull.

"Come out!" Leeanne bellows. The latch gives way, and the door flies open.

Leeanne's face is pure rage, red, wild-eyed, her hair a mess. In the split second before Leeanne lunges for her, Andrea can see the twin trails of tears down her cheeks.

Andrea does the only thing she can think of. The lighter flicks open with a soft click, and the little flame hisses out. It's too small to reach Leeanne but it licks the ends of her blond hair as they swing in Andrea's face.

Leeanne screams. There's a flash of heat, and an unspeakable smell fills the air. Andrea gags as she watches Leeanne spin across the bathroom, pawing at her hair that hisses as it's consumed, turning black and brittle. Leeanne plunges her head into the sink. A final hiss, accompanied by wisps of acrid gray smoke, and she straightens herself, gasping as she faces the mirror.

On the right-hand side, most of the length is gone—her hair barely reaches her chin, its ragged black ends curled up and burned to a crisp.

Andrea expects the girl to lash out, start screaming, beat

Andrea to a pulp against the bathroom tiles. But instead, her face screws up, and she begins to cry, racked by deep, horrible sobs. Not a thin, endless childish whine—adult tears. Quiet.

A sense of calm envelops Andrea then, a sense of control unlike anything she's ever felt before. And it feels good. She thinks that she would like to feel like that again. She exits the bathroom stall, putting the lighter away in her pocket.

"Keep your mouth shut," she says, meeting Leeanne's red-eyed gaze in the mirror. "And I won't tell your parents that you needed one of those. They wouldn't like it, would they?"

Leeanne tries to say something but tears choke her. "You bitch," she finally spits.

Andrea walks out of the bathroom and doesn't look back.

The next day, Leeanne comes to school sullen, with a short bobbed haircut.

No one calls Andrea to the principal's office.

# CHAPTER THIRTY-NINE

The first time Adele Schultz showed up at the shelter, I didn't realize anything was wrong. She wanted a place to sleep, she said, because she couldn't go home.

I never asked why—we weren't supposed to. She blended in with the others, a little unkempt, unhealthy looking, like she didn't get enough nutrients or sleep, with hollows under the eyes that had appeared too early. I took her phone, like I did the others'. It wasn't time to call Eli. It had only been a week since I last saw him.

I had long ago settled into this nonlife that had started when my brother got out of prison. I was acting normal—just normal enough to avoid questions from my boss, or coworkers, or Milton. At first, I chalked up my jumpiness and fitful sleep to the change in working hours. Now, everyone was used to it and no one asked any more questions.

You really can get used to anything. I was becoming accustomed to the idea that this is how it would be from now on—life as usual but with biweekly meetings with and payouts to my brother, who would tell me all about how he could barely get by because no one in their right mind would hire someone with his record. I believed him because I knew it to be true. I had seen similar situations at the shelter, and every social worker knows what it can be like for an ex-convict to try to reintegrate into normal life.

I managed to convince myself it was an adjustment period. That after everything, it was the least I could do. As I have always done, I floated along and hoped for the best.

The hope would prove to be short-lived.

It was nearing three a.m., and I was watching the clock, yawning into my thermal cup of coffee. Soon, Allan was going to take over, and I could finally go home, take a shower, and snuggle up next to Milton. I could already feel the softness of the Egyptian cotton sheets Milt favored, the warmth of his body next to mine.

Then I saw movement out of the corner of my eye. When I turned to look, she was standing in the doorway to the dormitory. At first, I couldn't remember her name. I was too tired, and frankly, I didn't care. I told her to go to sleep and turned my attention to scrolling through an article on my phone. When she didn't answer or move, I looked up again.

"Andrea," she said, "I'm Adele. Nice to meet you."

I'm really not here to fraternize, I almost told her. But she took a step closer and tilted her head.

"People call me Addie," she proffered. "Do they call you Addie too?"

In spite of the overheated, dry air in the shelter, I felt a chill. Nobody called me Addie—not anymore. Milton did as a joke, so that didn't count.

That left only one person.

"Look, Addie, I'm going to level with you," she said.

I wondered if she was on something—she was too animated and coherent. Ritalin? Coke? Her eyes sparkled in a way I didn't like. And the closer she came, the more I saw that she did, sort of, look like me—in the sense that we were both plain, nondescript, just shy of cute. The same dishwater hair, the same freckles.

"Did he send you?" I asked point-blank. "I just paid him. It's only been a week."

She grinned. "Yes and no. From now on, you'll be paying me too. Because he told me and now I know the truth."

In the back of my mind, I'd wondered, in my darker moments, what it would be like if Eli just walked in here, or showed up at Cynthia's, or worse yet, at Milton's, and casually told them. I pictured myself going berserk. Maybe reaching for the nearest sharp thing and stabbing him, melodramatically, through the heart. But in that moment, with Adele standing in front of me, I was calm.

"You should leave," I said. "Before I ask someone to help you leave."

"I'm not leaving," she answered. She took another step toward me, leaned closer, and whispered, "He told me everything. How much do you think that's worth?"

I gave her everything I had on me, not realizing what a

rabbit hole I had just fallen into. Not realizing that, unlike my brother, there was nothing keeping her from following me night and day, showing up just about anywhere, at any time.

When I called Eli, from another homeless kid's phone, for the first time ever he didn't answer.

Then Adele demanded a sum I didn't have. Only then, when I got caught stealing money from Cynthia and Milton noticed the absent ring, I knew I had hit a dead end.

Cynthia called me over to discuss something trivial, and I went, hoping for a chance to ask for some more money, supposedly to last me until the end of the month. Or failing that, to take some of her jewelry I could pawn. Instead, I walked right into an intervention. The whole story about drugs and booze was something I had to come up with on the fly, scrambling to find an explanation. My world was threatening to fall apart once again, fraying at the seams.

But this time, it was only my own fault.

\*       \*       \*

A while after Leeanne leaves, Cynthia brings me dinner. I'd lost track of time. By my estimates, it has to be past midnight, but there she is, still in her robe, carrying a tray that she maneuvers with surprising dexterity past the door.

I didn't think I had any appetite. I barely raise my head when she comes in. But the smell of food reawakens my survival instincts. My stomach rumbles. I sit up.

"You should eat something," Cynthia says. I can't discern any particular emotion in her voice.

On the tray are mac 'n' cheese, a glass of orange juice,

and two cookies on a little plate. The sheer simplicity of it is enough to make me cry. Appearances aside, the picture-perfect wife and mother has never been one for home cooking. Living in her house, I consumed more frozen meals and Hamburger Helper in one year than I had in my whole previous life. A "health kick" she instituted for Leeanne and me consisted of replacing these same pre-made meals with their inedible low-fat counterparts. So homemade mac 'n' cheese from the woman who lived by Kraft Dinner has to mean something. I can't throw that effort back in her face so I pick up the fork and take a bite. Before I know it, I've inhaled half the plate, and my stomach is cramping from eating so fast.

"Thank you," I say as soon as I swallow my mouthful.

"You know, all I ever wanted was to provide a decent home for you," she says, acknowledging my thanks with a dismissive half nod. "And, all right, I admit—I thought it would do Leelee some good to learn to share. I know you think it was some would-be political gesture but my husband was actually against the idea."

I look at her, confused. This goes against everything I previously thought. When Jim Boudreaux died, all I could muster was relief. It was as if the memory of that day at the burn ward died with him. Now I bitterly wish I could ask him myself, except it's too late. It's always too late.

"He was?"

"Yeah. He wanted to help place you with some nice foster family, maybe one of our friends. But I insisted you should come live with us. I had my reasons. You were your brother's victim too, after all."

I don't know what to make of this information that comes fifteen years too late. She sighs.

"I didn't think it would be easy," she adds. "And God knows you've done everything you could to make it as difficult as possible. But I thought I could understand your rationale, at least."

I can't help but wonder if she does now. Or whether she expects me to tell her—to give her the key to the questions of her own existence. *Who did I shelter in my home for more than half a decade?* But the problem is, even when you think you're acting out of self-determination, it's not always the case. Someone is always behind the scenes, pulling the strings. And living with someone like Eli makes you paranoid for life, always seeking out insidious motivations where there are none, mistrusting everyone who crosses your path, second-guessing every last little nice thing anyone does.

"I felt betrayed when I realized you'd stolen the jewelry that my husband gave me back when we got married. Or that the money I'd given you wasn't for groceries. But deep down, I didn't blame you, you know?"

"I'm sorry," I say, and I really mean it.

"But be sure, Andrea, that I haven't told a word of this to that woman. And I won't. As far as she's concerned, there never was any money. And I'm sure Milton will do the same thing on his end."

Now there's something I don't deserve. Cynthia shakes her head.

"I saw the CD was missing from my car," she says. "I know you took it. Why?"

I can only shrug.

"You've never read that book?"

"No."

"Maybe you should have." She sighs again. "Would have saved you so much grief."

If anything, I think the opposite is true, but I don't tell her.

"You know what? There's a reason they barely ever mention you in the whole thing," she says suddenly, and my head snaps up. "I was listening to it to make double sure. The lawyers had gone over it back in the day and okayed it, but I never checked for myself. I thought now was as good a time as any, right?"

I'm beginning to guess. "Lawyers?"

"Yes. My husband's lawyers. At my request, they made sure the book never mentioned you except in passing. No statements implicating you in a damn thing."

That explains a lot about that book.

"I thought it was the least I could do, to give you a fresh start. So you wouldn't have to be known as *that boy's sister* wherever you go. If only you'd been able to let it go."

But I wasn't able. Tears sting my eyes. Everything could have been so different, if only—

Cynthia unfolds her hands from her lap and reaches to pick up the tray. "Do you want me to leave the cookies?"

I shake my head. She gets up, bringing the tray with her. In the doorway, she stops again, setting the tray down on the dresser.

"We can only hope they catch the bastard soon. No. You know what I'm really hoping for? I'm hoping, and may God forgive me for these thoughts . . . " She chuckles and crosses herself half-heartedly. "I'm hoping he'll put up a fight when they finally nail him down. He'll put up a fight so they put a bullet or five right in his empty heart. Then it'll be over, once and for all, and all his lies can die with him."

She glances at me, searching for complicity, but all I feel is horror. I'm trying not to think about how much she knows and how much she understands.

But she closes the door, and then she's gone.

# CHAPTER FORTY

Adele came back to see me the day after the intervention.

It was in the dead of February, in the middle of a particularly bad cold snap. A few inches of snow had fallen, making the road slippery and paralyzing traffic. Not all of it had been cleaned yet, and a few of my coworkers called in absent.

I had contemplated doing the same. Except I needed the money. To pay back Cynthia. To try to get Milton's ring back from the pawnshop.

Adele did not come into the shelter, like she'd done up to now. Perhaps if she had, I would have reacted differently; perhaps everything wouldn't have turned out the way it did. Seeing her come through the doors would fill me with such dread that I was frozen to the spot, aware that she was holding my entire life in the palm of her hand. All she had to do was say one word, just one well-placed word, to anyone—another social worker, Marla, another homeless teenager. And my life would be upended.

But that day, she didn't come in. Instead, I found her waiting in the lot behind the shelter. I was walking to my car, drained and exhausted as usual, still jumping at every shadow. And just as I reached for my car keys in my pocket, there she was. Her silhouette detached itself from the bins behind the parking lot, the same spot where I met Eli when he got out of prison. She started walking toward me but instead of being paralyzed, I went to meet her.

"You happy now?" I snarled.

She didn't expect it. She recoiled, and for the first time in weeks—for the first time ever—that smug look she wore slipped from her face. She's scared of me, I realized with bafflement. She looked awfully young in that moment. Younger than her twenty-two years. My torturer was just a frightened young girl. Something in me clicked over, an understanding forming where there used to be only blind fear for my life.

She backed away, returning into the shadow of the recycling bins.

"I don't have anything else to give you," I said. "You're wasting your time. I suggest you go and get a real job."

"Don't you dare talk to me like that," she said.

She'd recovered herself and was trying to put on the usual arrogant air but it was too late. I was no longer afraid. "Tell Eli to come to me himself if he wants money. I'm not giving you another red cent."

"Eli doesn't know I'm here," she said. Her eyes were darting back and forth, never landing on my face; I could tell she was lying. Did he tell her to lie? I wondered. Or did he not know that she was asking for more than was the deal? Was she skimming the difference?

I may never have been quite certain what went on inside my brother's head, why he did the things he did. But I could see right through this girl. She thought she was like my brother but she didn't even come close. She was just greedy and perhaps a touch too arrogant for her own good.

Now she backed away until she hit the recycling bin behind her. The metal clanged dully.

"I'll go to the biggest newspaper in town," she said. "I'll go on TV."

"And tell them what?"

Her breath escaped from her in a puff of steam. She huddled in her greasy parka, pulling her head in between her shoulders, chin dipping into the stringy faux-fur collar. "The truth." Her voice wobbled.

"And why should they believe you? Do you have any proof at all?"

"I have your brother. He'll—"

"No one will believe him either. And I think you both know that, because otherwise, you would have gone to the media already. That story's gotta be worth more than anything I can give."

"The lighter—"

I laughed. It startled her, and she pressed herself into the side of the recycling bin, inching away from me. I threw my arms out, my unbuttoned winter jacket swinging open like a bird's wings.

"What lighter? Where do you see a lighter, Adele?"

"I'll—"

"You'll leave. And I'm never, ever going to see you any-where near this shelter again—you understand me?"

Her face twisted with a grimace of hatred, reminding me of an angry but weak little animal caught in a trap. Unex-pectedly, she spat in my face. I barely had time to turn my head before a big glob of her saliva hit the side of my jaw, and the spray landed all over my cheek.

"Fuck you," she snapped.

I hit her.

I'd never hit anyone before. And no doubt I would have done more harm to my own knuckles than to Adele, like every first timer. But in my right hand, I was still clenching my car keys on their keychain—my little lighthouse bauble. I wasn't even thinking about it. I just slugged her in the face as hard as I could.

The pain in my hand startled me but her reaction startled me even more. Her shriek cut short, she stumbled back, doubling over, her hand clasped over her cheek. In the half darkness, her eyes glittered like those of a rabid ani-mal; it took me a moment to realize those were tears. They streamed down her good cheek. I could see blood through her fingers. She let out a little strangled gasp and then backed away and away, deeper into the shadows.

I stood there, my arm hanging limply at my side, torn knuckles throbbing with pain—the only thing that kept me grounded. I clenched my fist around the lighthouse key-chain as hard as I could, even though that made the scrapes on my knuckles split farther open. It occurred to me that I should stop her, that I could be in big trouble. But I didn't move. I just watched her back away until she vanished.

Then I went back to my car, got in, and drove home. Or to the place that used to be—the town house that was now a mere husk of home, its most important part, Milton, gone. All because of her. Because of Eli.

That night, though, the solitude was a blessing. No one there to question what happened to my busted knuckles. Without fuss, without needing to hide, I got the first-aid kit and fixed them up as best as I could. Then I went to sleep and dreamed of nothing. I was ready to start anew, to be free. As if I knew, deep down, that she wouldn't come bother me again.

She didn't. Next time I saw her, her photo was on the news, and she was dead. Bludgeoned to death in my brother's apartment.

\*      \*      \*

When morning comes, I realize I'd passed out on top of my old bed, clothes and all. I know I can't hide in my old room at Cynthia's forever if I want to take back control of the situation. And right now, taking control starts with looking at my phone.

I'm not ready for the avalanche of texts and notifications. It takes several deep breaths and a minute or two of scrolling before I decide what I want to tackle first.

There's a voicemail from an unfamiliar number—if it's bad, I might as well get it out of the way. I don't know who I expected but when I put the phone to my ear, the man's voice erupts from it, poised and cheerful.

"Hello. This message is for Andrea Boudreaux. You might remember me—my name is Jonathan Lamb . . ."

I take the phone away from my ear and stare at it. The message continues, so loud that I can hear it regardless.

"You have all my sympathies about what happened with your brother." I'm not sure which exact thing he means—the one fifteen years ago or the most recent development. Either way, I hope he knows where I think he can shove his sympathies. "Here's the thing, Andrea. I feel like you're woefully underrepresented in the coverage of the whole story. I would love to get your version of events, from your point of view. I imagine you might have rather a lot to say after fifteen years. Give me a call at this number, and we can arrange a meeting. Don't worry—you can be assured of my discretion. Not a thing you say will find its way into print without your express permission. I wish you all the best."

I'm tempted to call him back just to have the pleasure of telling him to fuck off.

The next message is from Chris, asking me tersely to call her back. Not going to happen.

The last one is from Figueroa.

"Andrea," her voice says calmly. "I would very much like to talk to you. And please give my message to your lovely family and ask them to call you a lawyer and set it up. Because it's in everyone's best interest—especially yours—that you don't continue to avoid me. Elizabeth Jones has been found. She's dead."

# CHAPTER FORTY-ONE

*The one thing I had tried to ascertain was whether Eli did finally find some genuine remorse within him or if he was only sorry he got caught. If he had found remorse—which is not in the nature of a sociopathic individual—it is tragically too late. But if he hadn't, what does it say about him? About everyone around him? About society?*

*On the day of my last visit to him, I brought him a pair of brand-new sneakers. His face lit up when he saw them, with a childlike expression of excitement and wonder.*

*"You know," he said as he accepted the gift, with*

*the casual entitlement of royalty, "we're not even al-
lowed to wear sneakers in here."*

—*Into Ashes: The Shocking Double Murder in the
Suburbs* by Jonathan Lamb, Eclipse Paperbacks,
2004, 1st ed.

*FIFTEEN YEARS EARLIER: BEFORE THE FIRE*

Andrea throws a backward glance at the house every few
seconds, even though her mom has gone to the grocery
store and Sergio is in front of the TV, and he typically
doesn't get up until the episode is over. Still, she feels the
need to check. The sliding door leading to the patio remains shut so she reaches into her pocket and finds the
lighter there, its shape smooth and exciting beneath her
fingertips.

She crouches next to the wisteria her mom planted last
spring—or what's left of the wisteria anyway. The Denver
winter took care of it, and now it's nothing more than a
tangle of ropey brown tendrils. Her mom says it might still
come back—it's only April—but as far as Andrea is concerned, the plant is as dead as the decorative trellis that
holds it up.

The spider, on the other hand, is very much alive. One of
the first ones to emerge from hibernation or hiding or whatever hellhole spiders crawl out of, it's a small, sleepy thing
with a round black body and yellow-spotted legs. Those legs
move slowly, lazily, as it dangles in the center of a half-spun

web. Andrea isn't afraid of spiders exactly but they make her shudder; something about them is just wrong.

Nothing better to test this thing on.

She flicks the lighter open, delighting in the soft hiss that sends the good kind of goose bumps up her arms, and the pin-straight tongue of flame shoots out, almost all of it a beautiful blue with only a tip of orange.

She holds the lighter out, steadying her arm so it doesn't tremble. It's still too far below the spider to do any real damage, but the creature can feel the heat rising from the flame, and it starts to panic, legs moving faster, body spinning on the nearly invisible threads of the web that will never come to be. It pulls its body up, and she follows with the flame in her hand. The tip of it touches one of the spider's legs.

"What do you think you're doing?"

Her hand trembles, and she nearly drops the lighter before she manages to snap it shut. The spider disappears somewhere in the tangle of the dead wisteria's branches, but she's not watching it anymore. Guilt forms a thick lump in her throat, her face growing hot. Eli stands over her, and as she looks up to meet his gaze, she's ready to beg him not to tell Mom or Sergio. She'll do his chores, hand over her allowance. Whatever it takes.

But when she sees his face, she realizes his expression isn't anger—it's lively interest.

"Where did you get that from?" He reaches for the lighter, and she snatches it away as quickly as she can, knowing full well it won't be quick enough. They haven't looked like twins for a while now—he's taller, stronger, and strangers now assume he's her older brother. He's quick enough to catch her and strong enough to wrestle that lighter out of her hand.

"I found it."

"So you stole it. It's cool, Addie. Jesus, relax."

It feels like the last thing she should do.

"I don't care where you got it; just don't set the whole house on fire, okay?" He holds out his hand; the smirk on his lips is deceptive. "Lemme see."

She starts to back away but there's nowhere to back away to. And she's still crouching so she loses her balance and lands on her behind. Her favorite jeans, the ones with the rhinestones on the back pockets, hit the damp earth.

"Get away from me!" she snarls.

"Or what? You'll tell Mommy?" he sneers. "She'll take it away, and you know it, and since you're such a bad liar, she'll also know it's stolen, and you'll be in a ton of trouble."

"It's mine." She's ready to cry, and her voice betrays it, trembling treacherously.

"Yeah, yeah." Before she can draw a breath, he's upon her, and without effort, he catches her wrist and twists it. Her hand opens, and the lighter drops into his palm.

"Wow. Not bad. Might be expensive. If you stole it from someone we know, now's a good time to tell me."

That's when she lies. She doesn't know why—the opportunity is there, and it seems like the kind of thing that might make him give the lighter back, or at least make him not rat her out. "It's Sergio's," she says. "It was in his stuff. He thinks he lost it so it's cool."

Her brother's expression shifts so fast she's frightened, convinced that he saw right through her lie and that things are about to get worse. But instead, he tosses the lighter back to her with disdain. It traces an arc through the air but she fails to catch it, too stunned to move. It lands on the ground, and she dives for it before Eli can change his mind. She wraps it in the hem of her shirt to wipe off any dirt that may have clung to its perfect, shiny surface.

"You're not gonna—"

"I'm not gonna tell him," her brother says with a scowl. "God, even when you do have secrets, they're lame ones."

He turns around and storms up the stairs leading to the patio. She hears the tires of her mom's car on the gravel as it pulls up behind the fence, and she hurriedly puts the lighter back in her pocket. She's fuming. If you only knew, she finds herself thinking. If anyone only knew the things that go through her mind in the darker hours of the night. What she imagines saying, the things she imagines doing to Leeanne and the other girls, the prettier girls who will have it easy their whole lives because they happened to be born with a different set of genes. How she imagines smashing their faces repeatedly with a brick until lips split and teeth crumble and eyeballs burst.

She wants to tell him but then she'd also have to tell him that she hates him too, her own brother, her own twin. That she resents him, as if he took something that belonged to her without even realizing it.

Her whole life, everyone always liked him more, and she took it as the natural order of things. Only recently has she begun asking herself why. Watching him out of the corner of her eye.

Outside the fence, the car engine stops, and the door slams. Andrea goes to help her mom bring the groceries inside and then starts to put them away in the fridge without being prompted. She focuses on every item, lining them up just so on the shelves, pretending it's a game of Tetris: egg carton, milk, bologna.

"What's with you today?" Cass says, more affectionate than surprised. "You're never this helpful. Did you do something you're trying to make up for?"

Andrea pretends she hasn't heard, and the whole time, she avoids looking directly into her mother's face. All evening, she can't bring herself to meet her gaze. Later, she would wish she had.

After dinner, when she goes up to her room to finish homework, her brother is already there, sitting still and quiet on her bed.

"Hey," he says as she makes a beeline for their shared desk, doing her best to ignore him. Normally, he'd annoy her, throw her stuffed animals at her and then pencils and books. He'd needle her, saying increasingly cruel things until she had no choice but to pay attention. Eli isn't used to being ignored, and there's nothing he hates more. But after that first *hey*, it takes him another five minutes to speak again. She's had time to lay out her books and notebooks, pen hovering over a new page.

"Addie," he says, and something about his voice makes

her turn around. His eyes are red, she realizes with confusion. She doesn't think she'd ever seen him cry before—ever. Not even when they were little kids.

"I gotta tell you something. Can you keep a secret? A real one?"

She gives a terse nod, afraid he'll change his mind.

"The real reason I stole that money was...I needed it. I'm going to run away."

# CHAPTER FORTY-TWO

"I don't have anything to say to you," I tell Figueroa.

It's a nightmarish replay of the scene just days ago, except everything is different this time. Cynthia's lawyer, a prematurely gray man in his late thirties, stands behind me, an ominous presence that doesn't seem to bother Figueroa in the slightest.

"You don't have to say anything. Actually, as your mother's lawyer has no doubt advised you, it's better if you don't."

"Why do you hate me so much?" I ask. I'm staring right into her smiling face. Victory looks good on her: It's as if her skin has smoothed overnight, the fine lines and dry flakes all evened out. Another case untangled, I can practically read in her smug half smile. Another promotion looming. Or almost. The only thing standing between her and her triumph of the ego is this stubborn, ugly girl with her angry pink skin melted like wax.

Instead of answering, she tilts her head, inspecting me curiously. "I wondered about you from the start, Andrea. And I think I have you figured out."

"I seriously doubt that."

"The whole spineless thing," she says, as if she hadn't heard. "I just wasn't buying it. Eli Warren killed your mother and stepfather, made up a bunch of lies, disfigured you. And now he murdered another girl. A girl who, under slightly different circumstances, if it hadn't been for the Boudreaux family in any case, could have been you. A girl who even looks like you, who has a similar name! Why on earth would you continue to protect him? Is blood really that important?"

I draw a breath to retort but she silences me. It's probably for the best. "You know, let me tell you something. I'm an adopted child myself," she says. "My parents were upstanding people. They raised me and my sister to the best of their ability. They gave us values, they provided us with an education, and they taught us how to be good people. And it wasn't that I never wondered about my birth parents but I figured they had their reasons, right? Well, a few years ago, my birth father tracked me down. Spun some story about wanting to reconnect, the importance of family, and so on. Real tearjerker. Except it didn't take long for me to realize he owed serious money, something to do with gambling—I don't remember the details. I dropped him. Never spoke to him again. Perhaps some people would judge me for that, but in my mind, I did the right thing. I don't even know what became of him after that."

"I know what you're doing," I say quietly. "I do it too,

with the homeless kids from the shelter. Rapport. I'm supposed to open up to you now, or something?"

She leans closer, her eyes practically sparkling with glee. "No. I didn't expect it to be so easy. I simply wanted you to know that I do understand you, Andrea. It's just that, like with my biological father, I find the whole story a little on the nose."

"You don't have to talk, Andrea," the lawyer pipes up. I managed to forget he was there.

"She's not talking," Figueroa assures him. "She's listening." She turns back to me. "When things seem a little too contrived, a little too convenient, it makes me want to ask questions. Just how much is one girl willing to endure in the name of shared DNA? Unless it's not him you're protecting. It's something else."

"Is this what really brings you here?" A feeling of deep calm overcomes me. I think I'm even smiling. "Theories? Wow, you really have time on your hands."

"Andrea, please," Cynthia mutters.

"Not just theories. I'm looking for justice for a murdered girl. Two girls, as of late."

At the mention of Sunny, a lump blocks my throat, all my snappy answers dead and crumbling to dust.

"Elizabeth Jones. Found strangled in a bathtub, in an apartment with your name." The words ring out in near-total silence. "Where I will eventually place you at the time of the crime. You don't have an alibi for that either—I checked. Just like you don't really have one for Adele Schultz."

"I—"

"Don't say anything," the lawyer reminds me. As if I needed reminding.

"You clocked out of work fifteen minutes early. Your only explanation for the missing time is that car crash."

"Are you going to arrest me?"

"As soon as I can find motive. The reason you'd want Adele silenced."

"That's not what I asked. Am I under arrest?"

I start to get up, but Cynthia says my name, her hand landing heavily on my shoulder. The strength in her surprises me. I'm forced to lower back down onto the ottoman where I'd been sitting, perched on the edge like a nervous bird.

"This is absolutely, completely out of bounds," she thunders. "You come here to make wild accusations against my daughter, and with no basis as far as I can tell. It's unacceptable. Pray that we don't decide to take legal action against the police department."

"You can do whatever you want once the case is wrapped up," Figueroa says.

Childs murmurs something quick and nervous in her ear. She heaves a deep sigh and gets up. "Don't worry. We'll be going."

Watching her, it occurs to me that she never answered my question. Not really. She skirted around it in such a way that I didn't realize until it was too late. Why does she hate me?

As she's at the door, I catch her eye. If she's feeling disappointed with the setback, she doesn't show it. Her look is that of utter contempt.

I know what you're really protecting, I read in her gaze. You're a liar, as bad as your brother. Worse. Because he made a sacrifice, and you only care about yourself.

Except she has it so, so wrong. I ache to run and stop her from leaving, grab the collar of her sweater and shake her. I didn't kill them, I want to say. He's framing me. This was his plan all along—don't you see?

Too bad it took me so long to figure it out. And now it might be too late.

# CHAPTER FORTY-THREE

Since there's no point in continuing to hide out at Cynthia's, she called Milton and asked him to come and take me home. I've never been so grateful for anything in my entire life.

I'm upstairs changing out of Leeanne's sweats when I hear the doorbell, followed by steps, and, finally, his voice. I hurriedly pull my shirt over my head but already the steps are racing up the stairs; then the door swings open, and he bursts into the room. I'm still only halfway into my shirt, and I want to curse him out for not knocking but forget to.

He stops in the door, breathless. "Andrea," he says, and I cross the distance between us and return his hug. I want to stay like this forever, in his warm, powerful embrace where nothing can get me. "I was so worried. You didn't return any of my texts."

He could never, ever, understand what I did and what I

saw and the lies I told. If I told him, it would put the final nail in the coffin of what we once had. And as much as I realize he'd be better off if I released him, I can't bring myself to do it—not now. Not here.

So we go home. I look out the window while he drives back to the town house, like old times. Except instead of the classic rock he loves, the car is filled with silence. The weather is clear and beautiful. Rays of sunlight skewer the car, heating my skin in splotches.

As soon as he walks through the front door of the town house, he whistles softly. "This place is a mess."

"Sorry," I say. "Housekeeping was pretty far from my mind."

"I wasn't accusing you. I get it."

"I know."

"You didn't have to lash out at me. I was only trying to be there for you."

I turn and look at him, my eyes drinking in the sight. To have him in here again—it's almost enough to make me believe everything can still work out. He belongs here. I need to find a way to make him never leave, even if it's wrong and selfish and only delaying the inevitable.

"Milton," I say, taking a step toward him, "shut up."

He picks me up and kisses me, hard and passionately. I groan a little into his mouth. I don't think I ever fully realized how much I missed him—not just his presence by my side, his jokes, all the little things he used to do that drove me nuts. But also this. The purely physical.

My sex drive seemed to have crawled under a rock to die the day he moved out, and now that he's back here—even though it's not permanent, even though it's just a twist of fate—it's come back roaring, starved, demanding to be satisfied. I wrap my legs around him but it makes it hard to peel off his shirt. So I pull away and undo his belt buckle.

My already too-loose jeans, which have become even looser lately, fall without resistance around my ankles, and he lifts me out of them effortlessly, hauling me onto the couch. I kick my way out of my underwear and toss it aside. We don't even manage to undress all the way, forgetting everything in our mutual hunger.

It's over faster than I remember but I don't mind. I'm sweaty and panting, and so is Milt.

"Do you want to go upstairs, get into bed?" he murmurs in my ear.

"No." I don't want to move. I spoon against him, my body fitting so perfectly with his. My T-shirt and bra have ridden up and are bunched under my armpits, so his ripped six-pack presses into my back, slightly sticky with sweat. Milt is resolutely unkinky—doing it on the couch is probably among the edgiest things we've ever done. He's very much a bed / dimmed lights / no clothing kind of guy. It took him a while to convince me to have sex without a shirt on. I dug in my heels but he persisted, patient but pigheaded, until I gave in. At first I wanted the lights off, then got used to it, and then began to like it even. My tics, such as crossing my arms to hide some of the burn scars, gradually fell away.

The idea of having to relearn with a new person didn't appeal to me. If it didn't work out with him, I'd decided I was going to be dying alone.

We do move to the bed eventually. There we muster enough energy for another go. It's less frenzied this time, Milt as I remember him, taking his time, making sure I come before he does. Afterward, I kick off the blankets, content to bask in our combined body heat.

"Please don't push me away again," he says softly. "I know you needed your space. But all I ever wanted was to help."

"I wasn't pushing you away." If you only knew.

The silence lingers but it's no longer heavy. Downstairs in the kitchen, the fridge begins to hum. A clock is ticking. My house is once again a home.

"That money," he says. It's like having a bucket of cold water dumped over my head. "That you took. What was it really for?"

I sit up and pull up my knees. "Why would you ask me that?"

"A detective came to talk to me. Childs, something like that? He asked questions."

I squeeze my eyes shut. My head is starting to spin. How did I manage to forget about that?

"What did you say?"

When I open my eyes, he frowns. "What does it matter what I said?"

I swing my legs over the edge of the bed, reach down, and pick up a sheet from the floor. I tie it around my chest. Finally realizing this is serious, Milt sits up in turn.

"Just tell me," I say, making a knot in the sheet. "They asked you questions about me. I need to know what you told them."

"Why? What's going on, Andrea?"

I face him, furious, and realize that I can't answer this simple question. Not without lying again.

He gets out of bed, throws open the closet, and rummages through the scant selection of clothes he left there when he moved out. Finally finding an old, wash-faded pair of boxers, he pulls them on. I notice that he's thinner than before.

"I think I have the right to know," he says. "Tell me what's going on. Just what do you think is going to happen if you tell me?"

"You have no idea what you're even—"

"Why not? I'm on your side, Andrea. I'm your boyfriend. Your fiancé."

"Ex-fiancé."

The remark, meant to wound him, only fires him up. "Yeah. No wonder. What's surprising is that we lasted as long as we did, with you always shutting me out. Afraid to ever tell me what you're thinking, or feeling. Like if you say the wrong thing, I'll walk out or something. Is that what you think of me? That I can't be trusted?"

"It's not what I meant. You don't understand. Nobody can be trusted. Not with this."

We stand across from each other, the bed between us. I'm breathless. I have to turn this situation around, and I go for the only means I have left at my disposal. Attack.

"And speaking of shutting you out, what exactly was I supposed to do? Your freaking parents had a PI follow me around before we went on our third date, for God's sake!"

He groans. "You are not bringing that up again."

"You bet."

"I already explained it. And I apologized, over and over—"

"There were things I was going to tell you. On my own time. But your mom and dad deprived me of that! I was an open book to you from the start. How convenient."

"Andrea, you're being irrational. I'm not the enemy."

"Really? Or maybe the parents were just a good excuse. Maybe you did it yourself so you'd have all the dirt. Stealing the playbook before the game even started—very clever of you."

"Oh, is that what you think?" He's almost yelling now. "For fuck's sake. I loved you. You broke my heart. What more do you want me to say? And now you're clearly in over your head, and even now, you keep me at arm's length. Even though you have nothing left to lose."

This is too much. Just one step further than I can allow.

"What is that supposed to mean?" I ask, calm now.

"Nothing. I ... I'm sorry. I didn't mean that."

I storm past him, through the door into the hall. He follows on my heels. "Wait."

"You have something at stake here?" I snarl. "What is it? Are you spying on me for someone too? My brother? Figueroa? The police?"

"Are you insane?" he yells back. "What—"

"Or you just get off on fucking fucked-up people. Is that it?"

His nostrils flare, and I realize I went too far.

"I loved you," he repeats. "I still do." He steps toward me and reaches for my shoulder.

I move out of the way. "Don't touch me."

I start down the stairs, holding on to my sheet. He thunders after me, grasping at the edge of the sheet. "Let go!" I scream, trying to tug it free. "Let go of me!"

I hear fabric tearing, and part of the sheet comes away in Milton's hand. I stumble, and my back hits the railing painfully. I lash out from pure reflex. My arms outstretched, my hands connect with his chest before I realize what I'm doing.

Milt loses his footing, flails, grasps for the railing—but too late. He tumbles down the stairs, landing on the floor below. He groans and then goes still.

I clasp my hand over my mouth.

"Milton?" I don't really expect him to answer. "Milton?"

Not feeling my legs, I race down the stairs and crouch next to him. Oh God. He looks fine—nothing is at a weird angle, no blood. There's a big bump just below his hairline that grows and turns purple right before my eyes.

My first instinct is to shake him, to try to straighten him—no, I mustn't touch him. I remember from first-aid class that you should never touch anyone who fell because it might aggravate their injuries or even kill them, especially if the skull or spine is involved.

Oh God. What have I done?

As carefully as I can, I touch my fingertips to his neck. Thankfully, his pulse is thrumming strong and fast. He seems to be knocked unconscious.

What I should do is call an ambulance. Where the hell is my phone when I need it? I run to the counter where I remember leaving it, my feet slipping on the floor. But before I pick up the phone, I know how stupid it would be. I'm a murder suspect, even if Figueroa hasn't made it official yet. And now I've shoved my ex-fiancé down the stairs.

It looks worse than bad.

Shit. But I can't leave him. I can't. I pace for a few seconds before the solution comes to me. I look around and locate his jacket, which he left flung carelessly over the arm of the couch.

The side pockets are empty. When I reach into the inside pocket, my hand connects with something but it's not a phone. It's small, square, and smooth.

Bile wells up in the back of my throat, and I think I might puke. Holding my breath, I pull the object free.

My knees buckle, and I sit on the floor. The jacket slips off the couch's armrest, and I cradle it in my arms. Tears fill my eyes when I look at the little box again. I know what it is before I open it, yet I can't stop myself. It's there, the platinum band, the diamond winking like a star, impossibly clean and bright. It's not a copy or reproduction; it's the real thing, the one I wore on my ring finger for many months.

He got it back. He never told me. He got it from the pawnshop, and he was going to give it back to me.

On the heels of that realization comes another, and it makes me want to howl. He didn't betray me. He lied on my behalf. He told a lie to the authorities without even knowing what he was covering for. The only person in the world who really, truly loved me, with all my flaws and not in spite of them.

I suspected he might get hurt in all this. I just never thought it would be like this.

Even though it's all over, I can't get it out of my head. He loves me. He was going to give back the ring. He loves me. He was willing to lie for me...

Except those things never turn out quite the way you want. He doesn't know it yet; his life hasn't taught him. But when you lie for someone, they are in your debt. And the debt carries serious interest.

I'm numb with pain when I get to my feet. I pick up my clothes, pull my jeans up my thighs, throw on my T-shirt, and slip my feet into my sneakers. His phone is on the coffee table, right in my face. How could I not have seen it? I pick it up, unlock it—the passcode is my birthday. I punch in 911, my thumb hovering above the Call button, but instead of pressing it, I turn off the screen. I rush over to Milton and kneel on the floor and let myself look at him, for only a few moments.

*I love you*, I mouth, before leaning over and letting my lips touch his forehead.

Then I dial emergency services and wipe the screen with the corner of my discarded sheet. I leave the phone on the floor, near his hand.

Tears blanketing my eyes, I grab my purse, then exit the house, leaving the door closed but unlocked for when the ambulance arrives.

Then I start walking, leaving behind the only home I've ever known.

# CHAPTER FORTY-FOUR

*No doubt this is a question that crossed most parents' minds at least once: Are children capable of evil?*

*But Eli Warren's parents didn't realize anything was wrong until it was too late. Perhaps it was willful denial: We never want to think the worst of our own child, and it's easy to explain away or overlook the signs. Or perhaps Cassandra Warren, a single mother, simply got too caught up in trying to provide for her children to notice something was off about her son. In any event, the only thing we know for sure is that the Bianchis' failure to take action had fatal consequences for their family. The family home cannot be brought back up from the ashes, and the dead cannot come back to life. What was done can never be undone.*

*—Into Ashes: The Shocking Double Murder in the Suburbs* by Jonathan Lamb, Eclipse Paperbacks, 2004, 1st ed.

### FIFTEEN YEARS EARLIER: BEFORE THE FIRE

"I'm going to run away," Eli repeats.

Andrea isn't sure what kind of reaction he expected from her. It sounds so ridiculous it can't possibly be true. So the only response she can muster is a weird, half-stifled laugh.

But the angry tears that fill his eyes are real, and so is his furious scowl.

"What..." she stammers. "What about me?"

"What *about* you?" he mocks. "It's not about you, for once."

Nothing is ever about me, she thinks fleetingly.

"I can't stay here. Our mom and Sergio want to send me off to some reform school. And you, presumably, will go on with your insipid life. Getting Cs, hiding from Leeanne in the bathroom. Lucky you."

"Reform school?" she asks. Separate them? How is that even possible? How could their mom even think of doing something like that?

Unless it wasn't their mom. Unless it was Sergio. Andrea flinches as the brief flash of memory goes off in her mind, the sound of the slap so clean and loud it might as well be real.

Ever since the incident, everything changed, in a subtle, insidious way. Sergio became different—with her, with their mom, with everyone. He no longer brought Reese's Pieces from work to give to Andrea in secret. He was guarded. Distant.

"Why?" Andrea asks.

Her brother scoffs. "Addie..."

"I'm not too stupid to get it. I get it," she says breathlessly. Although she suspects that might not be true. But he has to tell her. He has to. Because they tell each other everything. They're two sides of the same coin...

"And what just kills me," Eli says, cutting off her train of thought, "what fucking kills me is that she's such a hypocritical bitch. You think she's some kind of a saint but she's anything but. Why do you think she lets Sergio treat me like shit?"

"Who? Mom?"

"They all want me out of their lives," he mutters. He stares at the floor in front of his toes, like he's talking to himself, not to her. Like he forgot she was there. "I'm in the way. Without me, they can all go back to pretending their fake lives are actually real. She can pretend she has it made, he can pretend his marriage is doing all right...Both of them can pretend we're all one big happy family."

He looks up, and his smile is nightmarish. "I mean, it's one thing to lie to everyone else but lying to yourself is pointless."

"What does it mean?" Andrea bursts out. "Eli, I don't understand. Just tell me. Please. Where are they sending you?"

He shakes his head, and a suspicion sneaks into her mind that this might be yet another one of his games. That he might be making this up to get a rise out of her.

"I just want them to die, Addie," he says, and his voice is so shockingly sad that she's taken aback. "I want them both to die. A horrible, painful, fiery death."

Much later, Andrea will repeat this exact sentence to the police. She won't wonder why she remembers it so clearly.

# CHAPTER FORTY-FIVE

Once I make sure—from a distance—that the ambulance arrives and Milton is cared for, I start walking and then break into a jog. My thoughts are a thorny tangle. Guilt still crushes my chest, and my temples ache from exhaustion and a budding migraine. Through it all, I try to think.

It looks bad. Figueroa has an inkling Adele was blackmailing me, and it's only a matter of time before she finds proof. Then she can pin the two murders on me. And now I attacked Milton. Something tells me she'll be turning up in his hospital room too. And after what I did, he has no reason to cover for me.

Only now it hits me how dire the situation has become. I realize I've run out of places to go. Whatever my brother was trying to do, he succeeded: I feel the world closing in on me. And like an animal in a trap, I become desperate.

Desperate is bad. Desperate people do crazy, stupid things.

I go over my options, which aren't many. I could always go back to Cynthia's and have her mobilize her legal team on my behalf but I'm no longer sure it's a good idea—or that the lawyers would be of any help to me now. At best I'd be a sitting duck for Figueroa and the police to descend upon when she decides she has enough proof to arrest me.

And then what? Bail, trial, siphoning money I don't have. And at what point will even Cynthia throw in the towel? When Figueroa produces my belt as Sunny's murder weapon? When she shreds my alibi for Adele for good? When they confiscate my lighthouse keychain and discover there's a lighter inside?

Meanwhile, my brother will be a thousand miles away. If he knows what's good for him.

The answer goes off in my mind like lightning. I stumble, break my stride, and cover my mouth to hold in a laugh. It's very simple and completely insane. But it's worth a shot.

I look around. The nearest ATM is in front of a convenience store down the street. I've hit both the store and the ATM on numerous occasions in the past so it won't raise immediate red flags. I jog up to the parking lot and then remember—the cameras. The ATM has them, and there's probably one over the front door of the store too. I stop, catch my breath, smooth down my flyaways with my damp palms, redo my ponytail. Wipe away the tear trails. I check myself in the side-view mirror of one of the parked cars and practice my fake smile until I get it right. I keep flashing back to the engagement ring in Milton's pocket but I banish the thought from my mind.

Normal. I'm normal; everything is fine.

*Suspect last seen on security camera footage, looking calm.*

I stop by the ATM and withdraw everything I can. It's not much, especially since at least half of it I'm going to need for what's next, but I can think about the rest later. When I'm not about to be arrested. When I'm free.

Once the ATM spews out the thick handful of bills, I fold them and put them away safely. Then I step away from the machine and take a deep breath. No taxis, no public transit—there are cameras all over the place in every bus. I'll have to walk. Good thing I know where I'm going.

All my years of working with the homeless and the disenfranchised, those who have nowhere to go, are finally paying off. I know how to vanish. How to fall off the radar, disappear from the system so subtly no one realizes I'm gone for days, maybe weeks.

The walk takes more than an hour, even though I'm trying to keep up the pace, breaking into a jog when I can. Still, by the time I reach the overpass, I'm freezing and exhausted. The hems of my jeans are soaked through with mud, splatters of it going as high as the knees. More of it squishes inside my once-white sneakers. The backs of the sneakers have rubbed my tendons raw, and I wince with every step.

I've never been here before. The place once had factories but those were long ago shut down and demolished, and since then the inconvenient stretch of polluted land has been semiabandoned. The closest I've come was a drive past on the overpass above, safe in my car and in my own little world, not giving a second thought to what might be going on far below my wheels. Which makes me no different from the thousands and thousands of others. But I've heard of the place, more than once. The teenagers at the shelter talked about it in hushed voices so we wouldn't overhear.

Now I feel the ground shudder as an eighteen-wheeler thunders overhead. The noise of cars is relentless. Directly under the overpass, I can hardly hear myself think. No wonder the whole area is pretty much deserted, the empty lots unappealing even to the greediest of urban developers and condo builders.

My destination is an abandoned house, from the 1930s or earlier, on the edge of the lots. It's the last stop for those who have nowhere else to go. It's a place where you can buy low-quality heroin and high-quality fentanyl, and everything in between. It's also the place where, for the right price, you can buy an ID with the name and birth year of your choosing.

Nervousness gets the better of me as I approach. I hide my sweaty hands in my pockets but I can't do anything about the thunderous thrum of my heart. I become aware of the folded-up bills hidden in my bra, their pointy corners poking my flesh. Here, someone could easily kill me for that much money. Stab me in the neck and leave me to bleed to death in the dirt. A death no one will investigate because, in this place, it's the kind of thing that happens. Anyone who has other options should have known better.

It's dark under the overpass, even though the sun has just started to set in the real world. In this one, it's perpetual gloom, like something out of a film noir. My eyes take their time adjusting. Then I see that I'm not alone, and my heart jumps. There are figures sitting up against one of the giant concrete beams. I see glowing cherries of cigarettes, and the smell of acrid smoke, too nasty to be plain tobacco, wafts through the reek of exhaust and motor oil.

I waver between stopping to ask which exact house I need and just walking on before they can notice that I don't belong here. I decide to walk on.

In the periphery of my vision, they raise their heads and follow me with listless gazes that burn the back of my neck. I dip my chin toward my chest and fight the urge to walk faster. I can't—I mustn't show that I'm afraid.

My imagination turns shadows into moving figures, making me hear steps that grow closer and closer. The roar of cars overhead fills my ears until I can't be sure what's real and what isn't. I stare straight ahead, forbidding myself to turn around no matter what. Soon, just a few more yards, I will be out of here—out in the open, in the dust and sunlight.

I was wrong, I realize with a pang of dread. I don't belong here—I wouldn't last through a week of this life. I thought I could relate to the people who crossed my path in my line of work. I thought we had a similar burden to carry through life, only mine was hidden and theirs was out in the open. I couldn't be more wrong. I thought I had the intelligence to lie where it counted and fake normal until I made it. How many times did I study my charges' files and find myself rewriting their lives in my head, changing one decision or turn of events, correcting and adding as if I were marking a term paper? I, who always thought, deep down, that it was only a matter of pulling yourself together, now find myself among the people I swore I'd never become.

Maybe that's my real punishment.

Finally. I emerge from under the overpass and let myself draw in lungful after lungful of polluted air. In front of me is an empty blacktop lot, to the right a chain-link fence, to the left an expanse of gouged dirt that serves God knows what purpose. Far ahead, I see the shapes of squat little buildings that might well be my destination. I start toward them, trying to calm the tremor in my legs.

"Hey!"

I jump and spin around, twisting my ankle in one of the potholes in the asphalt. My heart jumps into my throat when I see a figure in an oversize coat standing at the edge of the concrete under the overpass. It looks like a teenage boy. Immobile, he's staring right at me.

I should keep walking, I tell myself when the figure fails to say anything else or move. I'm just asking for trouble, standing here defenseless.

Reluctant to tear my gaze away from him, I slowly turn around. I take one step, another, fighting the urge to break into a run.

"Ms. Boudreaux?"

I stop in my tracks. The voice is young, oddly familiar. When I turn around, the figure is a little closer, peering at me with mistrust, and at this distance, I can see better. The shaved head, the stretched earlobes. It's not a boy.

"Ms. Boudreaux," she says as she advances toward me, uncertain, "it's you. What are you doing here?"

What's her name? I rack my brain but it slips away before I can grasp it.

"Are you looking for somebody?" the girl asks. And still, I am no closer to remembering her name.

She takes a couple more steps forward. I can see her well now. She squints in the fading daylight.

"Hey," she says, "don't freak out, okay? Are you looking for him?"

I should run now but I stand still.

"You're looking for your brother," she says slowly and holds out her hands like I might shoot her.

Cass. Her name is Cass, like my mother.

And Cass lied to me last time I saw her, at the shelter, when I asked her if she'd seen Adele around. The moment this fact surfaces in my mind I know I'm not going to run. Not until I get the truth out of her.

Instead, I come closer—close enough to touch her with my fingertips if I stretched my arm out as far as it could go. The smell of acrid smoke clings to her, wafting from her clothes. You shouldn't smoke that shit, Cass. You'll die before you're old enough to legally drink.

"What do you know about him?" I bark out. It comes out harsher than I intended but I feel like we're past polite introductions.

"He's not here," she says, talking slowly, cautiously, like I'm a child, or a cop.

"Do you know where he is?"

She shakes her head. "Did he really do it?"

"Do what?"

"Kill Adele." Her gaze flees, and her chin drops. She looks like she's about to cry. And understanding goes off inside my mind like the proverbial light bulb. She didn't just know her—they were close.

"What do you think?" I must tread carefully. I can't have her clam up on me now.

"Maybe. I don't know."

"What's not to know? She was found bludgeoned to death. In his apartment." I watch Cass wince. "I'm sorry," I add, even though I'm not that sorry. But I need to get her on my side. "Was she your friend?"

"No. Not really." She shakes her head vigorously, as if trying to get rid of a bad dream. "Sort of."

She sure is in a hurry to distance herself from the dead girl.

"We used to run together," Cass explains, visibly squirming under the weight of my silence. "We didn't do anything too bad. Believe me. Just small stuff. Steal wallets."

This doesn't help me. I'm trying not to lose my patience, waiting for her to say more. And I know she will. She has no reason to be talking to me unless she has something to get off her chest. "So what happened? She got in with some bad people?"

Cass shakes her head but she doesn't look certain. "I stopped hanging out with her."

"Why?"

"She did something bad, okay? And I didn't want to be dragged down with her when she got arrested."

If even Cass was afraid, it must have been something a

lot worse than just bad. My heart thrums like crazy, and I can't wait any longer. Even if it means risking losing her. "What did she do?"

Cass gulps and takes two tiny steps backward.

"You can tell me. I'm not going to tell anyone." Realizing what an easy, obvious lie that is, I backtrack. "I'm not going to tell anyone that you knew. And she can't go to jail anymore—there's no one to arrest."

The girl's head snaps up. "So what if I tell you?" Her voice, suddenly sharp, rings with angry tears. "Who's it going to help? It's not going to get your brother off, if that's what you think."

"I'm not trying to do that," I say.

Ten minutes ago, my only plan was to get a cheap fake ID and run for my life. But now I no longer want to.

"I'm going to make sure he pays for what he did to Adele," I say levelly. "But for that, I need to know what she did."

Cass appears to consider this. She wipes her eyes with the back of her hand and wipes her nose. Then she spits at the asphalt beneath her feet. The constant noise of cars fills the space between us. She must not notice it at this point.

"I wasn't there," she says. "I didn't see. I don't know exactly how she did it. But she pulled it off, because it's been more than a year now and no one's come for her. But then—but then she died."

"So you thought it might have been because of that."

"I did. Maybe. I don't know anymore."

God, just spit it out. "Who would have come for her? The police?"

"Yeah," Cass says. "But no one even came to ask questions. I figured she somehow did it without anyone knowing. But what I don't understand is why. It's not like anyone paid her or anything."

"Paid her for what?"

Cass finally meets my gaze directly. She could have been quite pretty, if not for the wear and tear of her lifestyle. Her chest rises as she takes a deep breath, as if she's about to jump headfirst into murky water.

"Adele killed someone," she says. "A year ago. It was on the news and everything but only for a while, and no one ever knew. She ran a guy down with her mom's car."

# CHAPTER FORTY-SIX

Adele ran someone over, a year ago.

No one but Cass knows this. And now, also me. And I'm willing to bet my life that my brother knows too.

Because my brother orchestrated it. Talked her into doing it.

I turn my phone back on the moment Cass and the overpass are out of sight. With the details Cass gave me, I have no trouble finding the news story. I find a whole handful. Hit and run, one year ago, unsolved.

Because when a prosecutor gets mowed down, on a street that happens not to have any cameras, close to where he lives, you think about recent cases. Not ones from fifteen years ago. That's ancient history.

The man's name, Jacob Collins, is generic enough not to ring any immediate bells, and if I wasn't looking for it, I would have missed it. He's not even named in the Wikipedia article about my brother's case.

But I know where he is named.

The book. Jonathan Lamb's book, the one that I foolishly hadn't read because I spent fifteen years with my head in the sand, thinking it would keep me safe.

I'm paying for it now.

God, I wish I still had the CD of that book. I wonder what became of it. Leeanne must have brought it back with her. Maybe I can rent another car, drive over there—

Then it hits me. Technology is on my side.

A short jog and I'm back to civilization, if you can call a small strip mall by the interstate civilization. But there's a coffee shop with fast Wi-Fi, and within a couple of minutes, the book is downloaded onto my phone. I get a coffee—decaf, thank you very much—and ask the girl behind the counter for a pen and a napkin.

Reading on the tiny screen is a pain. Fortunately, there's a search option, and I don't have to keep thumbing through page after dense page filled with ridiculously tiny letters.

The list on the napkin is short but to the point.

Jacob Collins, prosecutor. Killed in a hit and run a year ago.

The judge, according to my quick search, has retired a while back and is in a nursing home with advanced Alzheimer's.

Gregory Ainsworth, school counselor whose testimony helped seal my brother's fate, is dying of cancer, as I saw myself.

Me? I'm about to be arrested for two murders Eli pinned on me.

Two murders. Or perhaps three.

Because of all the people Eli hates, the people he blames for ruining his life, that leaves only one. One that hadn't even occurred to me at first because he was right there, out in the open, happy to sign his name to his own death warrant because it got him a juicy deal once upon a time.

The author/psychiatrist Jonathan Lamb. Whose expertise branded my brother as a sociopath and who made a mint off of it.

My options run through my mind, and I reject all of them. I could call the police and tell them to put surveillance on Lamb—but that would hinge on them believing me, which is a big if. Worst-case scenario, I'd just be contributing to my own downfall if he happened to be dead already.

I could still run, of course. I couldn't have murdered Lamb if I was on the bus to New York at the time. Except hiding my head in the sand hasn't helped me so far. Instead, I ended up playing into my brother's hands every single time.

He always was good at reading me. Fifteen years later, I'm still an open book.

I have one more option, but it's risky and reckless—and what's worse, it involves doing a thing I promised fifteen years ago I would never do under any circumstances. Telling the truth about what happened that night.

Eli will never see it coming.

I pick up the phone and scroll through my missed calls until I land on the right one. I tap the number and put the phone to my ear. It only rings three times.

"Mr. Lamb," I say, making my voice as bright and cheerful as I can, "it's Andrea. Thank you so much for calling me."

He buys it. "Andrea. Lovely to hear from you. To be honest, I'm surprised. I didn't expect to."

"Neither did I. No one's ever asked me my version of events before."

He gives a genial laugh. "When can you drop by for an interview?"

"Whenever is convenient for you. I think doing this as soon as possible will be in everyone's best interest."

He has no idea how much I mean it.

# CHAPTER FORTY-SEVEN

Here's what I plan to tell Jonathan Lamb:

I set the fire because Eli said he wanted our parents dead.

My brother went to trial and then to serve his sentence.

Now he's out, and he wants me to pay him back.

I wish it were more complicated than that.

No matter how many times I repeat my rehearsed confession over and over in my mind, it doesn't get easier. Letting go of a secret that's defined my life for fifteen years should be cathartic. But if I expected to feel freed, or relieved, or some other crime-and-punishment cliché, I was wrong. All I feel is fear—fear so intense my bones turn to cotton.

I use some of the money stashed in my bra to pay for a cab to Lamb's place. It's farther than I expected, buried deep in the heart of a suburb amid rows and rows of cottages set far apart. The house is at the end of a cul-de-sac, the offshoot of another bigger street. It looks like it might have been beautiful a long time ago but a house like that needs regular maintenance, and this one appears as though it hasn't had any care in years. The hedge has overgrown, hiding a good deal of it from view. The brick façade is spotted with moss, and the windows could stand to be washed.

Once I pay for the cab ride, the car does a sharp U-turn and is gone before I have a chance to rethink what I'm doing. I find myself wondering if he lives alone in there. Does he have a family? If he does, they could be in danger too. I try to shake the thought as I advance toward the front door and ring the bell.

I hear steps almost immediately, and the door opens, leaving me face-to-face with Jonathan Lamb.

He looks shorter and thinner than he did on TV. He has a pleasant look, I'm surprised to discover, maybe hailing from his days as a therapist. He's probably experienced at putting people at ease, getting them to relax and spill their problems. He lets me in without wasting time—if anything, he seems in a hurry to get me indoors and to close the door behind me.

The inside of the house is not much neater than the outside. I think Mr. Lamb is one of those people with hoarder tendencies who channel them into something more socially acceptable, like collecting everything they can think of. But he keeps all his clutter scrupulously organized and mostly dust-free. In the short foyer alone, there are masks on the walls and two end tables with African figurines.

In the living room, most of the wall space is taken up by bookshelves and display cases groaning under the weight of various unique knickknacks. A set of pre-Columbian (or just designed to look the part) figurines catches my eye: proudly erect penises, ceramic and wood, attached to figurines half their size. I peel my gaze away and scan the space for any indication of anyone else living here—photos, children's school trophies. I can't find any.

The place is shrouded in perpetual semidarkness thanks to a set of heavy, tasseled curtains that cover the enormous front window. Lamb flicks a switch and strategically placed spotlights illuminate the collections on the shelves.

"I have an office that I used to use for appointments," Lamb is saying. "We can go there."

"There" turns out to be a lot more like I pictured, thank God. A clean, spacious office, walls painted pale yellow, with a desk and two simple but comfortable-looking armchairs. I'm weirdly unsettled by the idea of doing the interview like this. Like I'm pouring my heart out at a shrink's office. Still, it beats the hell out of the penis figurines.

He invites me to sit, and I perch self-consciously on the edge of one of the chairs. He has a digital recorder that he puts on the end table next to the obligatory box of tissues. I eye it warily but he hasn't started it yet. I ask him if he minds if I record as well. He says he doesn't, and I set my phone down conspicuously on the armrest of my chair.

"Before we start," I say, "can I ask what this is for, off the record? Is there going to be another book?" Now that my brother killed two more people.

He tilts his head. "Are you familiar with the original book?" he asks, eschewing my question.

"I know what I need to know," I say, matching his evasiveness.

He smirks, which makes me nervous. "There's something you said on the phone earlier," he says. "You told me no one has ever asked for your version of events before. What did you mean by that?"

Convinced I'm being psychoanalyzed, I squirm in the armchair. "I was being literal," I say dryly. "No one ever asked me. I wasn't present at my brother's trial—"

"Because you were in the hospital," he interjects.

I nod. This is technically true. "I wasn't interviewed for any media features. My adoptive mother saw to it that I wasn't harassed."

"But you did talk to the police. You told them things about your brother, what he said and did."

Again, this is technically the truth. It's true that he wasn't in his bed that night. But he wasn't in the hallway when the fire started.

He did say he wanted our parents to die a painful, fiery death.

Technically.

I feel like this is the psychological version of a standoff—that we're circling each other like two cats about to fight, moments before the claws come out.

"Did you ever regret what you told the police?"

I tense but he quickly adds, "That you, to put it in more childlike terms, tattled?"

"Are you recording this?"

"I'll let you know when I start recording. I know how this works. The last thing I want is lawsuits when I publish," he says.

"So there will be another book."

"Maybe." He smiles. "You're avoiding all my questions."

"I'll have time to answer them when the recorder is rolling."

"I just wanted a quick snapshot of your mental state before we start. It can impact things quite significantly."

"Is this an interview or a psych eval?"

"A little bit of both. I am a psychiatrist by education."

A corner of my mouth tugs up in a grim smile. "An author by calling."

"It turned out that way." He shrugs. "I understand you majored in psychology?"

I have a bachelor's degree. We're not exactly equals. But I nod anyway.

"Every author is a psychologist a little bit. Every good one, anyway," he says. "Studying psychology helps you understand others, but first and foremost, it helps you understand yourself."

"So I heard."

"Then tell me. Did it help you better understand your brother? I mean, you must have drawn the obvious parallels and comparisons."

Oh, I understand my brother now. Better than I ever wanted. Too bad it's fifteen years too late.

"I think my judgment might be biased. After all, he's the only family I have left." I'd been hoping to throw him into confusion but he doesn't show the slightest hint of it. "You're the one who evaluated him," I say, shifting the subject. "What did you think then? Has that changed?"

He gives me a long look, and in his silence, I sense something. Something dark, malicious. He's trying to read me. And he's holding something back, something he doesn't want me to know yet.

I've read enough of his book to know his stance: Back when he wrote it, if Dr. Jonathan Lamb had his way, my brother would have been locked up for life. So what's different now?

"Depends," he says.

"On what?"

"On what you tell me, Andrea."

I clutch the wooden armrests of the chair, my hands slippery with sweat. Suspicion gradually gives way to understanding, then to certainty.

"You know that he's going to try to kill you, right?" I blurt out. "He's out for revenge against everyone he thinks ruined his life. And I bet you're pretty high on the list."

To my dismay, he doesn't look shocked at the revelation. He only sighs, shifting in his chair. "He's not going to kill me. Really, there's only one person on that list, when you get down to the basics. It's you, isn't it? And why would he kill me, when I can single-handedly tear you down and bring him back up?"

"You've got to be kidding me," I say. "You're working *with* him? Why?"

Lamb gives me a condescending look. "How do you

think he got through all these years, first at the institution, then in prison? *You* certainly weren't there."

I shake my head, incredulous. "You actually fell for his bullshit act. He's got you in his thrall too."

"Hardly.

"You can't be this stupid."

"He got used to me after a while," Lamb says. "He started looking forward to my visits, and I won't lie, so did I. He's a fascinating individual, after all. We talked a lot over the years. And after he got out of prison too. I helped him out when I could. He had time to tell me lots of interesting things."

"And you believed him."

"Was I wrong?"

My gaze darts to the recorder. It's silent and black, no little lights to indicate it might be working. But I know to tread carefully. An engineered confession is technically entrapment and can't be used in court. But in these circumstances, who knows anymore?

"So, Andrea, I know the real reason you're here. You're not going to surprise me. Should we get to it? It's what you came here to do anyway. Confess. Correct?"

"You really think I'm going to tell you everything now?"

"Of course you are. I'm still missing a few pieces. What was the real catalyst? It can't have been an offhand remark of your brother's. I don't buy it. I have guesses but it would be nice to find out if I was correct."

Careful. "I changed my mind," I say as calmly as I can. "The interview is cancelled. I'm going home now." I get up from the armchair so fast I get a flash of vertigo. He doesn't move, watching me as I storm to the door, only to grasp at emptiness as I realize the handle has been removed.

"Sorry, Andrea, but until we have your confession recorded on this device," Lamb says behind my back, "you're not going anywhere."

# CHAPTER FORTY-EIGHT

"After we're done," Jonathan Lamb goes on, "I'll open the door, and you're free to go wherever you want. No need for violence or coercion."

"That's an interesting way of putting it. Do you know where my brother is?"

"Yes."

"Then you're an idiot. You should have called the police."

"That wouldn't really be in *your* best interest. They think you killed those two girls."

So he knows about Sunny. Has it been on the news already? Or did Eli tell him? I try not to dwell on the second possibility.

"You know my brother is just using you, right? Isn't that what you wrote in that little book of yours?"

Lamb shakes his head. "But that book was based on

a lie. Which kind of throws everything else into doubt, doesn't it?"

"Yes. If you believe my brother. Who lies like he breathes." Stall—I must stall for time while I look for a way out. "You seriously think he's forgiven you for cashing in on his downfall? If you think that, you're in for a big disappointment."

He answers with an infuriating shrug.

"Where's the handle?"

Silence.

"It has to be in here somewhere. Is it in your desk?"

"There's only one way out of here, Andrea," he says calmly. Ignoring him, I go over to the desk and pull out the two small drawers. I yank them out and dump their contents onto the floor. Nothing even resembling a door handle.

Lamb looks on serenely, unperturbed as I turn his office inside out. It means I'm not even warm. Do I have to rip out the floorboards? I sweep his sleek, new-looking Mac off the desk in one movement. It drops to the floor with a clatter that makes me wince but Lamb looks bored.

"Just accept it," he says. "Save us the time. Think about it—what's the worst that can happen at this point if you confess? You were a child, and I'm sure you had your reasons. Say your manipulative sociopath brother made you do it. Or maybe you were just experimenting with some nail polish remover and the rug. Or hell, your stepfather touched you in naughty places. I don't know—I'm sure you can come up with something. There's no proof after fifteen years. They're not going to put you away for life because of it."

"Shut up."

"I'm putting you in control of the narrative," he says. "You should be thanking me. Who else has ever done that for you in your entire life?"

Jim Boudreaux did, if only for his own selfish reasons. Eli did, after a fashion. And I'm still paying for it.

"What does Eli think of that?" I throw volumes of psychology books onto the floor one after another. When I glance at Lamb, he remains unperturbed. Where is the door handle? I check each shelf—nothing but dust.

"You can't change what happened," Lamb says. "But you can decide what happens next. Just stop wrecking my office, sit down, and say your confession into the recorder."

"Not going to happen," I snap. In the middle of the destroyed room, I stop, panting, at a loss. There's nowhere else to look.

"Well, then. I'll just let your brother frame you for two murders. But it's a damn thin line between truth and a lie, Andrea. I'm asking you to see reason. You can't stop what's coming but you can control the damage. To an extent. They'll go easy on you."

"So what happens then? You go off into the sunset with my brother? You don't really believe that."

"You have a right to your opinion. But you're not leaving this room."

I look around and then back at Lamb's grim face. He's starting to look impatient; I notice the tremor in his hands, the way he drums his fingertips on his knee.

*Do you know where my brother is?* I asked him. And he said yes.

*There's only one way out of here.*

Things are starting to add up.

"There is no door handle, is there?" I say. His nostrils flare, a classic tell. I can't suppress a small smile. "The door is rigged, right? It only opens from the outside."

"Sit down," he says. "If you know what's good for you."

"The door only opens from the outside, and since the two of us are in the room, I'm guessing there's a third person somewhere in the house."

He opens his mouth to protest or threaten—I don't know, because before he can speak, I yell my brother's name at the top of my lungs.

"Shut up," he hisses. He jumps to his feet, eyes darting wildly from the door to me and back.

"So it is him. He's here. Doesn't that make you an accessory to something?"

"Don't be stupid. He'll only open the door once I give him the go-ahead. And I won't do that until—"

"Until I confess into your recorder. Got it. But the problem is you think you're playing him when it's really the other way around." I take a deep breath and yell, "Eli! I know you're out there. Open the door."

"He won't listen to you." Lamb's voice is on the verge of yelling.

"You can open it now! You hear me? I confessed."

Lamb lunges at me, taking me by surprise. My back hits the wall as he tries to wrap his hands around my neck. But he's weak, in bad shape. I hear him wheezing. In a simple trick I learned working at the shelter, I bend his fingers the way fingers aren't meant to bend, and he doubles over with a howl of pain. My knee connects with his forehead, sending him reeling sideways. He knocks the end table over, and the recorder clatters to the floor, breaking into three pieces.

He flails, trying to get up. His gaze, filled with pain and fury, lands on mine.

"You two," he gasps. There's a little blood in the corner of his mouth—maybe I knocked out a couple of teeth. "You are both completely fucked. You know that?"

It occurs to me that he's right. Maybe we are both toxic, doomed to never have a normal life no matter which one of us took the blame. Maybe it was spending the first couple of years of our lives watching our biological father beat the crap out of our mom. Maybe it's the bullies, or something we saw on TV or on the internet, or maybe it's video games or whatever people usually blame. Maybe it's because one, or both of us, was just born wrong.

I don't give a fuck, and who is he to judge me?

"You'll regret this."

"Probably," I admit.

We both hear the door rattle at the same time, and our heads turn toward it in unison, like puppets. His eyes widen in terror.

Eli kicks the door open and bursts in. He's holding something in his hand. A pistol, a strange-looking one.

Jonathan Lamb opens his mouth, and I hear the hiss of breath as he draws air into his lungs—to say something, or to scream. I don't have time to find out because my brother fires the gun one, two, three, four times, right into his chest.

# CHAPTER FORTY-NINE

*FIFTEEN YEARS EARLIER: THE NIGHT OF THE FIRE*

Andrea is blinded and deafened. All her senses seem to have deserted her—except for pain. Pain is ever present. Consuming her, devouring her mind the same way the fire raced across the carpet, merciless, leaving nothing in its wake. Dazed, she can barely see through the reflections of orange flames dancing in front of her eyes, burned into them. But there, on the other side of the orange specters, is a familiar face. Eli's face, his blue eyes wide and filled with terror. His cheek and forehead are smeared with soot, and underneath, he's pale as death itself.

"Addie!" It takes her a moment to realize he's yelling—she just can't hear through the roar that fills her ears. "Addie! What did you do? What the hell did you do?"

Her shirt. Her pajama top with the cartoon characters, the one that's too small—it caught fire too, and she needs to take it off. She fumbles with the hem, trying to pull it up, except her hands don't feel like her hands anymore. They feel disconnected from her altogether, like she's trying to operate one of those arcade machines where you fish out plushy toys with a claw.

And the shirt—the shirt won't come off. The shirt and her skin are now one. Melted into one another. If she tries to take it off, her skin will come with it.

She squeezes her eyes shut and tries not to think.

"Why did you do this? Why?" He's practically crying. She opens her eyes and sees his face again, the soot now streaked with white stripes where the tears have washed it away. He grabs her shoulders, which sends unimaginable pain coursing through her. Her mind winks out momentarily but flickers back in.

"Why did you do this?"

She tries to remember but she can't even remember how she made it out here. She remembers everything exploding into orange flames, and then—she thinks—she fell, facedown on the floor. Then someone dragged her, every inch of distance crossed echoing with pain in her upper body.

And then she was outside, back on her feet somehow. That's all she knows. She doesn't know what to answer him. She doesn't even understand the question. He shakes her again, and she raises her hands in self-defense. Her right fist unclenches, and something clatters to the ground.

Her brother lets go of her shoulders, which doesn't make the pain lessen in any way. She watches in confusion as he crouches and picks up the object, holding it aloft by the key ring. It swings on its short chain. The enamel reflects the flickering orange flames as they consume the house. Gold letters glimmer: COME BACK TO CAPE COD.

She blinks away the tears that blur her vision, and for just a split second, her mind is clear. "Because that's what you wanted," she whispers. Wasn't it?

"What?"

"You said you wanted them to die," she repeats, louder. Tears are pouring down her face now, and there's no stopping them. "You told me, and I did it. You told me. You told me."

"I never told you to do this."

She doesn't dare look back at the house—neither of them does. She just knows that there, in the fiery inferno, is their entire life. Their stepdad, their mother, everything they've ever known.

"Yes, you did." Didn't he? She's no longer certain. The pain is making her sleepy.

"I never meant for you to actually go through with it, you stupid little bitch."

Andrea shakes her head violently. She shuts her eyes but she's still seeing red.

"Don't you know the difference between what's real and what's make-believe? You were never supposed to do it for real."

She's weeping silently, tears seeping from under her eyelids that remain tightly shut.

"You know what's going to happen now? You're going to go to prison."

When he doesn't get an answer, he sighs. Andrea keeps

her eyes closed when he takes her hand and presses the lighter into her palm, closing her fingers over it. It's smooth and strangely cool, like a pebble.

"Fine. We're going to deal with this, okay? You won't have to go to prison. No one will know a thing. It's a fire; they happen all the time. All I need you to do is keep your mouth shut. Can you do it?"

Andrea forces a tiny nod.

"If anyone asks you anything, you know nothing. You woke up; the house was burning. That's all. And this thing." He squeezes her wrist, which only makes her hand clench tighter around the little lighthouse. "Keep it to yourself. Hide it, don't show it to anyone, and when you can, get rid of it. Got it? Get rid of it."

She starts to nod but a moment later sirens and lights descend on them. She's never seen fire trucks that close, and so many of them, lights blazing. They're as big as a house. And someone is running toward them, yelling something indistinct.

She doesn't remember how her hand ends up in the pocket of her pajama pants. Her fingers unclench and release the lighter, which nestles at the bottom of the pocket.

Then chaos breaks loose. She screams when someone drags Eli away while a paramedic pulls her toward an ambulance. More people, whose faces she can't see, surround her from all sides. She keeps asking where her brother is, where her mom is, but no one will answer her—it's like she's not speaking the same language and they can't understand a word she's saying.

She tries to remember her mother's face, the last words they said to each other, but like a wisp of smoke, they slip out of her reach. Where her memories used to be, now there are only fire and ashes, and the lighter in her pocket gets lost in them too.

Much later, at the hospital, one of the nurses will bring the lighter to her, never having figured out what it really is.

# CHAPTER FIFTY

Jonathan Lamb drops without a sound. I can't bring myself to look at the four jagged holes in his chest but I can't look away either. Blood soaks through his shirt. Death must have been instantaneous—there wasn't even a horrible last gasp as he realized this was it. No foam, no blood from the mouth. Just like that, here and gone.

My brother and I look at each other without words. Even if I wanted to speak, my ears are ringing so loudly I couldn't hear myself. My gaze wavers from his face to the gun he's holding in his hand. It looks off—something is strange about it. I can't quite figure out what. He's not training it on me, not yet, but he doesn't lower it either.

Compared to the last time I saw him, he looks even thinner and, not surprisingly perhaps, older. No one could ever tell he's only in his late twenties, or that we're twins. He looks like he has a full decade on me. Maybe more.

I watch his every move. He takes a couple of steps across the room and then nudges the remains of the recorder with the toe of his sneaker. "I take it you won't be confessing any time soon," he says. He's smiling but there's something cold and malicious in that smile.

"Where did you get the gun?" I ask through the ringing in my ears that has dwindled to a hum.

"His antique collection. It's from the forties or fifties, I think. Still had bullets in it and everything." He gives the gun an appreciative look, like a child with an expensive new toy.

"He just left it lying around?"

"Sure. In one of his display cases. He trusted me, the poor bastard."

"This was the plan all along then."

He shrugs. "More or less. My plan did involve you confessing though."

"I guess it's too late for that, huh?"

"It's not too late. You can always do it old-school, type it on his laptop or write it on a notepad..."

"It's not going to happen," I say, enunciating every syllable carefully, "because there's nothing to confess to."

He chuckles. "Oh God, Addie. Let it go! I'm not trying to trick you and record you. The paranoia is really getting the better of you."

"Was Sunny part of the plan too? Were you going to kill her all along?"

He ignores me. "Anyway, I have a contingency plan. Come on. Let's get out of here. This room reminds me of the loony bin."

"I'm not going anywhere."

"Just two minutes ago you were bellowing for me to come help," he points out.

"Put the gun down."

"No." He raises it, points it at me. Tilts his head and closes one eye. "Boom." He mimics a gunshot. "I'm kidding. I'm not going to shoot you. It's just insurance."

His gun points, unwavering, into the center of my chest. Slowly, I take a step toward him, and he backs out through the doorway until we're both outside, in the hall.

"What are you doing?" I ask. "You got them all. Everyone."

"Except for you."

"Except for me."

I gulp, glancing around for a means of escape. There are paintings and artistic photos behind glass on the wall. If I could get one and find a way to smash it over his head—

Without warning, he shoots. It's like a bomb going off inches from my ear, followed by myriad tiny bursts of pain like red stars blossoming on the side of my face. Glass flies everywhere, pointy little shards of it. Where there used to be a black-and-white photo of a vintage car, now there's a crater in the wall. Blood runs down my neck and behind my collar.

"You're fucking insane." My lips form the words but only a whisper comes out. "Eli, I'm your sister."

"As if that ever meant anything to me."

I struggle to get myself back under control. Blood fills my left eye, blinding it. I blink and blink, my vision tinted red.

"Then why didn't you just tell everyone back then? That it was me?"

"Would they have believed me?" He's raising his voice—maybe because the gunshot deafened him too. "I should have just let you burn too. Would have gone to prison anyway."

Finally, I dare raise my hand and wipe the blood out of my eye. I feel little bits of glass embedded in my skin like shrapnel. Don't panic, don't panic. It's what he wants.

"So why didn't you?" I ask.

He points the gun at my head now. His hand is trembling.

"But you did pull me out. And you kept my secret all these years. When you had nothing to lose. Was it all just so you could pull my strings for the rest of my life? Was that worth throwing your whole life away?"

He says nothing for a few moments.

"Go into the living room." The gun points at the dead center of my forehead.

"What—is this the contingency plan?"

"I don't care at this point," he snaps. "Go."

And I understand, from the way his voice wavers just for a split second, that he's desperate. The best I can do, to keep him from killing me, is to make him think he's still in control, that he still has a way out.

I hold up my hands. "You do care. You won't be able to get away with it if you shoot me. That was the idea, right? To frame me for Lamb's murder. It won't work if you shoot me in the head."

"I don't think it matters anymore," he says.

"Eli—"

"You were supposed to murder Lamb to keep your secret, then set the house on fire and die inside. But now I've changed my mind. We're both going to die."

I don't move a muscle. Just stand there, perfectly still, and look at him. "We don't have to die."

"I'm not going back to prison. I'd rather burn alive."

"Nobody is going to burn alive. Do you want me to confess to everything?" Stall, keep talking. "To the fire, to the murders? Sunny? *Adele?*"

I see a flicker of something pass through his empty gaze.

"Was it hard for you to kill her? Did you love her, in your own way?"

"Shut the fuck up," he says.

"She must have loved you too. She killed for you. You murdered a girl you loved just to screw with me—that's something."

He looks at me intently. The gun trembles and then lowers to point at my midsection. If he were to fire now, I wouldn't die on the spot—I'd probably bleed out from a gut wound.

"I can't take that off your conscience but I can take the blame for it. You were right. It's my turn to go to prison for you this time." I smile. Just let me have the strength to keep smiling, to keep being his sister. "That's what you want, right?"

He doesn't answer but the gun lowers just a tiny bit more.

"I'm so sorry she had to die," I say in my best social-worker voice. "I know you loved her very much."

To my surprise, he laughs. The sound is like claws on glass, so sudden and jarring that I reel back. The gun jumps back to my face level.

"You're so fucking dumb," he says. "You know why I killed her? I was ahead of schedule, actually. I had meant to do it on the anniversary of the day you killed our parents, as a special touch. But she threatened to tell about Collins, the prosecutor. I was pissed off so I snapped and killed her two weeks early."

I back away until I hit the wall. There's nowhere else to go.

"None of them mean anything to you," I whisper. "Just means to an end."

Eli shrugs.

"Well? Do you still want to take the fall for me?" He grins. "Didn't think so. Now be a good girl, Addie. Go to the living room. Face death with some dignity. After all, you won't be alone! It'll be the two of us, just like old times."

He's completely lost it. He's insane. And I don't have many options if I want a shot at leaving this house alive.

I hold up my hands and take a step toward him, then another. And then, just as he thinks I'm doing what I'm told, I charge at him with all the speed and energy I can muster.

The gun goes off.

# CHAPTER FIFTY-ONE

I roll on the floor, no idea whether I got shot or whether I managed to knock the gun out of his hand. I come to a halt when I hit a piece of furniture. The impact sends a jolt of sharp pain through my ribs but the pain brings me back into my body. Other than my shoulder aching from landing on the floor, I'm unharmed.

Fighting the dizziness that grips my head, I get on my hands and knees, and then on one knee. My brother is getting up slowly. I can see his hands but I can't see the gun. He feels around for it and, not finding it, jumps back on his feet.

Stumbling, my legs like cotton, I run from the room. He follows close behind.

"Come back, Addie," he calls out. "Don't waste your time. You're only making this more difficult than it has to be."

I need to call for help. And I'm betting there isn't a

landline—or if there is, my brother has disabled it. My phone! I feel around my pockets but there's nothing. Then I remember. I left it back in the office.

I can't get to the front door without passing through the living room again but there must be a fire exit. Or a window I can break.

A second-story drop doesn't sound too bad compared to being burned alive.

I race up the stairs and find myself in front of a long hallway lined with doors. I make my choice without thinking. I dart into the room, slam the door shut behind me, and—oh, thank God—there's a latch that I turn without wasting a single second.

The room is a guest room, or maybe a child's room that's been repurposed as a guest room some time ago. Everything is covered in dust. My every step raises small clouds of it that make my nose itch. I make a beeline for the window and start tugging on the window frame but it turns out the windows are as poorly maintained as the façade. The lock on the old latticed frame has rusted shut, and all my efforts can't budge it. I sink my nails under it, trying to loosen it, but one of my fingernails snaps off, sending such a jolt of pain through my arm that I lose my balance. I slip off the windowsill and land flat on my back with a gasp.

Behind the door, I hear steps. Slow steps, unhurried. I freeze; the only sound is my own ragged breathing and the beating of my heart in my ears.

The steps approach, followed by another sound I have a hard time identifying. Sloshing, like liquid.

The door handle rattles.

"Get away from me!" I bellow. "Help! Someone help me!"

But the neighbors won't hear me—I know it. He probably planned it that way. The next house over is too far.

The door shudders from a heavy impact. A few chips of paint go flying, along with a whole lot of dust.

"Just open the door," Eli's voice says on the other side. He sounds bored. "Unless that's how you want to die, cooped up in there."

I sure have a better chance here than I do out in the hall. I scramble to my feet and spin around, looking for something heavy. But the room is devoid of anything but the basics: a bed and an armoire I probably couldn't push. The door shudders again, and the doorframe breaks apart into splinters.

My brother crosses the room in one bound. He sinks his hand into my hair and yanks my head back. My scalp screams with pain, and the next thing I know, I'm drowning.

He's pouring something over my head. It burns like hell when it gets in my eyes, mouth, and nose, cutting my scream short before it can leave my throat. My airways are on fire, and I begin to sputter and cough for my life.

It's some kind of alcohol. Vodka, I think.

"Come on," he says, somewhere far above my head. "Let's go." His voice sounds almost tender as he drags me after him by my hair.

"Let go of me!" I howl once I've regained my ability to speak. My eyes are still watering, and I can barely breathe. He's dragging me toward the stairs. "Eli! Please. Please."

I hadn't even realized I'd begun to cry, and now I'm full-on sobbing. "Don't do this. Please don't do this. I'm your sister. You said we were—you always said we were two sides of the same coin."

When I look at him, he appears completely indifferent.

I realize how stupid I have been, to think that I was the one who made him like this. He was always like this.

"Eli," I blather, more to stall for time than anything else. "Please. It's me. It's Addie."

# CHAPTER FIFTY-TWO

A moment later, Eli is shoving me down the stairs.

I land at the bottom of the stairwell, the impact knocking the wind out of me. The thin carpet does nothing to cushion the fall. Everything reels. It feels like I've broken all my bones. I try to move my arms, then my legs, but I feel disconnected from them, from my own body. When I try to roll over, my shirt makes a wet sucking sound, and I realize the carpet is soaked through. The pungent smell of alcohol and something else—Acetone?—fills my nose and mouth.

Nail polish remover. He's doused the whole place. The smell sets off a chain of nightmarish memories.

A moment later, my brother descends on me. A scream tears from my throat, and I grab for him, clawing at him with my fingernails. He swats my hands aside with ease, flips me over onto my stomach, and then his hands are under my clothes.

I gasp into the booze-soaked rug, struggling to breathe. I can't even cry anymore. His hands are on my bra and then at my hips. I understand what he wants, too late. He finds the lighter in my side pocket.

My scream is so earsplitting that I'm surprised it came from me. I twist but he's straddling me, pinning me down.

"Your stepmother," he says. "She should be able to identify this. We'll both be dead but you'll be the criminal. You won't even have a real grave. Your ashes will be scattered through what's left of this place, along with mine."

Silent sobs shake my body. *Please*, I try to say but the carpet muffles my efforts.

"Any last words?" He threads his fingers through my hair once again and lifts my head up, straining my neck.

I see my chance. Or maybe I'm just imagining it.

"You have no idea," I gasp.

"No idea of what?"

"How much it hurts to burn."

His grip loosens. There's hesitation in his resolve; I can feel it almost on a psychic level. He never had a problem faking being hurt, if it got him what he wanted. But when it comes to real pain, real agony, he doesn't know a thing.

"It's the worst thing you can imagine. It's the most painful death there is."

He hesitates. My hair slowly slips between his fingers, and the pain in my neck lessens.

"I already know it," I say. "But you—you're in for the surprise of your life."

A chuckle escapes from him but there's something hysterical about it. "I'm not going back to prison, Addie."

"It's better than burning. Believe me."

He grabs my hair and slams my head into the floor. I didn't expect it, and I don't have time to draw a breath. He smashes my face into the carpet until I'm sure I'll suffocate. When he eases the pressure and air rushes back into my burning lungs, all I can see are black splotches.

"You liar!" he snarls, and I realize he's leaning close to my ear, so close that I feel the heat of his breath, the spittle flying from his lips. "What the fuck do you know about it? I've been in prison for half my life. Half my life, gone! And what about you?"

"And I"—I desperately gulp enough air to be able to speak—"I burned for you."

He lets go of my hair. My forehead hits the soaked carpet once more. I'm choking on sobs. "We're even, Eli. You don't have to kill us both."

Instead of an answer, I hear the lighter click.

"Fuck you," he says with a short, pained laugh.

I twist and kick out as hard as I can. He wasn't expecting it, and he falls off me, rolling on the floor. The lighter sails through the air, its blue flame nigh invisible until it connects with the heavy drapes, and then it clinks hollowly as it skitters across the floor.

Fire licks at the drapes' fringes and races across the drapes themselves with alarming speed. The heat blazing off it is enough to melt your skin off. From sheer instinct, I recoil, backing away and away, unable to stop looking.

Eli gets to his feet. His expression has lost all pretense of humanity. It's an insane mask, dead and hollow-eyed.

"See?" he says. "Now all we have to do is wait."

Under my petrified gaze, he picks up the lighter. The heat has singed his hair and eyebrows but he appears not to notice. Behind him, the fire is spreading, jumping onto the bookshelves. I realize with dawning terror this whole place is practically designed to catch fire like the head of a match.

"We have to get out of here," I yell. "Eli! We can still get out of here."

"No," he says. "We can't."

His hand closes over my shoulder, fingers sinking in like a vise. "You first," he says, holding the lighter inches from my face. He flicks it, and I scream, but all that comes out is a short burst of sparks.

He curses. I take the moment to claw at his face, aiming for his eyes. With a scream, he lets go, and I scramble to my feet. It's getting hotter and hotter, and I can't breathe. We'll suffocate before we can burn.

No. Fuck that. He can die. I don't want to.

He's yelling inarticulate curse words, his hand on his eye. I think I see blood. No time to take chances. I do what they taught us in self-defense class: I kick him as hard as I can.

He stumbles back, choking on a scream. "Addie," I think I hear him say but the roar of the fire drowns him out. He takes another uncertain step back, and in that moment, the burning drapes finally collapse, coming down in a fiery avalanche of sparks and charred fabric.

# CHAPTER FIFTY-THREE

My brother is consumed all at once. Everything bursts into flame, his clothes, his hair.

I'm paralyzed, unable to scream or move. I just know I can't look or the sight will stay with me for as long as I live, never fading, until it drives me insane. So I do the only thing I can—I shut my eyes. But not before I see his face one final time, the look in his eyes full of desperation and terror and pain. The scream that splits the air is hardly human anymore.

I didn't want this. Oh God, this is not what I wanted. I never meant for it to turn out this way.

Yet it doesn't really matter what I wanted, does it? This is how it played out. Intentions don't count for much in the end.

Please forgive me, I think. And I don't know who exactly I'm asking for forgiveness: my brother, whose scream will haunt my every living breath, or my parents, who perished, choking on smoke, before they could burn. Maybe God, if I believed in God.

Behind my closed eyelids, a memory comes back to me, but the more I try to hold on to it, the faster it fades, slipping through my fingers. My mother's face. Her smile that didn't match her eyes, always wary, always tired. I remember what she said—not her last words, just the last ones meant for me. I think it was, *Finish your dinner, Andrea.* Or something trivial like that. It's not that important anymore.

The scream dies. It's just the roar of the fire now. When I open my eyes, I can't find my brother, or what's left of him. He's become one with the flames.

In the distance, I hear sirens. So someone called the fire department—about time. I have to get out of here.

I draw a deep breath, though there's so little oxygen left in the room that it hardly feels like breathing. And I run.

With a hiss, the ends of my hair turn to charcoal. For a moment, I think I'm about to catch aflame and follow in my brother's footsteps but then I blindly collide with the door. The handle scorches my palm, and I'm pretty sure I leave some of my skin on it, but the door swings open, and I'm outside.

The air feels like ice on my burned skin. I breathe and breathe and can't get enough. I run down the street as fast as I can and don't stop until I can see only the rooftop of the house above the trees.

I stop dead in the middle of the road. My legs won't

hold me anymore so I indulge them and sit down, right on the blacktop. I assess the damage. It's not as bad as I thought; my palm has maybe a second-degree burn at worst, and my hair is a mess but it'll grow back. My shirt is singed at the edges but my skin underneath is just fine.

The pillar of smoke that rises into the sky is spectacular. The house is a funeral pyre my brother could be proud of. The sirens are growing closer, and I expect to see the fire trucks any moment now.

Good. I'm ready for them.

My brother always said we were two sides of the same coin but it never felt that way to me. The way I saw it, we were two sides of a mirror: He was luminous, shiny, containing within himself the entire world, reflecting onto people what they wanted to see and some things they didn't. I was the other side: dull and rough, always hidden because no one ever cared to look at it. And when the mirror broke, everyone was so fascinated with the reflections of their own fractured selves, their perspective and their comfort zones and their assumptions, that they forgot about me, like they always did.

And what does it matter anyway? Is it that important which one of us flicked the lighter? It was fifteen years ago. No one can be brought back from the dead any more than the waxy pink skin on my chest and arms can become smooth and perfect again. How long do I have to atone for a split-second decision? Leeanne was right. I was still on my brother's leash all these years, bound to him by our shared story.

But he's dead now, and the story is mine and mine alone. Figueroa may know, or think she knows, what really happened but what proof does she have? Nothing. Besides, my story is better—it's the one everyone already decided to believe. The story of the golden boy who became a monster.

They'll have to leave me alone eventually, and then I'll live my life however I want. I'll take all the media attention I can get. I'll talk Milton into forgiving me, we'll get back together, and then we'll get married like we always meant to. I'll find a new AA chapter where no one knows too much, and go to every meeting like a good girl. I'll earn my badges and be a shining example to anyone struggling with the demons of alcoholism. A good daughter, exemplary wife, model employee, dedicating my life to helping kids from troubled homes, victims of people like my brother.

I'll live in the town house with Milt, and I won't second-guess or question any of it. I won't spend sleepless nights obsessing over what I do or don't deserve. God knows I spent enough time on that. If nothing else, my brother put a stop to it once and for all—in dying, he freed me from self-doubt.

The sirens are deafening now. No doubt they'll get here in time to put out the fire before it rages out of control. Or before it can alter the crime scene inside the house: Jonathan Lamb, shot four times in the chest with his own gun, with Eli Warren's fingerprints all over it. And whatever's left of Eli, clutching a lighter in his fist. And me, out here, hair and clothes soaked with cheap liquor and singed at the edges. He tried to set me on fire, I'll tell the ambulance techs as I sob my heart out.

They're here now. A half dozen fire trucks, police cars, two ambulances. The police cars surround me, tires screeching, in a blaze of lights and sirens.

The final act, Addie, I tell myself. Let's make it a good one.

# CHAPTER FIFTY-FOUR

*FIFTEEN YEARS EARLIER: THE NIGHT OF THE FIRE*

Andrea wakes up alone that night. She knows it before she opens her eyes. Her brother isn't in their room. He's probably down in the rec room. Or maybe he did run away like he said he would, she thinks, and to her surprise, her main emotion is relief.

She gets out of bed, throws a sweatshirt on over her pajamas, and goes downstairs, her steps slapping against the floor. The house is still and empty. Sergio isn't home yet and won't be for another half hour according to the clock. But her mother is nowhere to be found either.

The kitchen is dark and drafty, ice-cold. She sees that the door leading to the yard is open a crack. Like someone left it that way in a hurry.

She pushes the curtain aside and sees the car, idling in the alleyway. Andrea can see the glow of its taillights through the fence.

She makes her way down the stairs and into the back-yard barefoot. It's cold, even for April, and within seconds, she can barely feel her toes. Her every breath is a puff of steam that rises into the dark sky in skinny wisps.

The gate is unlocked. Andrea clings to the fence and presses her cheek against one of the boards. There are voices. She glimpses a figure—only a silhouette against the intense red light of the car's taillights but she recognizes her mother anyway. She huddles in her robe. Her hair is pulled back sloppily, and wisps of it dance around her head.

"Don't do this," her mother is saying, her voice low but filled with urgency, verging on desperation. Andrea's heart starts to hammer, and she's afraid they'll hear it and catch her spying. "Don't do this, please. We can work it out."

"Jesus H. Christ." The man's voice mingles with the low rumble of the engine, and it's much harder to make out what he's saying. "Do you hear yourself, Cassie?"

It's jarring, hearing someone other than Sergio call her that. To everyone else, Andrea's mother is Mrs. Bianchi or Cassandra.

Her mother murmurs something pleading.

"After what that freak did to my daughter? How could I possibly keep seeing you? What kind of man would I be?"

"It can't end like this." The sheer anguish in her mother's voice is shocking. Andrea already knew she was witnessing something incredibly private but this adds a new layer. This is a secret, a shameful secret. "Listen. Please. We're sending Eli away. To boarding school. We're making arrangements. He'll be gone by the end of the week."

The man gives an exasperated groan. "Forget about it."

"Jim," she pleads. "You can't. You can't let my idiot son stand in the way of us."

It's like a slap. Andrea's ears are ringing.

"You bet I can. I have a family, Cassie. Think about it. If it were the other way around, would you still want to be with me?"

"Yes!" Her mother's voice rises in pitch, hysterical. For the longest time, there's only her frantic breathing, like she's crying or about to cry.

"There's something wrong with you," the man says. Even the noise of the car can't hide the disgust in his voice.

Her mother staggers back. Her silhouette is vivid in the red lights as she covers her mouth with her hands. The car door slams shut, and the car pulls away, leaving her standing there, motionless.

Andrea is numb, and not because of the cold. She doesn't remember reaching into her pocket, but her hand is there, curled around the lighter. The enamel has become hot and damp from her touch.

So it's all true, she finds herself thinking. The realization is like being punched in the stomach. Eli was right. He was right about everything. And that's what makes her angriest. Not her mother's betrayal, or the fact that everything Andrea thought she knew was a lie and the world was unendurable after all. It was that Eli had been right, just like always.

She hurries toward the house before her mother can notice her. She races up the stairs, leaving the kitchen door wide open. Cold April wind skewers the house. She thinks she hears her mother call her name but the bathroom door is already banging shut behind her. Her face is dirty, a gray streak where she leaned on the fence.

Andrea turns on the faucet and sees they're out of soap. She opens the cabinet to look for more. There isn't any soap but there's a bottle of nail polish remover, next to her mother's neat row of polish bottles in all shades of pink and red. Andrea isn't allowed to touch them but who cares anymore?

She takes the bottle of remover and hides it under her shirt and then makes her way to her room. The lighter is snug in her pocket.

How I hate you all, she finds herself thinking. But the thoughts are calm now. Steady. How I hate you. I want you all to die. A horrible, painful, fiery death.

She shuts the door of her room behind her, climbs into bed, and waits.

# ACKNOWLEDGMENTS

Thank you to my fabulous agent, Rachel Ekstrom Courage, for always being there with advice and help and nervous-author hand-holding. Huge thanks to Alex Logan, my editor, for dealing with my flights of imagination and to the entire editorial team at Grand Central Publishing for making my book sparkle! Thanks also to Kamrun Nesa and Tiffany Sanchez in publicity and marketing for going above and beyond.

A huge thank-you to everyone who supported me throughout the writing and publishing process. Alana, Marie-Pierre, Jessica, Nisha, Richard, and everyone who showed up with words of encouragement. Special thanks to Maude Michaud and everyone at The Ladies! You keep me sane. Thanks also go to my family for their support and cheerleading. And a separate thank-you to Patrick, for being by my side always.

Lainey has spent a long time peering into the faces of girls on missing posters, wondering which one replaced her in that basement. But they were never quite the right age, the right look, the right circumstances. Until Olivia Shaw, missing for one week tomorrow.

Please turn the page for an excerpt from
*Girl Last Seen.*

# CHAPTER ONE

LAINE, PRESENT DAY

Normal is something you can fake really well, if you try hard enough. You have to start by convincing yourself, and everyone else will follow, like sheep over a cliff. You act as normal as possible; you go through the motions. That veneer of normalcy may be tissue-paper thin, but you'll soon find out that no one is in any hurry to scratch the surface, let alone test it for weak spots. You can go through your entire life like this, from one menial action to the next, never breaking the pattern, and no one will be the wiser. At least, that's what I'm counting on.

The day I see Olivia Shaw for the first time, I know it's not going to last much longer.

Usually, I get to the grocery store at seven and leave at two, either to go for a run or to nap until my shift starts at my second job. At least two runs a week, usually three, and when I don't go between shifts, I go in the morning, getting up early. When I told this to another cashier, she said she wished she had my discipline, and I nodded along because what are you supposed to say to that? Since then, I try not to talk to people much about anything I do outside of work. I've had this job for almost six months now, which is a long time for me, and soon it'll become strange that I don't socialize.

That girl isn't here today. I haven't seen her in a while; maybe the manager changed her shift, maybe she got fired—I don't know. The manager is Charlene, and she looks like a Charlene, orthopedic shoes and perm and eternal frosty lipstick in a shade that should have been discontinued back in 1989. I suppose she thinks of herself as some sort of mother hen figure, but I noticed the look she gave me when I came in fifteen minutes late. The air outside is like breathing a swimming pool, and my hair is frizzing, stubbornly curling despite being racked with hot tools only an hour ago. I'm still cold and clammy even though I changed into my uniform, the purple shirt with the store logo over my right boob, my name printed underneath: LAINEY M., the M. because I'm not the only Lainey here; the chubby girl who had so innocently tried to be my friend was Lainey R. Still is, I guess, if maybe not at this store. That was her icebreaker: *Oh look, we have the same name—what are the odds?* I didn't tell her no one calls me Lainey, no one important anyway.

It doesn't matter. I didn't even choose the name for myself. They picked it at random at the hospital, some soap opera heroine's first name and a generic surname to go with it. As common and unremarkable as possible. Hiding me in plain sight—that was the rationale.

And it worked, the hiding thing, at least until today. Today, Charlene the manager pushes a slim stack of the usual flyers for me to put up beside the double glass doors of the entrance and exit. I'm still a little slow, and I take them, automatically, forgetting that it's not Sunday and I just did that, the specials for the week: ground beef, three ninety-nine a pound; condensed cream of tomato, three for four dollars. Only when my gaze slips down do I see what they are, and my brain grinds to a halt.

It's nothing unusual. Nothing that hasn't happened before, twice, in the time I've worked in this store. One was the six-year-old boy who was found a week later, whose dad skipped town in defiance of shared guardianship, the other the elderly woman who disappeared in the neighborhood and was feared to have killed herself. No one knows what happened to her, least of all me, except one day I came into work and the poster was gone, replaced by more of the weekly specials, by cantaloupes and broccoli and store-brand chips. For all I know, she did kill herself. But she's not the kind of missing person who interests me.

But today, I look down at the stack of papers in my hands and I see her, Olivia Shaw, age ten.

It's a typical Seattle PD missing-person poster, with the neat columns of stats underneath. The original picture must have been high quality, full color, but the printer was running out of ink, so the colors bleed into one another like one of those Polaroid photos.

Olivia Shaw has been missing since last Tuesday. She

was last seen outside the entrance of her elementary school in Hunts Point wearing a white spring jacket and pink boots. My brain registers the information on autopilot, searing every word into my memory, and in the meantime, a part of me is distantly, methodically, checking off the items one by one. Like pieces of a kaleidoscope, they all click together.

*If you have any knowledge of Olivia Shaw's whereabouts, or any relevant information, please contact...*

Images surface in my mind moments before dissolving into black dust, like a dream I'm trying to remember. I spent a long time in the last ten years peering into the faces of girls on missing-person posters, wondering which one replaced me in the basement. But they were never quite the right age, the right look, the right circumstances. Until Olivia Shaw, age ten, missing for one week tomorrow.

From my many sleepless nights of research, I know that most kidnapping victims are dead within forty-eight hours.

*You were lucky, Ella.*

I force myself to look at the face in the photo, into her slightly smudged features, and I can't bring myself to move.

Olivia Shaw could be my mirror image, rewound to thirteen years ago. She has a wild halo of dark curls around her head—like mine, when I don't torture them into submission with a hot iron. Dark skin, like mine. Her eyes—I can't distinguish the color from the blurry pixels of the poster, but the description says they're gray.

The sound of my name, my other, new name, takes a while to reach me inside my bubble. It's my boss. It feels like my spine has turned to brittle stone, and my neck might snap if I turn my head too fast. I register confusion on her face.

"The tape," she says, blinking her sparse, mascara-clotted eyelashes.

The tape? Right. The tape. Without realizing I'm doing it, I scratch the inside of my wrist under my sleeve. Charlene holds out the clear Scotch tape, her expression shifting closer and closer to annoyance. It takes five steps to cross the distance between us so I can reach out and take the tape from her hand. Doing this, my sleeve rides up and my wrist bone pops out of the fitted cuff. Her eyes flicker to it for just a fraction of a second, the same way people sneak a glimpse of disfigured faces: staring without staring, looking away with such intensity you wish they'd just glare out-right, get their fix of the morbid, and get it over with. I can't wear fingerless gloves here; "accessories" aren't allowed by the dress code. So I've developed a habit of always tugging my sleeves down, a tic that persists outside of this place too.

Probably not the worst habit to have, all things considered.

The sound of tape peeling off the roll raises the hairs on my arms, and I hold the poster in place as I tape its corners to the glass outside the entrance, taking too much care to make sure it's perfectly straight. As if that will help her. I know it's all an excuse for me to reread the text, examine the photo, burn it all into my retinas forever and ever and ever. To add Olivia Shaw to my ever-expanding mental collection of the disappeared. Except a part of me already knows one of these things isn't like the others.

The automatic doors of the entrance hiss open as I pass through, my muscles humming with tension. "Charlene," I hear myself say, "I'm going to go for a smoke."

She says something about opening the store in five minutes, but I won't take longer than that. I'm already on my way out, patting down my pockets before the door has a chance to slide aside and let me out, wondering what I did with my emergency pack of smokes. It might be in the pocket of my jacket, which is in the back of the store, stuffed in the shoe box–sized locker in the employees' lounge. Too bad. I don't think a cigarette will do it for me right now anyway. Instead, I take my phone out of my pocket, stare at the screen until it blurs, key in the code and screw it up three times until it unlocks. Open the browser and start feverishly typing in the search window.

Another thing I know from my late-night Internet forays: kidnappers, rapists, serial killers—they don't just stop one day. They are stopped. Whoever stole me—stole Ella—was never found. But in the last ten years, there hasn't been another girl.

And now there is.

# CHAPTER TWO

In the books and movies, the broken girl always dies at the end. Sometimes she's allowed one final heroic act, one last snarky line before she goes out. Maybe she sacrifices herself to save the real hero, or maybe her death is just a meaningless accident, an afterthought. But she always dies, because she's too tarnished to live.

Every time I see her die, I'm jealous. That should have been me, a long time ago.

It would have been better for everybody if I had just died, like they presumed I had—for years before I was found. Especially for me, the nameless, voiceless creature that was born out of Ella Santos's remains, an abomination. A living dead girl.

They had to give this voiceless creature, this Frankenstein's monster covered in scars and stitches, a new name at random because the creature couldn't speak to pick one for herself. The most I ever had the wherewithal to do was drop that last *y* from Lainey, turning it into Laine, one syllable. Sounds like something you'd find on a highway.

I will probably never know what exactly glitched in my kidnapper's mind that made him decide to take a risk, to allow me to live. I've never given up wondering, though. And I never could quite let go of the suspicion that some nameless force in the universe was saving me for something even worse.

Now, as my sneakers rhythmically hit the pavement, the shock of impact thudding in my bone marrow, I can't help but wonder if this is it.

I was spared so I could do something, help the next one. And a darker thought: I was spared so that I could watch it all happen again, unable to do anything about it.

I focus on the burning in my lungs, the steady fire kindling in my leg muscles, but it's not enough to keep my thoughts from drifting to the thing burning in my pocket, folded up next to my phone in half, then fourths, then eighths, until the layers of paper refused to bend. Charlene gave me four posters to put up, but only three are still there, next to the flashy yellow flyers advertising a discount on whole chickens. Charlene is of an exacting nature, just like everything about her suggests, and she will probably notice, but hopefully, she won't think it's me. She'll think one of the shoppers decided to snatch it off the wall and keep it for some unknown reason.

I catch myself with my hand in my pocket like a thief, when it's too late. The thick folded edge of the poster brushes the back of my hand, and to distract myself, I take out my phone instead and check the screen. Nobody ever calls me, and I'm not on any social media, unlike pretty much everyone my age. No one expressly told me to stay off it—it's just an ingrained instinct too strong to go against: the instinct to hide.

The first thing I see is the missed call, followed by the new voice mail alert. How did I not hear it? My heart lurches, and it has nothing to do with the exertion wringing my smoker's lungs. Another bit of ingrained knowledge: missed calls, and especially voice mails, are never good news. Fighting the tremor in my hands, I dial my voice mail and groan inwardly as the phone recites the date and time with agonizing slowness. A hiss, a snap of static, and then a familiar voice floods into my ear, heavy with its nasal accent, and a sweet balm of relief spills in my chest even though my heart hasn't gotten the memo yet and keeps hammering. It's my coworker from my second job. I didn't recognize the number because she's calling from the one ancient pay phone at work, the one they keep there for God only knows what reason. I'm so overcome with that feeling of having gotten away with something that I forget to even get mad about what she's asking. They need me to come in early, because so-and-so didn't show up. I hang up without waiting for the message to play to the end.

It means no time to take a nap beforehand, which is just as well because it's not like I'll be able to sleep now. But I had other plans for these two hours, plans that will have to wait until the end of the night—which, right now, might as well be in a hundred years. Ever since I saw Olivia Shaw looking at me from that poster, time shifted. It's no longer an ephemeral thing that trickles away while I look on with indifference. It feels voluntary, as if I forgot how to breathe and have to consciously pull and push every gulp of oxygen into my lungs if I don't want to suffocate.

Up in my apartment, I lock the door behind me and slide on the chain even though I'll be out again in under an hour, which leaves me just enough time to get ready. This is why I need the second job, sacrificing sleep and sanity, because I need this place. Living with roommates didn't work out so great—surprise, surprise—and it's impossible to get an apartment in this city on a single cashier's pay. Even a shitty apartment like this one, on the worst street in the worst neighborhood. And I don't just have to pay rent. I'm a twenty-three-year-old female who needs makeup and clothes and sometimes even jewelry, though my options are somewhat restricted here.

And other things.

I didn't do such a bad job making this place homey. It may be three hundred square feet, but every inch is mine. I have furniture from Goodwill and the great free market that is the curb on moving day: a narrow desk so old it verges on antique and a chair that almost matches it. The apartment has a built-in counter too small to eat on, so the desk doubles as a dining table. I have a cute little nightstand from IKEA. Well, not *from* IKEA but I think it's IKEA. Someone tossed it out because a corner is chipped, exposing the cheap plywood underneath. I don't have a bed frame but I have a decent mattress on the floor—the bed frame is going to be my next big splurge. Depending on how I'll make it through the next hours-days-weeks.

Whether or not I can keep reminding myself to breathe at reliable intervals.

I'm sweaty and consider jumping in the shower but reject the idea. I don't feel like being naked right now. So I run a towel under the tap and rub it in my armpits and across my chest, under my grocery-store sweatshirt. The water hardly makes the cloth less scratchy, and I feel like someone scrubbed me down with steel wool. When I pull the sweatshirt over my head, I realize my chest is covered with little splotches that will hopefully fade by the time I get to work.

The dress code at my second job is fairly simple, no uniforms—they either can't afford them or just don't care. You can wear what you want, but whatever it is it has to be white. The girls complain about the color, so unforgiving of spills and nearly transparent under black lights, but I think it adds an illusion of curves to my streamlined body, which helps with the tips. My two identical work dresses are cheap polyester, twenty dollars after the discount at one of the fast-fashion chains, but they have an appealing plunging neckline and the skirt hits midthigh.

Next, boots, knee-high with thick heels and blunt toes that boost my height by a couple of inches but are still comfortable enough, considering I have to be on my feet all night. I own lots of boots of all shapes, forms, and colors—boots are kind of my thing, although not entirely by choice. The other alternative is high-top sneakers, and I hate those. I never wear stiletto heels, and no sandals either, even in summer. Or ballet flats or those trendy platform Mary Janes with the delicate ankle strap.

Girls with scar rings around their ankles don't have many options. Some asshole I made the mistake of hooking up with still tells everyone I fuck with my boots on.

On my arms, fingerless gloves that go up to the elbow, and on top of that, three bracelets on each arm. Foundation, concealer under my eyes, eyebrow pencil, a touch of highlighter on my brow bones and in the Cupid's bow of my top lip, a beauty routine out of a women's magazine. I have a plain face without makeup, except for my big, brown eyes that some love-struck fool in another life might have called soulful, and I know how to play them up. I line my eyes with heavy strokes of dark-blue kohl, a little silver in the inner corners. Gobs of gloss on my lips, darkening their natural color to that of dried blood. Lastly, I pump the mascara brush in the scuffed tube that I really need to replace, if I can spare the ten bucks. The effect is clumpy, but I doubt anyone will notice in the dark.

Almost ready. I check my phone; I have just enough time, and the traffic usually goes the other way at this hour. The grocery-store sweatshirt is still where I left it on the bathroom floor, a puddle of cheery purple-pink, and I dive after it to get my keys and wallet out of the pocket only for the poster to fall out, landing at my feet.

My heartbeat thuds dully in the back of my throat as I retrieve it, unfold it, and smooth it out on the kitchen counter. With my fingertip, I trace the smooth, round outline of her face, the one ringlet of curls that springs off to the side, escaping from the elastic of her ponytail.

*If you have any knowledge of Olivia Shaw's whereabouts, or any relevant information, please contact...*

I should call the number, the thought crosses my mind. I even begin to reach for my phone. Call the number and say what? Everything's been said many years ago, and much good it did to anyone.

Before the temptation can become too strong, I grab the poster off the counter and race across the room to my bed by the window. Careful not to look at it, I lift up the mattress and slide the poster underneath, on top of the pile of printouts, folded yellowed newspaper pages, and other posters, weathered by time and faded by rain, that I collected all over the city over the years. Olivia Shaw is part of my collection now. As long as I can keep her there, maybe she'll stay out of my thoughts. Maybe her face won't flash in front of my eyes every time I blink, like it's been tattooed on the inside of my eyelids.

Enough. I'm running late. I put my wallet and my phone into the pocket of my pleather jacket then remember something and open the drawer of my nightstand. Grab the folding knife that sits there, under a pile of year-old tabloid magazines with frayed covers. Put it in my pocket, next to the phone and wallet.

Every single night I leave my apartment, I secretly hope I'll need it. But I never do.

# ABOUT THE AUTHOR

Nina Laurin is the bilingual (English/French) author of *Girl Last Seen* and *What My Sister Knew*, both published by Grand Central Publishing. She studied creative writing at Concordia University in her hometown of Montreal, Canada, where she lives and writes. You can learn more at thrillerina.wordpress.com and on Twitter @girlinthetitle.